THE INSIGNIFICANCE PARADIGM

JOHN HAMILTON

Copyright © 2023 John Hamilton.

All rights reserved. No part of this book may be reproduced, stored, or transmitted by any means—whether auditory, graphic, mechanical, or electronic—without written permission of both publisher and author, except in the case of brief excerpts used in critical articles and reviews. Unauthorized reproduction of any part of this work is illegal and is punishable by law.

ISBN: 979-8-88640-881-2 (sc)
ISBN: 979-8-88640-882-9 (hc)
ISBN: 979-8-88640-883-6 (e)

Because of the dynamic nature of the Internet, any web addresses or links contained in this book may have changed since publication and may no longer be valid. The views expressed in this work are solely those of the author and do not necessarily reflect the views of the publisher, and the publisher hereby disclaims any responsibility for them.

One Galleria Blvd., Suite 1900, Metairie, LA 70001
1-888-421-2397

DEDICATION

In memory of my mother, Nancy Lee (Malloy) Hamilton. Yes, mom, my poor, poor characters go through hell sometimes ... but a life lived without trial is a life deprived of what makes it worth living. Glad you got to read one of my books. Thanks for everything.

TABLE OF CONTENTS

Acknowledgements..vii
Author's Note...ix
Chapter One: Insignificant...1
Chapter Two: Rangers..16
Chapter Three: Intervention of Fate 31
Chapter Four: Along Comes a Woman..............................47
Chapter Five: Choices..63
Chapter Six: Luitgarde 78
Chapter Seven: Nature 93
Chapter Eight: Secrets Revealed 109
Chapter Nine: The Hole..125
Chapter Ten: Asch-Kur..140
Chapter Eleven: Know Your Enemy 155
Chapter Twelve: Clay 171
Chapter Thirteen: Rokka und Tramuta...........................187
Chapter Fourteen: Nice to Eat You..................................203
Chapter Fifteen: Puktah 219
Chapter Sixteen: The Change Within 234

ACKNOWLEDGEMENTS

First off, much appreciation goes to those who took part in the editing process. Philip Gallagher at Iowa State University was instrumentally huge in the early and late stages of the process, reminding me of all those nuances of the English language I tried hard to forget all these years! Much love my friend and college classmate.

    Also, much thanks to another classmate and fellow author, Zach Switzer. I'm glad this book had such meaning for you. Also, T. Coppery Keith spent many hours editing, despite recovering from cancer. Thanks to all of you for your time, commitment and passion in getting this book done.

    I would also like to acknowledge the influence of author Robert Bly (Iron John, A Book About Men). Reading his insightful look into one of the oldest stories ever told by mankind had a major impact in the writing of this story. I learned much from this book and it was a great help to me personally and in telling this story the way it deserved to be told. Lastly but not least, I would like to thank God for the divine inspiration and guidance that inspires the life and adventures of the main character, whose name literally means, "God has helped me."

AUTHOR'S NOTE

The Insignificance Paradigm is the beginning of the story of a young man, cast out of his homeland into a forgotten civilization of the past. The hope to someday return home and reclaim his father's throne is always at the edge of his mind, but it is the things one learns along the way to an end that shape who they become when they get there.

    His story takes place in the vast and magical world, which in his native language is called Zygia (ZI-yah), but as the series progresses, readers may find it more familiar to them than they first imagined. Regardless of place and time, his is a human story, which is what all truly great stories are. I hope his story touches you in some way and you, the reader, are able to see a little of yourself in his life, that of his companions, and their struggles.

—John Hamilton Nov. 11, 2016

Chapter One

Insignificant

Faith can be a real oddity; it is easy to speak of until a situation arises which requires one to exercise it. Eleazaar was having one of those moments. Faith derives from belief and belief is an assumption that fills in the gaps of that which is not fully known to someone. Belief forms the bedrock of one's reality in which faith is invested that the reality is true.

It was thusly so as Eleazaar found himself pinned by a magical web against the cavern wall that day, unable to free himself from its hold. The events of the day had rattled that foundation to its core and, at the moment, he was not certain of much of anything. What he was certain of was that the creatures were coming to take him, and there was little standing in their way.

His mind raced as he struggled against his bonds, desperate to regain control of his fate. He needed a miracle, but he could not envision how such a thing could now come to pass. All seemed utterly lost and that was how he felt as well.

Only a small, unlikely hope remained before him, between himself and the doom descending upon him. It required a faith the young man was no longer certain he possessed after he had already lost so much this day. In that waning moment, he reflected back on the events of the past two days that had brought him where he was now.

It all began innocuously enough with a visiting bishop that had come to the seminary to see his mentor. As Father Mannesh's scribe and student assistant, Eleazaar was asked to accompany them as they toured Warfall and discussed some delicate and private matters that were of particular concern to the O.I.L., or Order of Infinite Light.

Warfall was a pretty sizable human city, so there was plenty for anyone to see and do there. The seminary itself was an integral part of the local economy, bringing students and commerce from all across the regional provinces. There were not many schools of its size and grandeur to be found in the land. In most regards, it was the pinnacle of modern innovation for its time. There were also venues around town for traveling bards and other performers who frequented the area. Moreover, there were all types of ethnic foods prepared and served daily, reflecting the diversity of the city.

Also available were a variety of vendors and merchants that one could only imagine. From bath houses to barber shops, there were very few things not available in Warfall. In all respects, it had become something of a commercial Mecca of goods and culture from all across the region and beyond. As a consequence, there was always a lot of bustle in the streets and visitors ambling about from venue to venue.

As Father Mannesh and the Bishop walked along and talked at length, the young scribe Eleazaar's attention drifted off into the aforementioned bustle. After all, a couple of old priests jabbering about nothing and whispering about the rest got old fast. He could think of at least eighteen things off hand, he would rather be doing or that needed to be done. Then, as they came up to the main thoroughfare, something grabbed his interest.

He watched with curiosity as a wagon of dwarven goods pulled up in front of one of the shops along the street. A small, scrubby figure, another dwarf as best he could tell, was begging nearby and scuttled over toward the merchant wagon. A dwarf begging could only be a verloren or gully dwarf. That was the common, if not derogatory moniker, of a dwarf who was an outcast with no clan. He knew dwarves were less compassionate toward their outcasts than even humans tended to be. Furthermore, he knew it was not going to go over well.

The driver, a robust fellow who was most likely the merchant, rose from the bench seat while Eleazaar watched. He secured the reins as he stepped down from the wagon onto the street. There was also a guard with him, another dwarf, who stood up in the back of the wagon as well. The guard set his crossbow aside and picked up a wooden crate, handing it over the side of the wagon and down to the merchant. Even from across the street Eleazaar could see enough to guess it was artisan goods from one of the local hill clans that dotted the area. The crates that items were carried in were usually a good indicator of the type of cargo.

"An I told'im ya better quit faffing around, laddy," the guard said to the merchant. " 'Ol Roch 'il box'im 'round the ear'ole he will."

"Arse over tits he is. The chaps gone right naff if you ask me," the merchant responded.

"Please sir?" a softer voice, clearly female interjected. "Spare a coin and me's can help ya carry y'wares. Morish if y'fancy. Real good wit horses me is."

"Codswallop!" the merchant retorted. "Off with you! Diddle some other chap you bloody duffer."

"Go on slapper," the guard added. "You get nowt from us. Clear off, you."

The beggar recoiled, hurt and humiliated by their harshness. As she looked up at the guard, he made a disgusted face and spat at her. The two dwarves laughed at her as she slinked away, but this little dwarf was a feisty one; she was not going away silently.

"Don' hafta slag me off, ya wankers!" the beggar quipped back at them, shaking her fist. "Kiss y'mums wit'a mouth like that? Bust y'one right in the goolies, me should!"

The guard, obviously confrontational, started to jump down from the wagon. The merchant, being of a more moderate disposition, placed his hand up on the guard's chest to stop him. Then he began to laugh, diffusing the situation.

"Bloody well told you now, didna she?" he mused. "Juist let it be, lad. Forget the gormless."

The beggar shuffled away on up the sidewalk, disappointed and feeling embarrassed from such ill treatment at the hands of her brethren. Just then, as if to add insult to injury, a group of human boys came running out of an alley slightly ahead of her. They turned toward her on an arc as they ran, not slowing down noticeably. Father Mannesh and the Bishop were just beginning to cross the street at the time and Eleazaar continued to watch as he followed them into the street.

Seeing the beggar, who was looking back toward the merchant at the time, the lead boy purposely clubbed her with his forearm as he ran by. His elbow struck her in the head, stunning her and making her fall to the ground. Cruel and unremorseful, the boys just laughed and kept on running down the sidewalk past the merchant as she lay there. The beggar was slow to get up and tried her best not to cry.

Her life of poverty was humiliating enough, but for a proud dwarf the humiliation was worse than death. Father Mannesh and the visiting bishop crossed the street and passed not far in front of her without any notice. However, as Eleazaar passed, he let a coin fall from his pocket.

As if it had a mind of its own or an inherent destiny, the coin bounced and rolled right in front of her. Well attuned to the sound of a coin dropping, the beggar looked up and watched with surprise as it slowly rolled right to her. She scooped up the rolling coin quickly between two stubby fingers and looked at it. She hesitated for a moment, naturally thinking to pocket it as the scribe walked on, seemingly unaware of his loss.

But, even though the simple coin had little worth and probably meant little to the owner, she felt remarkably overcome with good will. In that moment, she had a change of heart and made a fateful decision.

"Sir? Sir!" she called after the young scribe as he walked away. "Me'thinks you dropped this."

Hearing her call, Eleazaar stopped walking and smiled, very pleased with her choice. He loved to test people when the opportunity presented itself. He often learned much more about people and society that way. Such circumstantial behaviors as exhibited by this dwarf today, he found to be a sign of extraordinarily good character. Carefully putting on an inquisitive expression, he turned to the little dwarf as if he had no idea what she was going on about. He looked at her briefly and began walking toward her.

As he walked back to her, she was unsteady about his approach as so many she encountered were often quite cruel to her. She trembled slightly as he stopped and stood over her. He was a rather tall young man, which only magnified her comparitively small stature. Bending down, he took the coin from her fingers. After scrutinizing over it for a moment, he smiled at her and she relaxed a little.

"Hmmm … it does indeed *look* like one of my coins," he noted. "I cannot be certain of that, however. I see no markings that would identify the owner. Tell me did you find this coin lying face-up or face-down?"

"Uh … face-up methinks, love," she replied.

"Mmmm … I see," he replied. "Well, then best *you* hold onto this one I think. Surely it shall bring you good fortune."

The beggar's face lit up, as she was moved by his display of kindness. She mustered a smile back at him in a silent showing of her gratitude. Suddenly however, there was a harsh voice from behind Eleazaar that shattered her smile. It seemed Father Mannesh and the bishop had stopped walking and were watching Eleazaar with curious scrutiny.

"Eleazaar!" Father Mannesh called gruffly. "Eleazaar. Stop your dawdle and come at once!"

Eleazaar gave the beggar a wink before discarding his smile. He turned around with a serious demeanor and hustled back to where the two men were standing. Minimizing his activity with the beggar, he tried to parlay his mentor reverently.

"My apologies father," Eleazaar said. "I thought perhaps I may have dropped something."

"Hmmm," Father Mannesh said, seemingly suspicious of him. "You have a strange habit of dropping things when beggars are around. You are still my assistant, are you not?"

"Yes, Father Mannesh," Eleazaar replied.

"Then assist, unless of course you would prefer the soup kitchen?" Father Mannesh retorted smartly.

"No … father," Eleazaar relented, pursing his lips to disguise the smile that was clawing its way out from the edges of his mouth.

"Good," Father Mannesh said at last, mostly satisfied he had gotten his message across to the young man. "Let us all continue on our way then, before you drop something else."

Father Mannesh and the bishop resumed walking and picked up their conversation where they had left off. Eleazaar followed obediently, leaving the beggar behind and took comfort in knowing he had done something that made a positive impact on another person. He did not get out much since he was always studying, but he tried to make a point of doing something good for someone else when he did get some time outside of the St. Gustav von Claus campus.

"He is really a good acolyte," Father Mannesh shared quietly with the bishop; a wry smile on his face. "A bit hard-headed and, arguably softhearted, but one of the finest students I think we have ever had here."

"So you have told me many times now," the bishop replied. "We could use a few more under the circumstances. The plague took an exorbitant toll throughout the countryside, both on the order as well as the people."

"Indeed," Father Mannesh said. "Were he not so promising, I might have risked him out in the field before now. I could have graduated him after his first year here, but I fear his unbridled compassion for others would ultimately be his undoing."

"And, what of this incident at Luitgarde?" The bishop asked. "Is there anything new coming from the town?

"We have very little information, outside of what I mentioned in our previous correspondence," Father Mannesh replied gravely. "Things being what they are, I am hopeful it will be a minor problem ... whatever it turns out to be."

"Certainly," the bishop agreed. "We will hope for the best, which is about all we can really manage until we get boots on the ground and assess the situation."

"Now, where was I?" Father Mannesh pondered aloud. "Oh yes, yes, the Ostium relic. With the break-in at the catacombs and the implications of a potential breach, there is a concern growing among many of us about its continued security."

"And you have reason to suspect this break-in was something more than petty thieves?" the bishop asked.

"Evidence? No, if I had that we would be having a different conversation;" Father Mannesh replied, "at least that is where we stand currently. But, given the profound nature and power of the item, I am genuinely concerned that we are taking the potential threat too lightly. It is far too dangerous to risk having something so powerful fall into the wrong hands."

"The consequences would be devastating; no question at all," the bishop agreed. "But, I think you are overreacting, Ben. Even those of us who actually know where it was hidden do not know exactly where. It was buried and hidden away well before any of us were even born. I feel quite certain that we have little to worry about from looters."

"I hope you are right," Father Mannesh said, relenting as he stopped and gave the bishop a troubled look.

"Come on, Ben," the Bishop coaxed. "Let us go have some of that famous coffee of yours."

The bishop and priest resumed walking, heading up the street, back toward the seminary school. Eleazaar followed along behind, trying his best not to eavesdrop while still catering to his mentor. For the life of him though, he could not imagine how coffee could somehow ease anyone's concern. He had come to know Father Mannesh quite well since he had come to seminary. If the father felt so strongly about his concern, he was pretty sure there was something to be concerned about.

There were times when it was difficult for Eleazaar outside of the seminary campus and Warfall. Being bi-racial, it sometimes drew scorn from others who frowned upon things and people who were not clearly of a *pure* race. Different was something to fear or distrust for some people and each, he always assumed, had their own reasons for that. He did not see nearly so much of it here in Warfall though, where many races converged for business and enlightened culture. Outside of the city, however, the attitudes of the small towns and remote villages could vary greatly depending on their exposure to outsiders.

The less exposure an area had, the more likely it was that trouble would be found. Thus, he was mindful in particular to hide his pointed ears, which betrayed his Elven blood. Outside of that distinct feature, he easily appeared to be about as human as anyone else. Being one or the other was fine; but not everyone approved of interracial breeding. That was true of the Elves in particular, not just a human condition. After returning to the campus, Father Mannesh dismissed him from further duty for the day. Eleazaar offered his respects to the bishop, and then headed over to the grand library where he spent much of his personal time reading.

He had been disinclined to do much of anything else since his friend, Jayden, had left for military training with the provincial army. Jayden had an appetite for adventure, and was always dragging him into some sort of predicament. The time away was actually a welcome break from what always seemed like trouble waiting to happen. In any case, he found the plethora of knowledge in books a more useful and, a far less dangerous way, to advance his ability to survive in the tumultuous world, should he ever have to venture out into it.

As night fell on the town of Luitgarde, things at least seemed to be normal. The town streets echoed with the song of crickets and shadows danced in the poor light from the torches that dotted the sides of the streets.

The pubs were full as usual, but there was increasing talk among the locals about the disappearances of other townsfolk over the past few weeks. Not surprisingly, the theories grew in number and grandeur with every drink. Fear and anger among those living there was growing as well.

As the number of those reported missing continued to increase, confidence in the town authority's ability to resolve the situation waned to the breaking point. A town hall meeting had been scheduled for the next day, in the hope of soliciting more patience and cooperation while an investigation into the disappearances continued.

Situated at the edge of Satoochie Forest, Luitgarde was something akin to the edge of civilization. It had its share of traders and travelers pass through, but they tended to be going somewhere other than Luitgarde. There were farmers who worked the land to the north, away from the forest, but much of the business in the town that wasn't oriented for local consumption was intended to serve those passing through too, like the Duchess Inn.

The Duchess Inn was pretty much the center of activity at night in Luitgarde. Complete with sleeping rooms for rent and a respectable kitchen, it was fairly busy even when there was nothing serious to talk about. It had sap-lacquered tables and benches scattered through the main floor, with a long bar at the back wall separating the kitchen and brewery from the rest of the room.

At the Duchess, a late-forties man with deep lines in his face finished off a mug of ale and stood up. He wobbled a little as he set his mug down securely on the table top and focused his eyes. Stepping over the bench at the table where he was sitting, he staggered toward the door to leave.

"Where you going, Frank?" A man at the table called out a bit smartly.

"Home, I think," he replied, waving his arm dismissively.

"You remember where it is?" the man called back as others around him laughed.

The man pulled open the door to the pub, and stumbled awkwardly down the steps into the street. He swayed a little as he tried to get his balance ordered and twisted around as he oriented himself for the walk back home. His gait was choppy at best and he stumbled frequently, seemingly over his own feet. There just was not a whole lot to do in

Luitgarde at night except eat, drink and sleep. He had gotten the drinking done in spades for sure.

Now, the only question for him was would he actually make it home before the sleeping part began. The night air was cool and refreshing though, and he breathed in deeply to improve his focus. After slogging along for a few blocks, he stopped in the shadow at the edge of a building. Seeing no one around, he took the liberty to relieve himself there. Standing still and straight proved to be a bit of a challenge, however, and he tilted over into the wall, spraying himself with his own urine.

"Verdammt alles!" he grumbled in disgust as he steadied himself.

Securing his garments again, he stumbled back away to continue home. Immediately, he passed a dark alley that sliced through behind four stone buildings. An odd sound, almost a kind of chirp, distressed his ears and he stopped immediately, leaning precariously toward the darkness therein. Then there was a clicking sound and another chirp.

"What in hell?" the man said aloud to himself.

Just for a blip of a moment, he thought he saw red eyes and a shadow of something move there in the deep darkness of the alley. The man swiped across his eyes with his sleeve and fumbled to the edge of the alley. He caught the stone block and mortar wall with his hand to steady himself and looked again, squinting into the dark.

"Hello?" he called.

There was only silence from the alley. He looked back down the street from which he came and around behind him. There was no one around to call to, but he could not contain his curiosity. Looking back into the alley, he hesitantly took a step in.

He crept forward, using the wall next to him for balance. As he scanned ahead, he saw what looked like the tip of a tail sticking out from behind a corner of the building on the opposite side of the alley.

Then, his foot kicked a rock which made a noise as it rolled across the packed gravel ground. He cringed at the sound, after which he saw the tail jerk out of sight.

"That you, Walt?" he called anxiously. "I have got a knife ... I do not want to hurt you. The joke is over ... okay?"

Still, there was only silence in response. He pulled a knife out of a sheath on his belt and nearly dropped it as he fumbled nervously. He took a deep, trembling breath as he edged closer to the middle of the alley where there was a nook between the buildings to either side. As he moved closer, he stretched his neck out to look, hoping really to see nothing there. From his position against the far wall, he thought he could see a shadow around the corner in the nook. The more it came into view, the more oddly shaped it looked. He cocked his head and strained to see, trying to figure out if he was seeing a real thing or some kind of trick of the shadows. Suddenly red, snake-like eyes appeared in the head of the shadow and there was clicking and chirping like he had heard before. Terror swept over his face. The creature rushed at him and he screamed out as it pounced upon him.

Eleazaar awoke from his sleep that night with a yell. He looked over at his roommates, still asleep in their beds, cotton in their ears. His nightmares were something they had already gotten accustomed to and they had immunized themselves from being disturbed. Even after arriving here four years ago, the nightmares persisted.

It was always the same; the DeGothian horde swarming the palace at Torkul and his parents slaughtered. Had it not been for the royal mage, the children would all have been slaughtered as well. With desperate magic, he and his siblings were hurled away to far reaches of the unknown, scattered at random. He had thusly arrived here, utterly alone and confused.

Where here actually was took some adjustment for him to understand. The unstable nature of the magic used had catapulted the boy not merely across space but across time as well; far into the past to be precise, and a past of which his own time scarcely even knew of. Tested by the Order of Infinite Light after he was discovered, he was found to be gifted, so the church took him in and he had been here ever since.

He closed his eyes and with an exhale of relief, he lowered his head. He could vividly remember the horrors unleashed by the enemy regularly on the towns and villages near the border. He had seen it all himself and in the faces of the refugees as they fled in droves from the embattled countryside.

It made nightmares difficult to avoid, for they were not the product of a child's overactive imagination. It was also, more than anything, why he was perfectly content with his life of study at seminary school. If he never left this campus, he would not be unhappy about it. He had his books and the endless supply of knowledge he found in them. They were his refuge from the pain of his past, though the memories of it still reached through time and haunted him.

He tossed his legs over the side of the bed and sat there for a moment, rubbing his face. The dreams were always intense and felt very real to him, like he was there in the chaos all over again. He was soaked with sweat and tugged at his garments, which felt sticky against his skin. Rising up, he walked to the door of the room and into the corridor beyond.

It was the middle of the night and the corridor outside of the room lay quiet and full of shadows in the dim light of the few sconces on the walls with their low burning torches. He looked both ways before turning right and heading down the corridor. He turned right again at an intersecting corridor and walked to a flight of stairs at the end.

He descended the stairs to the ground floor level below and turned right again. He walked for a short distance before turning right under an archway and left through a short hallway that opened into a room on his right. Among the wonderful amenities of the school were its interior bathrooms or guarded robe, complete with running water piped in from a large wooden tank that stood on stilts in the rear of the campus.

It was an ingenious innovation: collecting rain water and using gravity to create pressure to force it through pipes to the inside of the building. When they found early in its application that algae would form in the tank where the water collected and rested in sunlight, the order had used its vast collection of knowledge to create a chemical additive that would kill the algae without harming the people who came in contact or ingested the water.

Not only did this guarded robe have nice, comfortable wooden seats to sit on in private little cubicles, but there was also a trough to do your business quickly and conveniently. A valve at the end of the trough or behind the seats released water to flush the basins clean when you were done, which kept the heavily used place from stinking to high heaven.

Where all that stuff went he was not real clear on; someplace underground perhaps. He did not care to think much about that though. Such amenities were a great luxury that few across the land had ever experienced. There we even wash basins that were permanently affixed on the walls for the user's convenience.

In fact, students elsewhere were stuck with periodic duties of dumping the dreaded copper pots from the standard stool closets most schools used. He could imagine the opportunistic pranks of older students on the unsuspecting freshmen those pots would invite and the very thought made him cringe.

He stood over the trough and relieved himself, dismissing any further thoughts to that effect. After turning the valve to rinse the trough, he went to the wash basin and opened the valve there. He splashed the night-cooled water on his face and looked up into a mirror that was mounted just above it. It was a long oval encased in an artful alabaster frame that was secured to the masonry.

He looked pale and his eyes were a little bloodshot, but the water felt refreshing against his skin. Then, he was hit by a wave of guilt. Many areas of the world outside were still suffering through the worst plague it had ever known and he was here, enjoying the plush amenities of the church, and indulging his fears of facing the future. True, the plague was on the decline and seemed to be subsiding, but he was going to graduate soon whether he wanted to or not. Then he would be a proper cleric, and would have to go out there and face all sorts of new challenges. He only hoped he would be ready to meet that day head-on.

He dried his face with his garments, which smelled like sweat and were not all that dry anyway. He made an ugly face as he caught a whiff of them and looked back at himself there in the mirror. He rolled his eyes as if reacting to some internal lecture from himself.

"Beans," he said aloud, as he turned to walk back out into the corridor.

He trudged back up the stairs and down the corridor to his room. His roommates were still soundly asleep and so he crawled back onto his bed. He laid there on his back with his eyes open, just thinking. Though he was tired, he did not really want to sleep because it meant he would dream. He could not stay awake forever though. At some point, he would have to face down his fears if he ever hoped to get through the tough realities that awaited him in the world outside of the school. As hard as he fought it, slowly his eyes relented and fluttered shut. In practically no time, his eyes began to dart beneath his eyelids, back and forth. He was dreaming again, but this time it was something new.

It seemed he was on a dark street with no one else around, though he could hear the sounds of others faintly echo from somewhere far off. For whatever reason, he seemed to have a hard time keeping his balance and his vision got hazy from time to time. Was he seriously dreaming about being drunk? That was rather unexpected. He wanted to wake up, but the dream persisted and he just kept stumbling along.

Then the stumbling stopped and he found himself looking into a dark alley. His dream, like any bad dream of course, took him into that dark alley where nothing good could possibly happen. He tried to fight it, but he could not resist. He moved into the darkness where red eyes suddenly appeared before him. His body began to jerk in the bed as he fought desperately to wake up. He did not like where this dream was going. Then there was a horrible, growling hiss of sorts and the thing rushed upon him. Terrified, he sat up awake in bed with a gasp.

"Hoc ducit," he said, aggravated. "That is the very last time I eat the shellfish."

He clenched his fists in frustration and wrapped the blanket around him tightly. Curling up into a tense ball, he covered his head and gave up trying to fight sleep. A friend suggested that maybe he try thinking of good things as he was falling asleep; something that would encourage more pleasant dream experiences. It was worth a shot and he had virtually nothing to lose.

Outside of the library, his favorite place to spend time was in the campus gardens. He thus tried to focus on the flower beds and other plants he had seen while meditating there. Someone else had advised him to look down into his hands if in trouble when having a dream. He thought it was a little vague as to how that would help, but made a mental note to try it if he could remember. He closed his eyes and soon he was fast asleep.

CHAPTER TWO

RANGERS

The following afternoon, many of the people living in Luitgarde crowded together in the sanctuary of the St. Vincente church to hear what the local authorities, namely the Constable, were doing to stop the disappearances and find their loved ones. It was not typical for the church to host meetings for the town, but this was a clear exception. The town hall was not designed to accommodate such a large crowd, so the church had consented to the use of their sanctuary instead. Luitgarde was not the biggest of towns; maybe 1500 people lived there. It was small enough that the O.I.L. Church was really the only game in town. Thus, even St. Vincente had to offer multiple service times to accommodate everyone comfortably and effectively.

The church itself was an old structure that dated back hundreds of years and had been expanded multiple times as the town grew from the village it once was into a proper town. It had been through a fire and an earthquake, but its stone block frame was still standing strong. An iron bell rang out from the peak of a tower that rose from its roof as an altar boy pulled on long ropes that dangled far below, signaling to all that the meeting was soon to begin.

Inside the church, hardwood benches were lined up through the sanctuary beneath the glint of color cast by light passing through a single stained glass window on the west wall. Flickering candles stood in brass and pewter candleholders at both ends of the sanctuary and strategically placed torches shed their light from sconces on the walls. There was a finely worked wooden pulpit on a platform like a small stage just beyond the benches and an altar where the Holy book of Youja Shilud was blessed before service.

It had the biggest single-room structure in town, so it was the logical choice for such a meeting. A lot of frightened and upset people would be coming in to hear what the constable had to say, so it would have to suffice under the current circumstances. The people of Luitgarde packed the benches full and stood in the aisles, airing their opinions loudly amongst each other as they waited impatiently for the constable to speak to them.

Constable Spillman stood on the platform at the front of the sanctuary, having a private discussion with the priest, Father Torsten Kluge. He turned and looked at the crowd for a moment and then shook the priest's hand, appearing to thank him. Stepping away at last, he strode up to the front of the platform to address those that had assembled.

"Okay folks…….now listen up please… everyone!" he shouted over the din of voices.

Some of the talking died down right away in response, as most came hoping for some answers to the continued disappearances of their neighbors and loved ones. But, there was a lot of anger too and others carried on with their discussions unabated. Understanding this was a molten and heavily emotional issue; the constable tried his best to be patient in his approach. Some of those conversations were getting quite heated, however, so he whistled loudly to get their attention fully focused on him.

"Quiet please!" he yelled out. "Can I have your attention up here?"

Begrudgingly perhaps, the talking trailed off at last. As the full extent of the crowd turned its attention over to him, he waved his arms about in an encouraging way. Panning the crowd, he could scarcely find anyone he did not know reasonably well. They expected much from him and he did not blame them, but this unfolding of recent events had become a nightmare already. These people had no idea how much sleep he had lost over it or how the disappearances had affected him personally. As the number of missing grew without any progress, he was forced to ask for outside help to find answers. He took a deep breath and resolved to give it to them straight and let the chips fall where they may.

"This is a difficult time for all of us," he began. "I can assure you that we are doing everything we can to find those who are missing and what forces are behind their disappearances."

"And what does that *mean*, exactly?" a fiftyish man asked smartly. "People have been disappearing for weeks now and all you can tell us is you are doing your best?"

"I share in your frustration Henri," the constable replied. "This is a complicated investigation and we are bringing every resource to bear to get some answers."

"Sounds like a load of bollocks to me!" a heavy-set, sooty blacksmith retorted.

"Hear, hear!" many others in the crowd agreed.

"Please…..calm down," the constable urged them. "My own nephew is among those who are missing, so I can assure you I am as eager to get to the bottom of this as the rest of you are."

Grumbling arose and spread around the sanctuary. Few of them in their own distress had been aware that the constable's own family had been victimized. With roughly twenty known people missing in only a few weeks since the first disappearance came to light, it was easy to overlook how many families had been affected and who had personal connections to the losses. The constable understood that they were all afraid as well and, rightfully so.

"Now, we have called in some outside assistance to help us," the constable continued. "I have spoken with Father Kluge here about the church's help and we have hired a team of rangers to come in and try to pick up a trail or some kind of substantive lead for us to follow. Those rangers are out there right now, point in fact."

"But, what have you found out so far?" another man from the crowd asked. "I mean, it has been two weeks … surely you have found something."

"No, Merkl," Constable Spillman chagrinned. "That is the frustrating part about all of this. There has not been a shred of evidence, which we cannot really explain, and is the reason we have asked for help with this investigation."

"That is all fine, asking for help, but what are we supposed to do until these…..rangers find something?" a woman asked with concern.

"A very good question," the constable commended her. "From now on, wherever you are when the sun goes down, you need to stay there. That means if you are at the pub, you better have a pillow or be renting a room. *No one* is to be outside at night until further notice and *no one* goes anywhere alone in the day."

A collective groan rose up from the frustrated crowd. Public safety was always one concern of course and rightfully so, but word of the disappearances had gotten out and the effect on business was already becoming evident. Merchants were already hesitant to bring goods to the town and the travelers that frequented through had all but disappeared as well. Surely the appearances of such outwardly cautious behavior would kill any hope of a speedy return to normal in that regard. There was even a concern among the town authorities that some of those travelers or merchants could be missing too, though the constable took great care to keep that concern reserved amongst officials of the town.

"Now, I know…..I know, folks," the constable empathized. "I do not like any of this either, but it is what it is. If we can take precautions and avoid making ourselves vulnerable, then maybe we can keep any more of us from disappearing while we work to figure this out. I would even advise you to lock and bar your doors and windows at night, just as an extra precaution. Regrettably, that is really the best we can do until we have a better idea of what we are up against."

Satoochie Forest stood dark and foreboding as dusk settled that evening, with little light penetrating through its thick canopy down to the ground below. Within its shadowy confines, a ranger inspected the ground as he followed the trail of some kind of creature. There had been a combination of strange tracks left behind from its passing, though he was not exactly sure just what kind of creature had made them. With his hand, he carefully outlined a smooth disturbance pressed into the soil and separate clawed marks near it. He pursed his lips in thought, simultaneously intrigued and perplexed by what he was finding. Then he rose after a moment, continuing his tracking on deeper into the eerie darkness.

As he crept along in his search, picking his way through foliage that was growing across the shrinking trail, he found a tatter of clothing that had snagged on a prickly bush. He picked it up in his fingertips and reluctantly gave it a sniff after looking it over closely. The material was consistent with a typical workman's shirt; a light cotton garment. It had ripped away on a sharp, thorny branch and he made an awful face from the repugnant odor. It reeked of alcohol and urine.

The path of movement and tracks led away from the narrow trail into the thick of the forest from here and he continued to follow it, despite the darkness that had settled with the coming of nightfall. Finding prints was much harder in this part of the forest, not to mention it being dark, but there was more evidence yet to be found from leaves or plants that had been disturbed. He took some kind of object wrapped in cloth out of a side compartment on his backpack, which glowed softly from within so he could scan his surroundings without drawing too much attention.

Slowly he moved forward, continuing to track, night-be-damned. Finally, he came to a hill that rose-up oddly in the deep forest. He climbed up to the top and, after looking around and listening carefully, knelt down by a tree. Digging into his pack, he stuffed the soft-glowing object back in his pack for the moment and he pulled out two small stakes, each with a red ribbon attached.

He took one of the stakes and placed it between two roots of the tree and, crawling to the bushes directly across from it, he placed the second just under the cover of the leaves. The Ranger arose to his feet then and took a step forward, intending to continue with a quick search of the area before taking a brief rest. When his foot hit the ground, however, it made an odd creaking sound like stepping onto a wooden lid or old boards. Instantly, he froze in his tracks and carefully lifted up his foot again, gingerly taking a step back from the spot. He eased down onto his knees and probed the ground carefully with his hands. To his surprise, he found the edge of something that seemed to be a wooden door; a cleverly obscured trap door was set into the ground and covered by moss and leaves.

He clutched and pulled back a layer of the moss to reveal the weathered edge of the wood underneath. The door itself was about four feet wide and looked to be maybe twice that long; banded by twine and cut from young saplings. He unsheathed his scimitar and slipped the tip under the edge to pry it up. It lifted easily, which was not at all what he had expected. Initially, he assumed it was some old thief's stash or just on old abandoned secret storage someone had once made. It appeared to him clearly now that this was not the case; this structure was fairly recent.

Pushing it up, he looked down into a dark opening beneath. The opening dropped about four feet and descended at an angle away from him to somewhere deeper inside. He paused and then probed the side pocket of his pack. He again withdrew the lump of cloth with the glowing object and this time pulled back the folds, revealing it. In his hand, the luminescence of a moonstone lit up the immediate area and cast its soft light down into the foreboding darkness below.

He took a deep breath and exhaled; then, holding up the moonstone to light his way, he stepped carefully into the hole. He eased on ahead slowly and quietly through a tunnel about 12 feet long that ended at a short set of stairs descending to a stone floor. He pawed his lip, understandably apprehensive and a little confused at what he had just found. Pressing ahead regardless, he then crawled on down the short stairs there to an open area that lay below.

As he stepped down onto what appeared to be a cut stone floor, he was a little surprised to say the least.

Whatever this place was, it had been constructed elaborately and was no mere thief's stash or hole in the ground. He looked on carefully ahead for potential threats in the soft light given off by his moonstone. The area that opened to his left was actually a room constructed of relatively smooth, cut stone blocks. There were roots squeezing through between the stones in many places and it was dusty with a stale, sour smell like rot. Whatever it was, if it was anything, this part was very old.

"What in the holy hell?" he said under his breath; simultaneously amazed and concerned.

It appeared to him that he had stumbled onto some long buried and forgotten temple or citadel of some sort, but he could not be entirely sure of which just yet. He would have to see more to figure out what this strange place was and why it was out here in the middle of a dense, old forest. What he did notice right away was that there had been activity here recently, so it was either not abandoned entirely or something else had moved in and made it its lair. That might explain the wooden door he had stepped on, at least. No wood lying exposed to the elements in a moist forest would have survived so long.

The recent activity was in the form of notable disturbances evident in the layer of dust that had collected on the floor over the years. Looking up, he then spied another set of stairs across the room going down to somewhere farther below ground, so he began to creep quietly towards them. Moving closer though, he took notice of the familiar patterns in the disturbed dusty crud on the floor; it was the pattern of foot traffic akin to the tracks he had been following in the forest. The tracks lead between the flights of stairs and were much more distinct here than those found in the forest. They were absolutely not human prints; at least that much was for certain. What they did resemble clearly puzzled him.

"Serpent?" he said ponderingly, barely above a whisper. "Cannot be ..."

He looked around and tried to create a scenario in his mind where the details of what he had found in his search so far made some sort of sense. They did not, however. This was nothing he had ever seen before and the ranger had seen a whole lot of strange things in his lifetime.

He was an expert on things found in a forest, but this was new to him. What he *was* pretty sure of now was that these findings must all somehow be related to the disappearances happening in Luitgarde.

He eased over to the second set of stairs and looked down into the soft moonstone-lit area just below. The distinct and unmistakable smell of mold wafted up from somewhere down below and he pulled out a bandana to try and filter the spores in the air, covering his nose and mouth as he secured it behind his neck. Casting a glance over his shoulder at the stairs leading back up above ground, he seriously considered returning to Luitgarde at that moment and reporting what he had found.

But that was just it; what had he found? He had tracks he could not positively identify and a sunken structure with recent activity. It was something but he was not sure it was enough to go on just yet. He had to know for certain before he reported back because the only thing he really had was a circumstantial guess. If he jumped to conclusions and was wrong, it would reflect badly on the ranger's reputation. He needed evidence; perhaps an item from one of those who were missing, obtained from inside the structure. Thus, he resolved to continue on down the stairs, descending into the unknown that lay in wait for him below. He crept down to the bottom where the stairs ended and opened up into another dank, stone room, adorned eerily by shadows cast across two doorways and a hall passage from the moonstone's glow.

As the next morning unfolded, the constable finished his breakfast anxiously and walked down the street to the town hall. He pulled open the front door and walked straight down the central hall of the building to the conference room where the town elders conducted their meetings. Today the room was being used by the constable to meet with the ranger team the town had hired to help with their investigation of the disappearances. Inside, the head ranger, Captain Jahko Silger, stood at a long table waiting for him. Seated around the table was his team of experienced rangers who had assembled to report on the previous day's search activities and to get their daily briefing on their respective assignments.

"Good morning, Captain Silger," Constable Spillman greeted as he entered.

"Morning, constable," Captain Silger returned cordially.

"Your search turned up something ... I hope?" The constable inquired apprehensively, but hopeful.

"Not exactly," the ranger captain admitted before pulling the constable aside in a hushed discussion.

As the two spoke, the frustration of the constable was evident. He shook his head in disbelief and looked around for a moment as if wondering what he had to do to get a break in this case. After speaking privately with the ranger captain, the constable then turned to the others and addressed them.

"Ok... up here fellas," he directed as the ranger captain clapped his hands together loudly in tandem ... "Let me have your attention for a moment. Am I to understand that *no one* found anything significant in their assigned sweeps yesterday?"

"Well ... yes ... and no, constable," one of the rangers said finally after a short silence.

"What the hell is that supposed to mean, Quinn?" the ranger captain quipped back. "Elaborate please."

"I am um ... not really sure how to explain it, cap," the ranger replied. "None of us found tracks of brigands or some kind of hungry monster stomping around or anything. It is just that ... um ..."

"What he is trying to say, I think," another ranger interjected, "is that many of us found similar impressions across our search radius that we could not quite identify."

"Impressions?" the constable asked blankly.

"Movement patterns; tracks, sir," the ranger quickly added.

"I would say that was pretty significant, Stack," the ranger captain then said.

"Why could not any of you identify them and *why* are you just now bringing this up?"

"Honestly cap, we did not feel like telling the constable that the town having a snake problem was relevant at the time," Ranger Stack explained. "Once the boys got to talk about it though and, once we realized we were seeing the same things all over. We are not really so sure that it is not relative now … in some way at least."

"Snake problem?" the constable inquired, skeptical.

"You have seen a lot of snakes lately?" the ranger captain asked the constable.

"No, nothing," the constable replied confidently. "To tell you the truth, I am not even sure the last time I saw one."

The ranger captain put his fingertips to his chin, rubbing with a look of concern as he puzzled for a moment. This new information seemed very strange and did not make much sense to him, but surely it had to be more than a mere coincidence if the team was seeing the same pattern all over the area. In any case, it was the only lead of any substance they had to go on at the moment. Finally, he turned to the others, hoping to glean something else that might shed more light on the mystery of the disappearances.

"What kind of snake makes tracks that none of you could identify? He said at last, seriously bothered. "You are all well trained and none of you are new to the bush."

"Maybe a kind of giant python or some other constrictor," Ranger Stack guessed blindly. "The movement pattern is not consistent with anything we have ever seen though. Whatever this is, it is something new."

"A hybrid of some sort, maybe some new kind of species," another ranger at the far end of the table, Bo, interjected. "A giant species for sure."

"Preposterous!" the constable exclaimed. "Giant snakes are *not* eating the people of this town."

"You have got a better explanation, constable?" the ranger captain said in retort, defending his team. "And, no one said anyone was being eaten. Am I right, boys?"

"No sir," Ranger Quinn affirmed. "No signs to indicate that, cap. Even if snakes were only swallowing parts of people, they would not be able to go far and we would have found them resting somewhere or found a nearby lair at the least."

"I do not believe this," the constable said, frustrated.

The ranger captain frowned. He found the snake relevance a bit of a stretch himself, but it was the only angle they had to work with at the moment. Until the finding could be eliminated as a possible catalyst for the disappearances, it was still going to be suspect number one. Then he suddenly noticed that one of his team members was not present. It startled him that he had not noticed before, despite his being busy with other matters.

"Where the hell is Ritter?" he asked the others.

"Have not seen him cap," Ranger Bo admitted. "We just figured you had him off on a special assignment or something."

"No," the ranger captain replied with concern. "He never reported in after his sweep yesterday. He did not come in last night?"

"No cap," Quinn revealed. "We did not see him after we split up. We thought maybe he came in late and reported directly to you."

"Shit," the ranger captain said angrily; mostly at himself. "Get the map out on the table."

Two rangers in the back got up and went to a wooden rack that hung on the back wall of the room. The rack, cut from polished oak, held a score of maps wrapped in protective covers, detailing the town of Luitgarde and the surrounding areas. They grabbed a large map of the whole area and spread it out upon the tabletop in front of them. The ranger captain came around the table to look at the map, shadowed closely by the constable who peered over his shoulder. Captain Silger leaned over it and studied it closely, mentally identifying the division of assigned areas designated for their search radius. Singling out the area assigned to Ritter, he traced with his finger from their current location to a forested area on the map.

"Okay then," the ranger captain said finally. "Ritter covered the forested area right here; designated section four."

"That is Satoochie Forest," the constable noted. "It is some heavy forest too; more like a jungle in most places and there are swamps farther south."

"Bo?" the ranger captain inquired. "Your area skirted the east part of that forest. What did you see there in section 3?"

"Just the same snake patterns, cap," Ranger Bo replied. "There were lots of them too."

"Constable?" the ranger captain inquired.

"Not too many people venture off into Satoochie," the constable relented. "It is a dangerous place; honestly, there could be pretty much anything lurking in the dense cover of Satoochie."

"Well," the ranger captain said finally in response. "I think we have ourselves a target area to focus on, boys: Satoochie Forest."

The ranger captain pounded his pointer finger down onto the map area of the forest and looked at the constable, who reluctantly nodded his agreement. Now, Satoochie was a very old forest that had claimed its fair share of lives in the past. On occasion, remains of a hunter or some kind of vagrant had been discovered there or someone had gone missing and never returned, but such things were not too abnormal, if uncommon. Those who lived near the forest, the smart ones at least just avoided it.

There were plenty of deadly creatures and plants to be found in an old forest; everyone knew that. Not all of the animals and plants in such forests had admittedly even been catalogued. Also, the dense forests of the sub- tropics were far more dangerous than those of the north. There were many more species of life to be found there and the food chain was less agreeable that humans were at the top.

The constable stepped away from the table to the door of the meeting room and pulled it open. He stepped through the open doorway and outside of the room into the hall, closing the door behind him. Next to the door stood a town guard; an older man in his late forties. The constable turned to him and gave him the news.

"Sergeant ... it's Satoochie Forest. A ranger went missing there. Go tell Father Kluge that it is time to assemble the church's team of volunteers," he instructed the man.

"Right chief," the guard replied.

"Oh," the constable added. "Keep this under your hat too. No one outside of Father Kluge needs to know anything."

"Certainly," the sergeant agreed.

The constable returned to the room and closed the door behind him as the guard headed down the hall and off to find Father Kluge. He hung his head low, still unsure whether they were making the right call. When he looked up again, the ranger captain was looking at him.

"Are you alright, constable?" the ranger captain asked.

"I will be fine when this is all over with," the constable replied. "I have a community that I'm trying to hold together ... it's a lot of weight for one man."

"I can appreciate that," the ranger captain replied. "I have a team I'm trying to hold together and I am a man down already."

"Captain," the constable countered calmly, "people disappear in Satoochie: always have, probably always will. That team may not come back out and we may not get a second crack at this. I just hope your hunch is right."

"You have any better ideas, constable?" the ranger captain asked pointedly.

"No," the constable replied, "nothing at all."

"Well then, for everyone's sake ... I hope we are right too." the ranger captain said.

The guard, Sergeant Scheper, exited the building straight away and walked briskly across and down the street, heading for the rectory at the St. Vicente church. Like everyone else there in Luitgarde, he was just as eager to put the stress and terror of the past few weeks behind him and get on with a daily life that resembled something normal. The town had lost two guards already and finding volunteers to replace them for street patrols was proving difficult. The townsfolk may have demanded results from them, but few were so keen as to put themselves in danger to protect everyone else.

Fear was eating the town alive and, in some respects, was worse than the problem that had spawned it.

As he walked along, he whistled aloud nervously. He took great care to keep the matter to himself as he exchanged pleasantries with those he passed along the way, but he wanted to tell everyone in the worst way. With so little to hope to hold on to as of late, any kind of hope, even a fool's hope, would be a big boon to the town's morale. Still, there was probably no sense in exciting anyone and maybe causing them to foolishly let their guard down either. They would know all they needed to know when the time was right. When the team of volunteers arrived at their little town armed for battle, they would know.

Scheper crossed the street again to the church and made his way around to the rectory on the far side of the grounds. He looked around to see if anyone was watching him, concerned someone might ask questions or see though his pretense that nothing important was going on. By his own admission, lying was not really his strong suit. He reached the rectory door, relieved that he could finally tell someone, though he realized that he still had to make it back to the town hall without cracking. He would feel much better after the constable had made an official announcement. He knocked on the rectory door and waited anxiously. When the door creaked open at last, it was a postulant, not Father Kluge who stood before him.

"I ... I have an important message for Father Kluge," Scheper stammered, a little surprised to find someone else at the door.

"He is resting at the moment," the postulant explained to him. "Give it to me and I will see he gets it as soon as he wakes."

"NO ... no," Scheper panicked before calming himself. "I must give it to him and it must be now. Wake him at once ... it is very important."

"Ok ... I will tell him," the postulant replied after a moment, a bit taken aback by the sergeant's odd behavior. "Wait here."

The door closed again and Scheper nervously waited. He fidgeted as the minutes passed by, eager to just deliver the message and be done with it. Then, the door opened again at last, this time with Father Kluge standing there before him.

"Sergeant Scheper," Father Kluge greeted, curious.
"Thank heavens," Scheper said, relieved. "I bring news from the constable, father."
"Malvay?" Father Kluge called behind him to the postulant who appeared beside him shortly.
"Yes, father?" he responded.
"Go to the market and fetch us some fresh fruit," Father Kluge ordered gently.
"Now, father?" The postulant asked.
"Of course now," Father Kluge responded, less gently. "Go on."

The young man slipped past Scheper and walked away, off toward the market. The two of them watched him go, until he was out of earshot. Then the priest turned his attention back to the sergeant.

"Come inside quickly then," Father Kluge replied, glancing one last time across the grounds. "Tell me everything."

Chapter Three

INTERVENTION OF FATE

Eleazaar awoke in the morning and poured water into a clay basin to wash himself. He could vaguely remember that strange, new dream that had befouled his sleep, but it haunted him nonetheless. He had read once that dreams sometimes have meanings, though he was not too sure about such things. Perhaps, he thought, he would do a little research on it at the library today if time permitted. He set the basin down against the wall and began to dress. His roommates had already gone off to somewhere and the hall just outside echoed with voices as the school came to life with activity. As he pulled on his boots, a more distinct voice captured his attention.

"Eleazaar," the voice addressed him.

He quickly turned his head to the sound. In the doorway stood the floor monitor; a fiftyish man with a frequently sour demeanor. He did not seem particularly cross standing there, but then he always appeared a little cross so it was hard to tell.

"Me?" Eleazaar said, confused.

"Of course you;" he growled, "unless there is another Eleazaar around I know not of ... God help us. Report to Father Mannesh's office at once. He wants to see you."

"I will go straight away," Eleazaar replied. "Well, as soon as I ... uh ... as soon as I get my boots on anyway."

The gruff man rolled his eyes and disappeared into the hallway. Sometimes Eleazaar wondered why someone who seemed to dislike young people so much continued to stay here at the school surrounded by them.

Surely there was some other line of work to be done if being here made him feel so miserable. But the bigger question for him at the moment was what Father Mannesh could possibly want with him that was so urgent?

He tried to think of some fool thing he might have done recently, but since his friend Jayden had joined the military and left town for his training, he had not really done anything remotely dangerous or even forbidden that he could think of.

After pulling on his other boot, he rose up to his feet and headed out through the door into the hallway. Abruptly turning left, he walked to the end of the hall and turned right down the long hall that ran along the east side of the dormitory. Half-way down the long hall, an enclosed causeway connected the dormitory with the offices and personal quarters of the provost and the priests who taught at the school. Eleazaar turned and crossed the causeway where a central hall ran through the building to a set of stairs which lay in the center.

He went to the stairs and descended to the level below where his mentor's office was located. At the immediate bottom of the stairs was an intersection of four hallways. He made a left turn off of the stairs and stopped before the second door on his left; a heavy wooden door that was curved at the top and fit snugly under an identically curved stone archway. He knocked gently on the door, listening for a moment before easing it open to peer inside.

"Ah, Eleazaar," Father Mannesh said, looking up from his work desk. "There you are ... come."

Eleazaar felt a little unsure as to what he was in for. He squeezed inside and quietly closed the door behind him. He turned around then and looked at Father Mannesh for a moment, still curious as to whether he was in trouble for something, but he could not sense anything to that effect from his demeanor.

"Come and sit down," Father Mannesh instructed reassuringly, looking up from some parchments on his desk. "We have something to discuss."

"Is there something wrong, father?" Eleazaar probed as he slowly sat down in a chair across from the desk. "Have I offended?"

"Quite the contrary," Father Mannesh replied. "In fact, you have excelled at every task since you arrived here some four years ago. But, like a vapor or a rush of wind, it grows harder to contain you within the mundane tasks these walls have to offer."

"I am not sure I understand, father," Eleazaar responded slowly, surprised and even more uncertain now as to the intent of the meeting.

"Hmmm ... perhaps not," Father Mannesh observed, pausing to consider the proper words to explain what he desired to say. "Eleazaar, you are a top student of our faith; a good scribe, an exemplary healer ... perhaps a bit over-adventurous at times; some had even told me that your combat skills are unsurpassed among your peers. You are very knowledgeable, instinctive and well diversified in the skill sets you have acquired here at seminary. I must say, it is a disservice to you and this order to continue keeping you here."

"But I enjoy my work here. My studies, father," Eleazaar said in protest, a little dismayed. "St. Gustav is my home ... life; it is all that I know. I cannot even imagine being anywhere else."

"I can appreciate that," Father Mannesh empathized. "I have enjoyed teaching you, enjoyed watching the man emerge from the boy we found in that garden nearly four years ago ... but one *needs* new experiences to continue to grow ... to become all of the things they are meant to be. The things that you must now learn are those which I cannot possibly teach you. The things you need now are those which you could never learn from within these walls and the tomes we study here."

"What then would you have me do, father?" Eleazaar asked, somewhat perplexed but opening up to his mentor's line of logic. "Do you want me to say that I am afraid of what lies out there? Well, I am."

"You have every right to be," Father Mannesh conceded. "Among all of your fellow students here, you probably know far more about what awaits out there; you have seen and carried the weight of more than any child should have to. Your fear only makes you human, Eleazaar. That is precisely why I am sending you now on an errand of great importance."

"Errand?" Eleazaar asked, caught off guard.

"A sugar-coated way of putting it, perhaps," Father Mannesh replied thoughtfully. "There has been a series of unexplained disappearances in a nearby town for some weeks now: Luitgarde, to the far southeast of us. As you already know, the order is short-handed at the moment because of the plague. We have nonetheless agreed to assist the town with their peculiar problem."

"And you want to send *me*, father?" Eleazaar said, completely shocked. "Surely there are others far more qualified for such a thing. I do not even graduate for a few months."

"Yes, there probably are;" Father Mannesh agreed, "but I think you are ready. Even if you are not ready, our options are very limited, I am afraid. You, Eleazaar, certainly possess the appropriate knowledge and intuition for this task, and right now we need you to fulfill the promise of your potential. Thus, I have decided to graduate you early."

"I do not know what to say exactly," Eleazaar said. "I *am* truly grateful for your confidence, father. I will try to serve the order well, though I know not for certain what you ask of me."

"*That* is a very good question and unfortunately one not so easily answered," Father Mannesh said. "What we do know, beyond what I have already told you, is that there is a deep wooded area that has been identified as the probable source of these disappearances and some unusual snake activity?"

"Unusual?" Eleazaar inquired. "In what way, father?"

"*That* is really the heart of the issue, *young cleric*," Father Mannesh said.

"The rangers hired by the town cannot identify what they have found. So, I am sending you to join a team to find the problem and fix it. You are to go to the town hall here in Warfall and contact Manuel Yost. He is a mercenary working for the town guard and has agreed to assemble a volunteer group for this task. He will fill you in as to what will be expected of you."

Eleazaar released a sigh and arose slowly from his chair. His head was spinning with doubts and uncertainty and, doubts about his uncertainty. He felt very confused. It was one thing to have great knowledge and another to put it in practice when mistakes could cost you your life and the lives of others. He offered his mentor a respectful, if trepidatious bow of his head and turned away, walking to the door and pulling it open.

"Eleazaar?" Father Mannesh called to him.

Eleazaar stopped and turned back around to him there in the doorway. His face looked troubled and he felt so heavy and slow at that moment. The weight of the world had suddenly seemed to just plop squarely upon his shoulders. He knew that he was gifted and he was pretty sure he knew what he was capable of, but the anxiety of finally doing it was overwhelming him at that very moment.

"I know that your young eyes saw much war and suffering in your homeland," Father Mannesh began, encouraging him, "that it is easy to hide within these walls from the terrors of the world. But, I also know that you will be a great cleric one day."

"I will be that which God wills, father;" Eleazaar replied, somewhat distant, "nothing more."

With that, Eleazaar turned away again and walked out into the hallway, pulling the door shut behind him. He stopped there and took a breath. He was in it good alright, just not in the way he had imagined. Anything worth doing was worth doing well, so he resolved himself to be confident in what he had learned here and to go forward boldly. How he would manage that was something he would have to figure out as he went.

Father Mannesh sat there behind his desk for a moment with his hands folded before him on his desk. He truly felt like he could have graduated him a year early; the kid was that good in comparison to his peers and even many of those he had already graduated. Still, he felt he had a personal stake in the boy, like a real father. He believed in the boy but worried too. If only he could find a way to tilt the odds a bit in the young man's favor.

Eleazaar turned to his left and walked down the hall to the foyer at the end and the heavy, iron reinforced doors that led outside. Pulling them open, he stepped out into the morning sun and descended the grand stone steps of the school entrance to the street below. He turned to the west and headed up the street, walking for three blocks before crossing over to the town government building and jail.

The single entry door to the building appeared unimposing from the outside, but it was as thick as an outer door of a castle and had a portcullis inside that could be lowered to seal the building in case of an attack on the facility or some other emergency. The building itself was two stories high with a secure sub-level below where prisoners were housed. Inside the front entrance, a protective wall with arched windows separated the clerical staff from those who entered while allowing them to engage in official business. Eleazaar entered and approached a female clerk at one of the service windows.

"Can I help you?" the clerk inquired.

"I was sent by the church to find Manuel Yost?" Eleazaar said. "I am to meet with him."

"Oh, yes," the clerk recalled. "Manny said the church was sending someone over. He is down in the detention level. Just go down the hall, take your first left and then the second right."

"First left, second right," Eleazaar repeated back to her. "Thank you." "Oh! I almost forgot," the clerk added excitedly. "He left this parchment for me to give you when you arrived; some kind of background on your assignment."

"Great," Eleazaar replied. "Again, my thanks."

"We aim to serve here," the clerk returned pleasantly.

He walked into the open corridor to his right until he reached an intersecting corridor. Turning down the left wing, he passed the closed door of a room to his right and then came upon a corridor branching off to his right. He had rarely ever been inside the building before, but it seemed so dull and bland inside. The church, of course, had art of all types and sacred symbols everywhere. Perhaps it was as it should be, he thought.

Government's mission should be the effective and efficient service of its duties, not admiring its status like the aristocracy.

As he turned down the corridor to the right, a single, secure iron door guarded the way to the detention level below, monitored by two armed guards. As he approached, the guards stopped him and checked his person for weapons or other prohibited items. Finding none, one of them inquired as to his purpose for being there.

"Alright, you are clean," the guard acknowledged. "State your business."

"Manuel Yost," Eleazaar said.

"So you are the one the church was sending over, eh?" the guard asked.

"Yes," Eleazaar replied.

"Right then," the guard noted as he unlatched and opened the heavy door. "Check in with the clerk down below."

The flight of stairs beyond the door descended until it reached the entry to a room on the right. Inside, he could see a thin man with a scarred face sitting at a worn wooden table. The room was a gloomy dull gray and lit by torches on the walls all around the room. Behind the man was a heavy iron door with a barred window that he figured led into the detention area.

The man looked up at him as Eleazaar approached.

"I am here to see Manuel Yost," Eleazaar announced.

The clerk did not respond right away. He looked the young cleric up and down for a moment, and then he slowly began to rise from his chair.

"Scraping the bottom of the barrel, are they?" the clerk questioned with touch of scorn. "Sending boys to do the work of men?"

"I have been adequately trained," Eleazaar returned, trying not to take offense.

"I am sure," the clerk replied. "Follow me. He is expecting you."

The clerk led Eleazaar to the iron door and took a ring of keys off of his belt. The metallic clank of the key turning in the lock echoed down the corridor beyond. The clerk pulled open the heavy door, which whined painfully, and Eleazaar stepped into the cell block. The clerk closed the door behind him, locked it once again and reattached the key ring onto his belt.

Near the opposite end of the cell block, he could see two men standing at one of the cells. As he walked toward them, one of the men turned and walked past him to leave the cell block. He said nothing as he passed, so he assumed the man was not Yost. As he approached the other, the man slammed the cell door shut as he argued with someone inside.

"Everybody is innocent, hack," he heard the man say. "Save it for the Master of Laws."

"Manuel Yost, I presume?" Eleazaar inquired after taking a deep breath. "I am Eleazaar. The church sent me."

"You are just a boy," Yost noted in a tone that was less than flattering. "I ... am getting a lot of that lately," Eleazaar returned, becoming annoyed. "You were expecting an old bishop in a fancy headdress perhaps?"

"Mmm ... you got some onions," Yost replied. "I will give you that, but I have no time to wet-nurse some k ..."

"Why is *she* here?" Eleazaar cut him off, realizing that the person in the cell was the beggar he had met the day before.

"What?" Yost asked, at first confused. "You mean that dirty, thieving little hack?"

"I mean that woman in rags ... yes," Eleazaar affirmed with a corrective tone in his voice.

"She stole from a merchant in town and we brought her in," Yost explained.

"And I assume you retrieved this item from her that she allegedly stole?" Eleazaar probed.

"Nothing of the sort, he did!" the beggar Grunda retorted.

"Shut up you!" Yost yelled back at her before attempting to scold the boy for interfering in official matters. "And as for you, I don't see that this is any of your business, first off."

"It is absolutely my business, sir," Eleazaar replied confidently. "I know this woman. I dropped money only yesterday and she brought this to my attention and returned it to me."

"Listen boy," Yost snarled. "I do not care what she did or did not do yesterday. It is *my* job to enforce the law. You stick to whatever it is you do and leave the law to me."

"On the contrary," Eleazaar countered; a wry, gratifying smile emerging on his face. "Section 4, article 2c of the criminal code states clearly that no one may be detained for non-violent offenses without the possession of physical evidence associated with or first-hand witness account of actions pertaining to a violation of non-violent criminal statutes. Someone did then see her physically take the item, I assume?"

"They saw enough," Yost said defensively.

"Could you define *enough*, as it relates to the aforementioned statutes?" Eleazaar continued smartly.

Yost pursed his lips, displeased. He was not used to being challenged by anyone and he did not like it at all, particularly when they were technically correct. Grunda, who had been scrunched up as she sat on the cot inside the cell, released her legs and sat up straight, smiling at last.

"She ran from us when we went to question her," Yost added, desperately grasping for a tenable position.

"Men with weapons tend to have that effect on the weak and unarmed," Eleazaar again countered him.

"Alright," Yost relented through his teeth, agitated. "Are *you* gonna vouch for her then? *You* gonna take responsibility if I release her to you?"

"Yes," Eleazaar replied. "That I will."

"Fine," Yost said, relenting bitterly. "She ... is you're problem now."

"Fine," Eleazaar agreed, undeterred.

"Come on," Yost grumbled to Grunda as he took the keys off his belt and unlocked the cell. "Out with you."

Grunda did not have to be told twice. She jumped up, but treaded carefully as she stepped out of the cell past a scowling Yost. He closed the cell again behind her and turned to the young cleric again.

"Not a good way to start off kid," Yost said.

"I will take that under advisement," Eleazaar returned, unwavering.

"Be at the armorer's at first light tomorrow," Yost then said, moving on. "We will be meeting there before we leave for Luitgarde and ... try to be less of a pain in the ass, if you can.

"I will be there," Eleazaar affirmed, "bright and early."

Yost stared at him for a moment, but Eleazaar did not back down. Maybe he was a boy and maybe he was a little scared about going out into the real world, but when he had to or felt that he was right about something, he was not scared to stand his ground with anything or anyone. It was just something one had to do. He grabbed a hold of Grunda's shoulder and turned away with her, walking back to the iron door leading out of the cell area of the detention block.

As they approached, the guard who had returned there earlier pulled open the iron door. It whined as it swung open and Eleazaar stepped through followed by Grunda. The detention clerk and the guard just glared at them as they walked past. He led her to the table and turned to the clerk who just stood there staring.

"Her walking papers?" Eleazaar requested with a raised eyebrow. "Please?"

Yost appeared in the doorway of the cell block just then. The clerk turned to look at him and Yost nodded, confirming he was to grant the request. Reluctantly, the clerk walked across the room to a rack with small wooden shelves and retrieved two sheets of parchment.

Returning to the table, he sat down and began to scribble away on both of them with a quill pen. When he had finished, he shoved the parchments across the table to Eleazaar. The clerk slapped the pen down against the table with his hand and stood up, stepping back behind the chair with scowl upon his face.

Grunda wisely remained silent all the while, ever mindful that these seemingly unscrupulous men might use any excuse to keep her from leaving the detention block. Eleazaar looked over at Yost and then across the table at the dour clerk, but avoided making extended eye contact with them. They were clearly trying to intimidate them, which he thought was wholly unnecessary and made them into little more than thugs.

He skimmed over the words on the parchment and signed the release. After Grunda, who was largely illiterate, had made her mark, he eased one of the copies across the table. Rolling the other copy up and clamping it firmly in his hand, he turned sharply with Grunda and headed for the door to the stairs that would take them back up to ground level.

No one said anything as they walked briskly away and Eleazaar was quite relieved. He had surprised himself a little, being so bold under the circumstances. It was not a behavior from him that he was accustomed to and was not something he was sure he wanted to or *should* make a habit of. All that aside, he was pretty proud of what he had done nonetheless.

He ascended the stairs with Grunda to the secure iron door leading out of the detention area. Knocking on it to get the guard's attention, he waited patiently until the guard opened the viewing slit. He held up the parchment for the guard to see.

"Pass it through," the guard advised him.

He pushed the parchment through the slit in the door and waited. After a moment, the sound of the tumblers in the door lock clanked and echoed down the stairwell. With a high pitched creak, the door swung open as the guards let them pass. The guard handed the parchment back to Eleazaar as he stepped through the doorway and acknowledged Grunda.

"Looks like it is your lucky day, miss," he offered.
"Jus' a wee cock-up love," Grunda replied as Eleazaar hurried her on. "Right," the guard returned, seemingly indifferent as he turned and shut the door again behind them.

They continued walking briskly down the hall and then turned left into the main corridor. Eager to be back outside again, the walk seemed longer to Eleazaar in leaving than it did upon entering. All the way his heart was racing and he felt short of breath.

"Are we to leg it then?" Grunda asked, unsure why he seemed so anxious in leaving. "Went rather tickety-boo, me thoughts."
"Colander's law," Eleazaar replied sharply, not slowing.
"Colander?" Grunda asked. "Is that the magistrate or something?"
"Far worse," Eleazaar explained.
"It is the *unwritten* law that says anything bad that can happen, will. I will feel much better once we are outside."

They turned the corner to the right which led them back to the entrance area. Eleazaar stopped once again at the window to show the clerk the parchment he had brought up from the detention level. The clerk took the parchment and scribbled a record of the document into a registry book.

"You have been recorded, your grace," she noted respectfully. "May you be blessed," Eleazaar responded humbly.

Eleazaar turned around and went to the door straight away. He opened it for Grunda and urgently ushered her through, then followed her likewise. Once outside at last, he shut the door behind them and breathed out in a heavy sigh of relief.

"Yous alright, love?" Grunda asked, looking curious at him as he seemed quite pale.

"I am now, I think," Eleazaar replied, taking in a deep, cleansing breath. "Next order of business ... let us be on our way then."

He walked away from the government building, crossing the street where he turned left heading west once again. Grunda scurried right after him, not at all certain of what she was to do next or if something was expected of her. She was certainly grateful to be free again, of course, but had not even considered what might come next. Eleazaar stopped abruptly in front of her and turned to face her.

"You know, I just stuck my neck out for you," he reminded her. "So what in grace is your name, anyway?"

"Grunda, love." she replied.

"Grunda ... no clan, of course," he said aloud to himself.

"Once had a clan I did," Grunda explained, "But, they rans me off ... the lot of them; says I was bewitched."

"Bewitched?" Eleazaar asked with surprise. "They still do that? Really? In what way?"

"I was but a wee lass upon them days," Grunda reflected. "Not so oddly from the other wee ones methinks. Just there was times when I was emotioned and all; odd things seemed to happen a wee bit."

"Odd things?" Eleazaar probed further. "Such as ... what?"

Grunda was hesitant to reveal too much. Though she really liked talking ... a lot actually, she learned a long time ago that it was sometimes better to keep her mouth shut and not reveal too much. Those "odd things" never seemed to be received well by others and gratitude aside, she was not too sure if she wanted to risk the scorn of her only friend just yet. It was a fearful juxtaposition, but she did feel he was owed some kind of explanation.

"Not meanin' to skive an all," she said at last. "Just wouldnae want-yas to think me a right barmy."

"Well, I have surprised you twice already," Eleazaar said, encouraging her. "There is a good chance I will do it again. Come on now. Out with it."

"Alrights," Grunda humphed begrudgingly. "Me moves things without touchin' them sometimes ... and other things too."

"Oh ... OH ... I see," Eleazaar remarked with surprise. "That *would* probably tend to frighten others, I think. So how many people around these parts know about these ... *things* you can do?"

"Not many me thinks, love," Grunda replied with a shrug. "Real careful to hides it me is."

"Well, that much is good, at least. Smart," Eleazaar said. "People do get very put off by things they do not understand ... including that, certainly. It is called telekinesis. I have never actually seen it before, but I have read accounts of it in the great library. It would be best, for the immediate future, to keep that carefully away I think ... just for now at least. I will need time to understand this gift of yours a little before I can help you. So now tell me, why *did* you steal from that merchant?"

"Dinnea know whats you mean." Grunda dodged, toeing the ground in front of her.

"Grunda," Eleazaar returned in a critical tone of voice.

"Alrights!" Grunda quickly relented, unable to contain the lie any longer. "The bloody prat was mean to me ... so I went and took somethin' I did."

"That is better," Eleazaar then said, relieved at her choice to be forthcoming. "So then, we will keep that just to ourselves as well ... *this* time. But, I will not tolerate any such behavior from now on. Am I being clearly put?"

"Yes, love," Grunda replied, subdued.

"Now, what did you do with this item you took?" Eleazaar inquired of her.

"See, me heard the guards a comin'," she said, gesturing with her hands, "so me hides it up on the roof."

"Now, how in the relic of Sardif did you ...," he began before putting the pieces together in his head, "no no, do not tell me. One of those little things you can do?"

"Yes, love," she acknowledged.

"Mmmmm ... I think I get the idea now," Eleazaar said, noting his affirmation.

Nodding his head and succumbing to the acceptance of this bizarre revelation, he turned away again and headed back up the street to the west. Again, Grunda scurried behind him, trying to keep up with her short little legs and strides. She had not really ventured to the west end much, so she was a little confused as to where they were going now.

"So where is we off'ta now, love?" Grunda queried.
"I am taking you to the bath house and I am paying to have you cleaned up," he informed her. "You are filthy dirty and ... not to be mean ... but you smell rather unpleasantly."
"Oh how posh," she replied, thrilled by the idea. "Yous be just the mole's bollocks, you be."
"I am the mole's what?" Eleazaar said, humored.
"Just means yous really ace, love," Grunda explained. "We dwarves dinnae bathe so much, you know. Too fancy for the lot of us, methinks."
"I ... kind of gathered that, actually," Eleazaar said with a touch of sarcasm.
"You are not exactly the first dwarf I have ever met. I know quite a few, actually."
"And you know what else?" Grunda said.
"What is that?" Eleazaar replied.
"Me knows you was a good person ... first time ah saw you, me did," Grunda said as they walked on.
"And how is that, pray tell?" Eleazaar asked, hardly daring to imagine what her answer would be.
"You had a glow all about yous y'did," she said, "a glowin' white you was."
"It was probably just sweat in your eyes and the bright sun," Eleazaar posited, shaking his head.
"Oh no, no," Grunda said. Me sees all kinds a' glows about people sometimes, when ah puts me mind to it. Some be not so bright and all, like that mean old guard. Ugly red, that be what he was."

"Interesting," he pondered aloud. "Well, you are just full of surprises then, are you not?"

"I can do other things too," Grunda said.

"And something tells me you are going to tell me all about each and every one of them," he said with a roll of his eyes.

"Well," she continued unabated. "Sometimes I can do other things, but not unless I have to ... you knows ... scares meself sometimes ah does."

"Yep, going to talk the whole way." he said aloud to himself, shaking his head. "Nice."

Chapter Four

ALONG COMES A WOMAN

Eleazaar escorted Grunda over to the bath house, the Hitzig Himmel baths, and turned her over to the attendants. They were less than thrilled to see to her needs, but they were respectful nevertheless. He bade her farewell and promised to return to take her to the seminary shelter after visiting a trinket shop down the street. He was infatuated with unusual things and never missed an opportunity to drop in to see if anything new and interesting had arrived.

The bath house had both community and private baths available, but the staff was gracious in offering Grunda an upgrade to a private one to bathe in. In truth, they were more concerned with the potential chaos and panic a little naked bearded woman might cause if she entered one of the public baths. In particular, one that was as grubby and dirty as this little dwarf.

Grunda could have cared less though and was giddy at the sight of bubbles; perhaps the first she had ever seen in such abundance. Everything to her was just posh from then on. Eleazaar meanwhile, had her clothes brought to him by the staff.

They smelled horrible and he cringed at the thought of even touching them, but he had expected the staff to do so and he could hardly refuse after what he was subjecting them to. He then left and promptly looked for the nearest disposal point to be rid of the stinking rags. After successfully disposing of them, he scuttled up the street where he popped in through the doorway of a small shop.

"Anything good come in for me?" he asked the shopkeeper with a boyish and hopeful excitement.

"Ah, Eleazaar," the shopkeeper said, looking up. "I have not seen you in a week. The father must be working you extra hard ... or perhaps you are in trouble again, maybe?"

"It is the workload, I can assure you," Eleazaar replied, smiling. "I have not been in trouble even once since Jay left town."

"Good," the shopkeeper said, smiling. "It has been a rather slow week here anyway, so you have not missed anything important. There has been nothing special, to speak of."

"Nothing at all?" Eleazaar asked, quite disappointed.

"Well, as I recall there is a set of loaded dice," the shopkeeper said.

"Well no, I do not gamble and I certainly would not cheat," Eleazaar said with a sigh. "Is that all?"

"Let me see," the shopkeeper pondered for a moment as he looked around behind the counter. "There were some artfully painted, baked clay sling bullets ... oh and a fellow gave me a handful of corn he said was magical or whatnot. It is supposed to make reindeer fly or something silly like that."

"Reindeer?" Eleazaar said with surprise. "That would be pretty useless. There is not a reindeer for a thousand Li probably, at least. What in the world would you do with flying reindeer?"

"I have no idea," the shopkeeper said. "He seemed pretty downtrodden, so I gave him something for them to be nice. Like I said there has been nothing special come in."

"Beans;" Eleazaar lamented, "maybe next week then?"

"Hard to say, kid," the shopkeeper said. "Keep checking when you are around."

"Always, Mr. Doudlebager," Eleazaar replied as he turned back to the shop's open door to leave.

"Oh, and let me know when your buddy is back in town," the shopkeeper called after him as he left, before finishing under his breath. "I will be sure to take a vacation; a nice long trip somewhere … far, far away"

Over on the other side of town, Jayden, a young man wearing the insignia and leather armor of the provincial army's light infantry, strode up the main street with a swagger. He distracted a shopkeeper at the market and stole an apple behind his back before walking on with a satisfied smile as he took a bite. Life was good, he thought, and he was living it. As two girls walked together across the street towards him, he puffed up his chest and got ready to deliver one of his characteristically unimaginative icebreakers to them.

"Hello, ladies." he said, beaming in his own self admiration "Yeah, I just got back from a terrible battle with giant ogres and I am really lonely. Maybe you could keep a poor, dedicated, freedom-loving soldier company for a while, eh?"

"Come on you two," a deep and rugged voice from behind him said gruffly to the girls.

"Yes father," the girls replied quietly as they shuffled on past the surprised boy.

Jayden turned and looked behind him. Standing on the walkway in front of one of the shops was a robust bearded man in typical farm worker's attire. He stood with narrowed eyes scowling at him until the girls walked past, before he turned at last to follow them.

"Paynim lackwit," Jayden grumbled, flailing his arms in disgust at his misfortune. "Those were a nice pair of chalices too."

He just shook his head as he watched them go; then looked all around. Seeing no alternative targets to pacify his fancy of the moment, he continued on, disappointed but not so much as to dwell much on it. Always living for the moment, Jayden was not given to dwell on much for very long anyway. His attention span was short, his ambition was huge and he was always sure the next great thrill was just around the corner. He thus turned up the street and continued on toward the seminary school which loomed ahead in the distance.

Now, Jayden had a big ego to go with that ambition and it could be rightly said that he thought himself to be pretty special ... special in that the rules did not really apply to him. That often led to him, and often by default Eleazaar, getting into a lot of trouble. He had gone months without causing any trouble while away for training, so of course he was eager to track down his friend and make up for lost time.

Jayden strutted and flirted all the way up the street to the seminary school. He ascended the front steps and entered the main building where the offices were located, looking to find Father Mannesh. The good father, to whom Eleazaar served as a student assistant, would know where Eleazaar most likely was and then he could track him down more quickly. He went to the office straight away and scarcely even knocked before barging in.

"Surprise," Jayden announced upon entering.

"Jayden Ulrick?" Father Mannesh said with an uncertain grin as he looked up from his troubled thoughts. "Has it been four months already?"

"The longest four months of my life," Jayden replied with a big smile. "Four whole months without getting into any trouble."

"A new record I am sure," Father Mannesh chuckled.

Then, at that moment, a wave of clarity overcame Father Mannesh. He had been deeply worried about Eleazaar going on this assignment. Not that he had any reason to worry, but he just had a sense of foreboding about it that he could not quite shake off. The return of Jayden seemed like an omen to him.

The two of them had went off adventuring many times together and, despite the dangers they always put themselves in, they had always come out of it safely together. Perhaps, he thought, teaming up with

Jayden again, the newly trained soldier version, would be a good thing and help the young cleric acclimate to the situation.

"Come sit down," Father Mannesh said.

"I am kind of in a hurry actually," Jayden replied. "I just wanted to track El down before I went home."

"Oh, there will be time enough for that," Father Mannesh said. "I have a very important matter that requires your special skills. It is probably quite dangerous, of course. You interested?"

"Uh ...," Jayden began, surprised at first since he was not used to being offered trouble.

"You and Eleazaar ... just like old times," the father continued to entice. "Well, except you will not be in my office facing punishment this time."

"What did you have in mind?" Jayden asked as he slowly took that seat he was offered; a delightful, almost naughty smile stretching across his face.

After making a few other minor stops, Eleazaar returned to the bath house to retrieve Grunda. Since he had decided to dispose of her dirty clothing, he had stopped and purchased clean clothing for her. He did not have to, of course; it was entirely charity on his part. On the other hand, he could not see putting filthy, stinky rags back on her after having her cleaned up, so he was largely compelled to purchase them. He had guessed on the clothing as to size, but measured her ragged shoes before disposing of them.

He entered the bath house with her new clothes hanging across his arm and a pair of low cut, soft leather boots in his hand. He was not always quite this charitable; he had to take money away from what he had been saving for new armor. Still, he thought if something was worth doing in the first place, it should be done right all the way. For better or worse, Grunda seemingly had become his ward.

"Ah ... there you are," a staffer at the bath house said as he entered. "Will the ... uh ... client be leaving us now?"

"There is a problem?" Eleazaar asked with concern.

"Uh, well ... no." the staffer began in reply. "It is just that ... see, we will have to clean the bath before we can let someone else use it."

"I get you," Eleazaar said, nodding. "You can tell her it is time to dress then. I have fresh clothing for her if you would be so kind to take them to her for me."

"Thank you, of course," the staffer replied, eagerly taking the new clothing from him and walking off to the baths.

After a short while, Grunda emerged from the baths wearing her new clothes and boots. The shirt and breeches were a little loose and she had to tug at her waist to keep the breeches from sliding down as she walked. One of the staff found a small rope she could use as a belt to tie the waist tighter, so that solved the present problem for now.

"Turn around," Eleazar said as she emerged into the room before him.

"You mean like this?" Grunda asked, turning away from him in her confusion.

"Ha ... no I mean all the way around," Eleazaar elaborated more clearly, shaking his head. "Well, you are looking more like a respectable dwarf now. Are they comfortable enough for you?"

"A bit loosey, methinks," Grunda assessed, "but theys quite nice really."

"And the boots?" Eleazaar pressed.

"Oh, thems wonderful, they is; nice and squidgey," Grunda answered, elated. "M'feets havenae felt s'good in ages!"

"Very good," Eleazaar concluded. "Let us be on our way then."

Eleazaar paid the bath house for its services, plus a little extra for the cleanup. He was a little aggrieved at doling out his hard-saved cash, but the values he espoused were not much good if he could not back them up with his own actions. Thus, he decided finally as to how Grunda could make good on his charity. He pulled open the door of the bath house and stepped outside. As Grunda followed, he turned and headed back up the street to the east, toward the seminary school. Grunda scurried to catch up and inquire of what was to happen next.

Considering how good her fortune had been so far, she was almost afraid to ask.

"Wheres we goin now, Mr. Cleric?" she asked.

"Well, we will be stopping at the school's armory for a bit," Eleazaar explained as he continued to walk. "Then, we will go to the shelter and get you set up with a sleeping area."

"Oh," Grunda returned. "Whys we goin to the armory?"

"I am so glad you asked," Eleazaar replied, smiling. "I am going on a potentially dangerous task for the church and uh ... I ... *we* ... could possibly use the services of a thief."

"Pbbbbbt," Grunda fired back, stopping. "Mes' be n'good at fighting, love. Dinnea thinks mes' even been in one before!"

"I would not ask you to fight, Grunda," Eleazaar said, clarifying as he too stopped and looked at her. "You might conceivably have to defend yourself, yes. But, on the outside chance I might need you to steal something, for the common good of course, you can repay me by coming along and helping."

"Well, dinnea rightly know what good little mes could do," Grunda replied, unsure of the prospect, "not havin n'armor or weapon an all."

"Come along," Eleazaar encouraged her as he returned to walking. "I will take care of all of that."

After walking for a while, they arrived back at the school. Eleazaar escorted her to the armory and found the quartermaster. After a short, private discussion with the man, the quartermaster nodded and disappeared for a moment. When he returned, his arms were full of what Grunda could only guess was a stack of strangely shaped and ugly pillows of some sort.

"Is those for me t'sleep on?" she asked innocently.

The quartermaster smiled and nearly chuckled. Eleazaar smiled too and just shook his head. He then took the fluffy pile from the quartermaster's arms and turned to Grunda.

"This, Grunda;" Eleazaar began, "is called padded armor. You wear it for protection."

"Cor ...," Grunda expressed, finally understanding. "So mes *t'wear* that pile of fluffies then?"

"Yes indeed," Eleazaar confirmed. "Now we need to show you how to strap yourself in it properly."

"You sure it goint'a fits me now, love?" Grunda asked, skeptical.

"I am pretty sure it will fit you," Eleazaar said. "I made it for a dwarven friend of mine so we could spar safely. He might be a tad larger than you, but we can always adjust the fit. It just needs to be snug and not too restrictive with regard to your movements."

After adjusting the main body piece for a snug fit, Eleazaar and the quartermaster began fitting the pieces for the legs and arms. The last pieces were pretty easy to secure as there was little difference in the girth of the arms and legs. Once all the pieces had been fitted, they stepped back to get a look at the finished product.

"Well," the quartermaster thought out loud with a chuckle. "I have seen worse ... I doubt she comes back with too many bruises."

"Definitely fluffy," Eleazaar agreed. "Now all you have to do is strap yourself back into it tomorrow morning. That much should be easy since the adjustments are already done for you. How does it feel, Grunda?"

"Oh ... it be comforted an all," Grunda elaborated, "but me feels a bit silly in it."

"You will get used to it," Eleazaar countered. "Now, un-strap yourself again and let us get over to the shelter before it gets any later. Beds can be a hot commodity there some days."

After getting out of it and collecting her pile of *fluffies*, Eleazaar escorted Grunda over to the church's shelter for the needy. After registering her with the priest administrator there, he led her over to her assigned sleeping area for the night. Beds were indeed in short supply on this particular day, so she had to settle for a cushioned sleeping mat in the overflow area.

"Well?" Eleazaar said, verbalizing his thoughts. "It is not much, I am afraid."

"Pbbbbttt!" Grunda said in counter. "Beats a stack'a hay an old rags it does!"

"Very good then," Eleazaar replied, satisfied that she was content with her lot. "You do know where the armorer's shop is on the main street, right?"

"Sure me does." Grunda said. "Been past that ways many a time me has."

"First thing in the morning then," Eleazaar instructed. "Be there to rendezvous with myself and the rest of the team and be ready. We have a good, long trip ahead of us."

"Be there me wills, love." Grunda replied, assuring him. "Dwarf's honor."

Taking his leave of her with a respectful nod, Eleazaar headed back to the school library to do some research on the situation they would be entering into. He was no expert on animal life by any means; certainly not comparable to the rangers already there in Luitgarde searching the area. However, he hoped that maybe they had missed something or that he could find something in the great library which would shed some light on what evidence they had found there.

The great library at St. von Claus was truly worthy of its moniker. There was a massive collection of all kinds of knowledge; something one would expect from a seminary library of the O.I.L., organized in a dizzying expanse of bookshelves in long columns. The high arches, expansive multiple floors and the grand staircases were something to behold as well. It was a big ... big place. The library was the biggest building on campus in fact, and maybe in the whole region short of the provincial castles. No one could be faulted if they found themselves lost within it. Colorful banners draped down from the balconies of the upper floors giving it a majestic feel to those entering.

After a good, long search for books or tomes on reptillia, reptile lore, mythological creatures and sub-tropic forests, Eleazaar buried himself in reading at a long wooden table on the ground floor. Surrounded by stacks of these books, some left open for cross-referencing alongside parchments, he flitted between them all, occasionally taking notes and softly reading aloud to himself.

"Largest normal snake officially recorded was about thirty feet in length ... yikes," he annotated under his breath. "Hmmmm ... *normal* snake. Able to eat larger prey such as Caiman-class reptiles or medium to small mammals, but no human victims known of. Few such snakes are known to exist near human settlements. Giant varieties, possibly of more ancient origin, reported on rare occasion in subterranean areas, estimated to be over fifty feet in length."

He paused for a moment and looked up from his reading. That would be a seriously big snake, though he was skeptical anything so massive could suddenly appear on the mainland here without being seen by anyone. As expansive as Satoochie Forest was, it could not hide a creature which left the veil of its cover to attack. The tracks the rangers were finding were not described as being massive either. Thus, he felt reasonably confident he could rule out any of the truly giant snake varieties.

The history and lore of Satoochie Forest appeared sketchy too. It was dangerous and known to be a killer at times, but because it was so dangerous there was still much that was not known. Thus, he turned his search toward serpent lore. Serpents and snakes were often generalized in the same group, but were really more like close cousins. Unlike the snake, the serpent tended to have fins or even legs, but was more the product of myth than any official science. Ship's logs had recorded sea serpents for centuries and adventurer's had reported occasioning land or subterranean varieties in remote areas, but no physical evidence had ever been brought forth and studied. Thus, serpents remained mostly confined to legend.

That did not mean that serpents were the product of imagination by any means. They could be a rare species or ones which breed slowly, which would account for their lack of frequent observation. The best accounts of such creatures came from drawings or glyphs left behind by ancient peoples.

"The people of the Isle of Otsland would, as a spring ritual, pound the ground with staves until the serpent arose from the ground," Eleazaar read aloud with fascination. "The behavior of the serpent upon its rise was said to tell them how much frost was left in the season; interesting. Glyphs on an ancient, buried temple found in Atacama in the deep southern continent also told of rituals where the blood of the serpent was ingested. The ingesting was supposed to cause the participants to assume the traits of the serpent and pictographs showed people in various stages of transformation from human to serpent-like humanoid states. Thus, the process has been termed Ritual Polymorph by lorists. Wow, that is crazy."

Indeed, he could not imagine why anyone would want to do such a thing; not that anyone ever really had. Lore was a funny thing when trying to separate fiction from fact. One just could not really know for certain because no one was around when these ancient peoples lived and created these stories. The elves were a long-lived race, of course, but it was a big world. They knew a lot about their own ancients but were not so curious and driven to adventure and to seek obscure knowledge quite like humans were. The dwarves and similar races had ancient roots as well, but race relations and knowledge sharing was more of a product of the modern age.

Taking a break from snakes and serpents for the moment, he opened a tome entitled, "*The Unusual Properties of Psionics.*" He had never had more than a passing interest in telekenetics and other mentally manifested powers before, but then he had never met someone who apparently had possessed such abilities either. There was very little to find in the great library concerning the phenomena, outside of references in stories. Many of those were in relation to horrific creatures who seemed to have such terrifying versions of those abilities, not so much the sort affecting the common humanoid races.

He read the lone academic tome in earnest, eager to know as much as he could and hopeful to further help Grunda manage or at least better understand her abilities ... whatever those abilities turned out to be. Then he cross-referenced a parchment detailing an encounter with a human who had purportedly wielded such bizarre powers. Setting it aside after a few moments, he looked off in thought before his eyes rolled down again to the tome in front of him. As his finger traced along a paragraph therein, he read aloud to himself.

"Unlike the mage who captures and molds the energies of the world around them," he read, "or the clerical channeller who divines the external power of their god in the natural world through them, these individuals seem to draw upon inner energies that manifest in unusual and remarkable, if unpredictable ways."

Just then, a shadow cast down upon the table in front of him as a figure walked up to where he was sitting. Eleazaar looked up slowly where his eyes met a pair of breasts snugly squeezed into a low-cut, buttoned tunic. A bit caught off guard at that moment, he quickly looked up from them to find they were attached to a slender young woman with big, brown eyes. The woman stood before him in studded leather armor, with a brown cloak cast over her shoulders and a green hood upon her head. She pulled back her hood and shook loose long, wavy dark brown hair. Eleazaar felt suddenly awkward and his mouth dropped open involuntarily.

"You must be Eleazaar?" The young woman inquired. "I was told that I would find you here."
"Awa ... ukummm," Eleazaar began, nervously clearing his throat. "Who is asking?"
"I am Kalise," the woman said, curious at his demeanor but extending a friendly hand in a formal greeting nonetheless, "The animal specialist assigned to the Luitgarde team?"
"Right ... of course you are," Eleazaar replied as he struggled to recover himself. "You are a druid."
"Nice to meet you too," Kalise noted with a raised eyebrow and sarcastic edge to her tone, pulling her hand slowly back. "You have a copy of the ranger's report ... correct?"
"Yeah ... yes," Eleazaar replied as he fiddled through all the materials on the table before him and scooped it up in his hands. "I uh ... I got it right here."

An awkward silence immediately followed as Eleazaar held the ranger's report in his hands and just sat there staring at her. She stood there before him, expecting him to hand it to her, which he did not. Thus, she took it upon herself to break the stalemate.

"Can I have a look at it? She asked him finally, a little annoyed but still withholding any judgment of him just yet."

"Yes ... yes of course," Eleazaar responded apologetically, gathering his composure. "Sorry. My mind was just somewhere else when you walked up. I ... I was not trying to be rude. Please sit down."

Kalise looked curiously at him, unsure of what to make of him just yet. She slowly walked around the table and Eleazaar pulled out the chair next to him for her to sit. He handed her the parchment on which the ranger's report was written as she sat down and she looked at him again as she took it.

"Have you discovered anything notable?" She inquired.

"Not really ... no," he said with disappointment. "This is not all that surprising given that the rangers were not so sure of what they had found either. They know the woodlands better than most ... certainly better than I do at least."

"Well, that is why I am here," Kalise said smugly.

"I gathered that," he replied, a little taken aback by her seemingly strong personality before continuing on. "The common theme is snake-*like* indicators in the soil, which are most heavily concentrated in the area near the Satoochie Forest. Most of the reports indicated sizeable three-toed prints as well; perhaps made by a roughly man-sized lizard. I eliminated rooks as a possibility, since they have webbing on their feet which I think would be apparent in their tracks."

"I am sorry ... rooks?" Kalise queried, unfamiliar with the term.

"Oh, uh.... that is just what we called the race of lizard men back home," Eleazaar tried to explain before finishing. "It appears they also lost a ranger in the target area, so it seems to me a good bet that we have a solid search radius."

"Have you tried researching the archives for data on serpents; particularly ancient varieties and supposed mythological accounts?" Kalise subsequently asked him.

"I followed the logical progression there, yes," Eleazaar affirmed. "There is limited useful literature to speak of in the mythical category and nothing really jumped out at me from what else is here at least not in terms of natural species."

"By that, are you inferring the possibility of something *unnatural*?" Kalise probed, perhaps skeptical but more so attempting to quantify the young man. "Perhaps you would suggest a magical phenomena or extra- planar life form?"

"No," Eleazaar responded flatly. "I am merely suggesting that when common explanations have been eliminated, whatever uncommon possibilities are left must be considered feasible."

"How very academic of you," Kalise observed smartly, but with a smile. "I suppose anything is theoretically possible, however unlikely they may be. You might also consider that an entirely new species may have been encountered, or it is an obscure and invasive life form that has entered the ecosystem from somewhere else. It would have been most helpful if they could have retrieved a bio for us; a skin tissue or scale sample."

"Under normal circumstances, I think they would have," Eleazaar said. "That is why I feel like this might be an anomaly."

"You jump to conclusions too quickly, cleric," Kalise advised. Some species rarely leave much biological evidence behind, or only do so seasonally. But, then again, I specialize in animal life."

"I ... never said I had concluded anything;" Eleazaar said in defense, "it was more of a gut hunch, really."

"Well;" Kalise concluded firmly, "let us leave the animal kingdom to me from now on and you ... you try and opine about your own area of expertise, okay?"

"Sure," Eleazaar replied, a bit disappointed.

He did his best to try and not show any hurt feelings because of her. He loved to research new and different things and he thought he was pretty good at it. His grades at the school, at least, and the feedback from his instructors had always indicated that he was very good when it came to research. He forced a smile and did his best to assist her, despite her opinion of his analysis.

What he could not seem to do well was figure her out, in the sense as to what kind of person she was. He tried not to look at her too much because it made him feel anxious and uncomfortable. It was not because he thought she was mean or terribly unpleasant, but he found her very distracting. It was like her presence, so near to him, had made his brain inexplicably short out. Now, Eleazaar had seen plenty of females while attending seminary. Being friends with Jayden made that unavoidable as he was always flirting and putting on a display for them. But, this female was magnetic, pretty, and utterly confusing to him. He was attracted to her and it was invading the fortified sanctuary of his thoughts. He tried to block it out and focus on the literature that lay before him … total fail. Every time he looked at her it started again, so he tried not looking at her … epic fail.

"Why do girls have to be so confusing," he thought distressingly to himself. "*WHY* am I talking to myself about *THIS*?"

It was not just this particular female so much. Girls were all pretty confusing to him. They were nearly the only thing he had much difficulty understanding. He tried to calm himself and find a quiet place in his mind. She had an ego, which was fine since she was obviously a confident person. He did not need special intuitive skills to know she was not exactly as she seemed; rarely was anyone who they seemed to be at first meeting them.

Oddly, he thought he sensed pain for a brief moment; emotional pain or baggage as some might call it. He had no idea why he thought that he sensed such a thing. It was a sensation that was new to him. It was something that emanated from deeper within her that did not show clearly in her outer demeanor. The feeling soon passed though and he felt a sense of relief, like he could finally focus a little more effectively. She *was* a drastic improvement over that thug Yost in every way. He hoped the others would be more like her. Then again, he thought, if they were all like her, he might be confused the whole time and be utterly useless to the group.

"Ugh ..." he lamented quietly to himself.

Chapter Five

CHOICES

Eleazaar arose just before the dawn to make his preparations for his trip into the wild unknown of Satoochie Forest. He was eclectic in his choices and thorough when it came to readiness and survival; anything he imagined he could conceivably need and be able to carry, he found a pouch or pack to put it in. Father Mannesh impressed upon him early as a student that those who prepare the best often survive the longest and, he took it to heart.

He carefully secured some vials of potions and a few other chemical mixtures in their protective bag. Vials were delicate things and therefore, needed extra protection, because broken vials were useless and the spilled contents could be dangerous, even more so sometimes if mixed. He also checked the pouches of his belt to make certain they were attached tightly.

To him the only thing worse than over-preparing, was reaching for an item when he needed it, only to find that it had dropped off somewhere or was broken and useless. Finally, he checked the straps on his splint mail armor; he was probably as ready as someone was ever going to get for their first real adventure.

Eleazaar stepped over to the window, pushed open the shutters and looked out across the courtyard below him. The sun was starting to rise by now and was chasing the shadows from the campus grounds. Scanning around the room one final time for anything he might have forgotten or overlooked, he was anxious about what lay ahead for him.

Whether it would be good or bad he could not be certain, but what he did know was that his life was about to change dramatically and probably permanently. Not wanting to start off his first day with the group bound for Luitgarde by being late, he stepped out into the hallway and headed off down the corridor for Father Mannesh's office as the campus began to come to life. His mentor had asked for him to check in before he left to meet up with the group. He assumed that, if for no other reason, the father just wanted to offer him some final encouragement before leaving. Eleazaar hurried down the stairs to the lower level and knocked on the father's door.

"Come," he heard Father Mannesh call from inside the room.

"I was just," Eleazaar began upon entering before realizing someone unexpected was there waiting for him. "Jayden? W-what are *you* doing here?"

"Hey El," Jayden replied with a smirky smile.

"Jayden is also going to be accompanying the team to Luitgarde;" Father Mannesh informed him, "and I thought the two of you could walk over together."

"Wow, I ... Jayden!" Eleazaar exclaimed excitedly, at last getting past the initial shock. "I thought you were still training in Fenzig-Kurg."

"We finished up earlier in the week," Jayden said. "I had just got home to see my parents when I heard about the disappearances and had a little time to spare, so I volunteered to come along."

It was a lie, of course. Father Mannesh was the one who had told him about Luitgarde and asked him to join the team. But, the father did not want Eleazaar to think that he did not have confidence in him either. So, he had instructed Jayden to lie. A lack of confidence would be a bad way to start off the trip and could get you killed in the dangerous world he was bound for.

"Well now," Eleazaar chuckled, "is this not a switch?"

"What?" Jayden asked.

"This is actually a mess that *you* are not dragging me into," Eleazaar said with a grin.

"Hmmmph!" Jayden said, clearly disagreeing. "I never did have to drag you very hard!"

"Whatever," Eleazaar replied dismissively. "Look, we better head on out. We have about ten minutes to meet up with the rest of the group."

"I am packed and ready;" Jayden said, "just lead the way."

"Boys," Father Mannesh interjected quickly as they turned toward the door. "Hold up just a moment. I just want to say this before you leave."

Father Mannesh paused to marshal his thoughts. He was about to act like a real father, but he could not avoid it. Eleazaar's parents were dead and he had mentored him from the beginning a little differently than he had other students because of it; more like a parent might have. Given that similarity, he had come to feel the same kind of concern that a parent would experience in sending their child into what was likely harm's way.

"There are a lot of people who have gone missing down there;" he reminded them, "including a seasoned ranger. This is not going to be some backwoods frolic like when you were kids. You get me?"

"Yes, father," Eleazaar replied solemnly.

"I will try to keep him from hurting himself," Jayden said smartly, earning a stern look from the father before correcting his tone. "I mean yes, Father Mannesh."

Eleazaar gave Jayden a moment of the *squinted eyes of death* too. He then gave the father a quick wave as he and Jayden stepped through the door. Subsequently, the two of them engaged in a sporty shoving match as they entered the hall.

"Hurt myself?" Eleazaar asked with a good shove, agitated. "Really?"

"Ha ha ha ha ha!" Jayden laughed, before feigning seriousness.

"Watch it now! I am a trained fighter of the province!"

"And professional jerk!" Eleazaar said.

"Ouch!" Jayden fired back in dramatic satire. "Wounded by words."

"I hope that army thing works out for you, Jay;" Eleazaar said, critiquing him smartly, "because dramatic performance … totally *not* in your future."

The boys exited from the rear of the building this time to cut across the campus grounds. It was a shorter distance to the armorer's that way and, determined to be on time, they were in a hurry. Thus, they walked along at a quick pace also. Though they had been friends for nearly four years now, they seemed to be heading in different directions since the beginning, which was fast becoming evident as they grew older. Those growing character differences had increasingly created tensions between them.

"How crazy is that … you just showing up here … now?" Eleazaar said, just tossing his thoughts out for conversation. "You might even have time to catch up and graduate."

"I just cannot believe you are still here," Jayden replied critically in response. "I mean … really … how much studying can a person realistically do? It is not natural; even healthy."

"Ha!" Eleazaar countered sarcastically with an edge. "Okay … you want to be like that … the only thing *you* ever *studied* was someone else's notes … and that Mary Fontaine girl!"

Jayden smirked as he reflected about that. Oh yes, Mary Fontaine; the girl who was filling out faster than others her age. Jayden never missed anything when it came to girls. He then made an impression of large breasts with his hands, mimicking his most notable recollection of her. Eleazaar rolled his eyes away and frowned at him.

"There! Right there!" Jayden exclaimed. "*That* is your problem, El; you are a *stiff*!"

"Am not!" Eleazaar said defiantly in response.

"Please," Jayden replied smugly. "It is not natural, chap ... *you* seriously need a girlfriend!"

"Phhhh!" Eleazaar scoffed dismissively. "I do not have any time for ... for that stuff. I am happy ... quite happy with my life here, thank you."

"El?" Jayden asked, determined to make his criticism sink in. "You are b-o-r-i-n-g! *That* is what you are. You sit around ... hiding all day in that stupid library reading books. Life is meant to be lived ... and *felt* and *experienced*, right there on the edge!"

"Mmm Hmm," Eleazaar agreed mockingly. "The edge is a cliff, Jay. You take one wrong step and it is a long way down. No no no, I will go to the edge only when I have to."

"Were you dropped on your head as a baby?" Jayden said, lamenting in disgust with him. "You are like talking to a wall."

"I am not like you Jay," Eleazaar added in reply as he stopped for a moment to emphasize his feelings clearly. I will not live like that; like you. I refuse to be so reckless with my choices. I would rather be boring."

"Phhh! You are hopeless," Jayden said as he began walking on ahead, away from him.

They reached the main street and turning to their left, walked toward the central area of Warfall where many of the town's shops, and specifically the armorer, were located. Eleazaar could not remember ever seeing so little bustle here in this part of town. Then again, he had never really been down here so early in the morning either.

As the armorer's shop came into view, they could see three people standing just outside of it. Eleazaar was pretty sure the one was Kalise ... the flowing hair was a dead giveaway. He figured that Yost would be another, but had no idea who the third person was. He had been told that a sorcerer of some sort was expected to be included as part of the team, so he surmised that must be who the other one was. As they got closer to the three people, he saw that the unidentified person was wearing what he thought was a rather gaudy-looking robe.

He imagined only a magic-user could wear something so blatantly absurd, so he was sure now that it was a sorcerer. What he did not see anywhere was Grunda. He hoped that she would show up as promised, although he knew he would surely go another round with Yost over it. He hoped he would somehow come away from that argument as cleanly as he did the previous one. As they approached the others standing there, Yost turned to them.

"Good ... you are both here," Yost noted approvingly. "Go on in there and get fitted, Jayden. It looks like our cleric here is already ready to go."

"I ... try to be prepared," Eleazaar said with a shrug.

"Good then," Yost said. "You go on in too and have a look around in the shop while you are waiting; maybe see if there is anything else you might need or be able to use."

"Okay ... thanks," Eleazaar replied, amicable. "I will do that."

As he walked to the door of the shop, he took a good look at the chap standing there in the robe. He was a well groomed man in his late forties, if he was guessing, and made no attempt to disguise his snobbishness.

Eleazaar figured he must have a lot of money and was probably a nobleman of some sort. He could not remember anyone poor having their nose so blatantly stuck up in the air, or being so outwardly dour. Then again, he could not imagine anyone who was not filthy rich wearing anything so seemingly impractical on a quest such as this one. Eleazaar just figured 'to *each his own way*' and entered the shop to look around.

Now, this armor and weapons shop was not spectacular, but it was adequate. It was certainly not on the level of the one in Palmus, which this shop sometimes ordered specialty items from. This one had suits of several types of armor displayed on mounts, and arrays of weapons were hung on the walls or lay in display tables in the middle and around the edges of the room. It was the suit of plate mail that always drew him closer though. There it was, mounted elegantly on a stand before him, beckoning him from afar ... longing to be worn.

He stroked his hand across the shining surface of it almost lovingly. As he lifted his hand away, he looked down at his serviceable but rather unremarkable splint mail armor and sighed. He then puffed up his chest as if posing for a painter's heroic portrait, imagining fleetingly how grand he could look if wearing such a fine suit of armor. If only he had a king's ransom to pay for it, he could have it for himself some day. For what it would cost him, he could buy a small house in town.

He put his fingertips up to his forehead in disappointment, internally chastising himself for entertaining such covetous thoughts. It was no use daydreaming about something he lacked the means to possess and such thoughts could poison the mind. So, he turned away from it and occupied his mind with the weapons that were on display instead. There were a few swords of good quality to be found there and he took out his own long sword to compare them against it, but he did not find anything that was such an improvement over what he had that it would warrant him the trouble of switching them out.

While his own interest in those weapons remained but a casual distraction for him, he did need to find one weapon that would be suitable for Grunda to use when she arrived … if she arrived. He was not quite sure if she would show up, or even if she *should* show up. He had some mixed thoughts on whether or not it was a truly a good idea for her to come along. Yes, he was pretty certain she had skills that could be useful to them and yes, it would be an opportunity for her to earn what he had spent on her … money that could have been saved for that fine armor.

He would also feel badly if something happened to her, but after their second chance meeting, he could not shake the feeling that she was supposed to go with him. On the other hand, she had been surviving under dire conditions for probably a long time. In the end, he considered, she might be more likely to survive whatever situations awaited them than anyone else in the group. Yes, he had at last concluded; if she were to show up for the trip then it would be clear that it was God's will.

There were three short swords lying next to their sheaths on a display table before him. He picked each of them up in turn and gave them a good look down the blade from the hilt. As it was a piercing weapon, it was important that the blade was very straight and sharp if it was to be effective against an armored opponent. He did not know if they would encounter one, of course, but he thought it was important regardless.

It was also a very common weapon among those of short stature; mostly because it was lightweight and it was not too awkward for them to wield in combat. Each of the swords appeared to be well crafted and of a roughly equal quality. Looking around at the other possible choices, it seemed to be the best option among those available for her. He could not imagine sending her into danger with a slingshot and bullets or something like that.

Ranged weapons had their benefits, sure, but nothing gave a sense of security like a sword. Besides, it took a lot of skill to use something like a slingshot in a deadly manner and he had no way of foreknowing if she had any such skills. The short sword would just have to do.

In the back room of the shop, the armorer was fitting Jayden into armor for the excursion. With his arms raised high in the air, Jayden watched as the man tugged the straps tight on a suit of banded mail. The suit had a base frame of chain across the shoulders and around the neck with strips of leather woven through it. Sheets of leather hung down from rings with thin bands of overlapped metal attached across horizontally.

It was not great armor, but an improvement on mere studded leather and about the equivalent of Eleazaar's splint mail. In fact, it was quite similar, though the splint mail had vertical strips of riveted metal. Both types would usually keep your organs from being sliced open by a slashing sword at the least. Jayden made an uncomfortable face as the man worked diligently, trying to make it fit, though the suit seemed to be slightly bigger than it would have been if it had been specially made just for him.

"How is that?" the armorer asked with a concerned look.

"No ... still not tight enough," Jayden replied, twisting his upper body around. "It pulls away right ... right there."

"Well, this is as close to your size as I could get," the armorer admitted, pursing his lips with frustration. "I will keep working at it."

Eleazaar took the short sword, sticking it under his arm and he then turned to walk back outside to rejoin the others. He was thinking that it would definitely be better if he was out there when, or if,

Grunda actually showed up. The disdain Yost had displayed for her at the jail was not likely to have changed in less than a day. As he began to walk toward the door, however, something caught his eye that he had apparently overlooked before. There was a small weapon with a crescent-shaped blade and a shiny white handle that lay on a display table against the other wall of the shop.

He went to it straight away, picking it up carefully and looking at it with marveling eyes. He had never seen anything quite like it before. The handle was hard and smooth to the touch, with a glossy finish he thought was very impressive. He was not certain, but he thought the handle could be made from bone.

Looking behind him, there was a curtain hanging down to the floor in a doorway, blocking off the back room of the building where he could hear the voices of Jayden and the armorer. He went to the curtain and pushed through it, taking the unique weapon with him.

"Excuse me?" he said respectfully to the man working on Jayden, holding the item out for him see. "What is this?"

"Oh, *that*?" the armorer replied, looking up and smiling before returning to his work. "That there is called a hand scythe, or, some folks call it a garden sickle. It is the hand-held version of the more traditional scythe used by wheat farmers at harvest … or those just wanting to trim the grass."

"But what do you use *this* for?" Eleazaar pressed on in his query.

"Ha!" the armor chuckled, amused by his interest. "That would be used mostly by nobles for trimming the verge in the gardens. It is probably more ornamental than practical for *your* line of work, young cleric."

"It is a beautiful piece," Eleazaar commended him, still smitten with it.

"The handle is actually carved from donkey bone," the man added, proud of his craft. "I shaped and polished it myself."

"I can see it now," Jayden said, interjecting smartly. "Surrender … or I will trim your garden!"

"Very funny," Eleazaar retorted disapprovingly. "If it is alright, sir, I would endeavor to have it. I am certain that I could find a use for it."

71

The armorer stopped what he was doing and looked up at Eleazaar with surprise. He was getting paid for outfitting the team and, seeing that the kid would not be getting any armor from him, he would surely be getting compensated for it. What items they chose, even if they were impractical, were not really his concern as it were.

"Well ... it is not cheap;" the man began in response, "but you do have a stipend from the town for equipment. If you want to spend it on that ... that is entirely up to you."

"Thank you," Eleazaar said, delighted. "Oh, you would not happen to have some kind of holster or sheath for this which attaches to a belt or something?"

"As a matter of fact there is," the man replied, shaking his head. "It should be down in the cabinet, just below where you found it."

"Great!" Eleazaar replied exuberantly, thrilled with his new oddity.

Eleazaar offered Jayden a smug and thoroughly satisfied grin. Jayden had always made fun of his obsession for the unusual and he was not about to let his friend's belittling ruin the indulgence of his passion. Of course, he was not quite sure himself as to what he would use it for ... cutting herbs for his personal needs perhaps. He just thought it was really cool looking and different. He resigned to figure out the rest later as he swept the curtain aside and left them, re-entering the front of the shop.

"I never dreamed anyone would seriously want to carry it," the armorer said aloud to Jayden as he continued the fitting, puzzled.

"Yep;" Jayden agreed, "he is a weird one."

Eleazaar returned to the display table and knelt down. He pulled open the cabinet doors below and spotted the sheath right away. It was hard to miss, being so oddly shaped to accommodate the grossly curved blade. Nothing else looked even remotely similar to it. He lifted it out and carefully inserted the blade of the hand scythe into it. The sheath, or possibly holster; he was not sure which it really qualified as, fit nicely upon it. That was very important to him if he had any real plans to use it; it would be impractical to carry if it hung awkwardly.

He unlatched his belt and slipped the holster on before securing his belt once again. As he stood up and closed the cabinet doors, he heard loud voices and shouting just outside of the shop. He was pretty sure he knew what that meant. He quickly opened the door and found Yost yelling at Grunda. She had indeed showed up for the trip after all, it seemed.

Of course, Yost had not been forewarned she was coming, so Eleazaar had to intervene quickly before things got ugly. Perhaps it was just the abrasive Yost, or that she was not much of a morning person, but she seemed to be much less willing to play the victim to him today than yesterday. She was wearing the padded armor he had given her, so it was obvious that she had every intention of going along.

"Just get your grubby ass on down the road!" he bellowed at her. "You are not going anywhere with …"

"As a matter of fact;" Eleazaar quickly interceded over him, pulling out a small parchment from his belt, "she *is* coming with us. I have a contract for her services … right here."

Yost turned immediately and glared at him. He really did not like being told what he was going to do by some kid, particularly this one and especially when *he* was in charge. Being in charge and having his commands obeyed was what he was used to and he was averse to changing the way he did things. On the other hand, he was not an ignorant man and could, on occasion, be reasoned with.

"That filthy, little wretch?" he asked, fuming with anger. "I do not care what you have … no; absolutely not!"

"You yourself said she was a thief," Eleazaar countered smoothly. "Anyone else here have that skill set?"

"Ohhhhhhh;" Yost fired back smartly, "so *now* she *is* a thief?"

"I never said she was not a thief," Eleazaar clarified. "It was you who said she was a thief. I merely pointed out that you were holding someone without evidence against the provincial statutes which govern incarceration."

"Manny," Kalise suddenly interjected. "If she has any skills at all, it might be a good idea. A thief could be of some use to us."

"And now you too?" Manny lamented gruffly at her before looking back at Eleazaar. "I really do not like you, cleric."

"Be that as it may;" Eleazaar said firmly in reply, "she *is* my hireling and she *is* coming with us."

Yost breathed out of his nose in a loathing huff. He could imagine a few scenarios where a thief would be useful and had worked with professional thieves on ventures a few times in the past. It was this one that he had a problem with. If she was going to be allowed to come along, he was going to make sure that he set the ground rules.

"Okay, kid;" Yost said at last, relenting begrudgingly through his teeth, "she comes along, but let me be perfectly clear about the rules. If she lags behind or does something stupid, I will leave the both of you behind without a second thought. You got that?"

"A person owns their own conscience, Mr. Yost," Eleazaar replied calmly. "I will leave your conscience to you."

Yost just gave the cleric an icy stare. He was willing to tolerate the kid for now, but that might change if he kept pushing. Adventures into the unknown were dangerous and if the kid got himself in trouble, he just might not be inclined to help him out of it.

The man in the fancy robe, Stanislov Barrister, eased up next to Yost as he stood there glaring at the boy.

"That is what you get with all these damn half-breeds running around these days," Barrister whispered smugly. "Damn monkeys. The whole world is going straight to hell."

Yost glanced up at Barrister briefly as he spoke. Society was changing and he was not real fond of it either. Just then, Jayden emerged through the front door of the armorer's shop. Yost broke off his stare when he saw him and let everyone know it was time to leave for Luitgarde.

"Alright, that is all of us now," Yost said. "Everyone get into the wagon."

The group of them turned and started to shuffle to the step at the rear of the wagon. Eleazaar took his time, lining up at the rear of the group. Jayden stopped to whisper in his ear as he passed him in line, and patted him on the shoulder in mock approval.

"I see you still have a way with people," he whispered sarcastically. "However do you do it?"
"I learned from you, jerk," Eleazaar said softly in retort.

As he looked up, he saw Kalise as she was about to step up into the wagon. She looked back just then and their eyes met. They exchanged a look for a moment. She smiled at him briefly and turned away, climbing into the wagon.

"I sure wish I could figure her out," Eleazaar annotated in his thoughts. "Every time she looks at me … my head starts swimming. It is maddening."

As Grunda walked past him, his train of thought was broken. He quickly grabbed her arm and handed her the short sword he had picked up for her. In the heat of arguing with Yost, he had almost forgotten about it.

"Hey … take this," Eleazaar said. "You will need something to fight with if it comes to that and it should not be too unwieldy for you to use. How is the armor; still fitting ok?"
"Oh, it be comfy enough an' all;" Grunda began to elaborate, "but m'feels like a ruddy *pastry* in it!"
"Ha ha ha!" Elazaar laughed in reply. "Let us just hope that whatever we find out there does not like eating pastry then! It may not

look too flattering, Grunda, or even protect you a whole lot, but it was the best I could do; certainly better than nothing."

"You sure you wants me a comin' wit you, love?" Grunda asked, concerned about the problems her presence might be creating for him. "You keep a stickin' y'neck out on mes accoonts an somebody 'il chop it right off they will ... startin' wit that blimey brute right there."

Grunda pointed right at Yost as she spoke. She did not like feeling guilty for causing problems for those who showed her kindness, even if it was in the process of repaying that kindness. Even Eleazaar had to admit that things did not seem to be starting off well for him. The lack of cohesiveness in the group did concern him, but he was not going to let that show ... or dictate his decisions.

"Do not worry your self about that, Grunda," he said, reassuring her. "I can take care of myself."

"Ah be grateful for y'kindnesses an all;" Grunda replied, "dinnea gets me wrong now, love. Jus it be a coincidental meetin' an I wouldnae wants t'put ya outs for it."

"Listen," Eleazaar said, attempting to relate the personal motivations from his beliefs. "Everything my faith has taught me, Grunda, is that there is no such thing as coincidence. We rarely know the reasons why things happen the way they do or even why we make certain decisions at a certain moment. But, I believe that things all work themselves out in the end and make some sort of sense. To me, that is the meaning of having faith."

"Canna say me gots much faith for anythin' meself;" Grunda reflected, "but *you* sure takes the biscuit, y'do."

"Well, I will take that as a compliment, I guess," Eleazaar chuckled lightly. "Most people believe in something; believing in your self is a good start. We will have to work on that a little. For the moment, however, how about we get on that cart before they decide to leave us here ... hmmmmmm?"

"Aye, love," Grunda said. "If yous insistin'.

"I am," Eleazaar replied. "Get moving."

Eleazaar gestured toward the wagon as he finished and Grunda just shrugged. If he was going to be set on her coming along, then she was going to go. Sometimes a dwarf just had to do what she had to do. She climbed up into the uncovered wagon and took a seat on one of the benches next to Kalise. Eleazaar followed her up and sat down on the opposite side of the wagon, next to Jayden.

Yost, who was going to be riding with the driver on the trip to Luitgarde, looked back over his shoulder from the driver's bench in front and saw that everyone was in the wagon finally. He tapped the driver with the back of his hand to let him know it was time to go. It was going to be a long ride to get there and with clear skies and the air still, it would probably be a hot one too.

Chapter Six

LUITGARDE

The wagon driver took his cue and tugged sharply on the reigns of the horses. The wagon lurched as it slowly started forward on its iron-wrapped wooden wheels, rocking its passengers. The next town they would see on the trip would be Luitgarde, but only after a very long, rough and bumpy ride. The incessant clopping of the horses' hooves was almost hypnotizing after listening to them for awhile. Even for the first thirty minutes of the trip, Eleazaar thought the ride was fairly tolerable, but that was not going to last. He had ridden horses plenty of times wearing armor, but sitting on a hard bench in the back of a wagon was completely different.

As the sun rose higher and higher above them in the still air, the ride got hotter and they all began to sweat, making it increasingly uncomfortable. Eleazaar in particular began to shift his sitting position and noticed each little thump more when the wheels of the wagon ran over small, jagged rocks in the road. There was really very little around them to focus on as a distraction.

Notably, no one in the group was really talking either, which made Eleazaar feel awkward. He was very sociable by nature, at least in his own opinion, and always seemed to be talking to someone if he was not in the library. Then it hit him; that was what he had forgotten. He should have brought a book to occupy him during the ride.

Sometimes it was the most simple things that eluded him and it disturbed him because he was afraid it would happen one day when it actually mattered to someone other than him. It was never a good thing for a young person to feel like they had to be perfect all of the time. It was an impossibility for sure, but he had yet to learn that. Bored and uncomfortable with hours of the same looming ahead still, he tried to initiate some conversation to pass the time.

"I do not believe we have been introduced," Eleazaar said as he stretched his back and looked at the man in the gaudy robe.

Dead silence ensued. The man did not even turn his head, continuing to watch the road ahead of them. No one else said anything either, which aggravated him even more. Thus, he tried again.

"I am Eleazaar;" he began, "a cleric of the St. Gustav Sem …"
"He knows who you are, kid," Yost grumbled as he turned around toward him. "This is Lord Barrister."
"The Evoker!" Eleazaar said excitedly. "I have read about your adventures … in the library."
"Good!" Barrister suddenly and harshly remarked. "Then I expect that you will not mind allowing Manny and I to make the decisions on this trip while reserving your own frivolous thoughts unless or until otherwise solicited!"
"Uh … uh," Eleazaar stammered in response. "I was just trying to introdu …"
"No one cares who you are kid, okay?" Yost scolded him. "This is the real world out here that we are going into. If you can somehow manage to bandage a wound without hurting yourself or anyone else … that would be great. Are we clear now?"
"Yeah, I guess so;" Eleazaar said in a subdued voice, "sure."

There it was: that *hurting yourself* line again. He found that he hated it even more when someone other than Jayden was saying it. His pride nagged at him to tell those pompous jerks, Yost and Barrister that his father was a king and he had seen more of war and atrocity of their "real world" than the whole of the others combined. But, he did not. Tales of a kingdom they had never heard of in a land and time, far away no less, was not going to change the perception anyone had formed of him. If anything, he could see it becoming worse. He had relented to tell Jayden of it once, only to be laughed at and made fun of as a liar. Frankly, he still felt resentment for Jayden over that. He was definitely not going to tempt that here.

Eleazaar quickly realized, however, that he was out of his element and that, at least to a point, Yost was right. While he may have seen many of the horrors of the real world in his childhood, he had not really had many experiences of his own and had to survive or make tough decisions in such a world. He had a lot to prove to others before people who had been in those kinds of situations would begin to respect him. All he had were fanciful stories, nothing more.

It was easy to assume that he knew everything when he lived in the safety of a proverbial *ivory tower* like the seminary school. There was a lot of knowledge to be found there but little risk involved in applying it academically. Perhaps it was that notion that frightened him the most and made him hesitant to leave the seminary; the fear that the knowledge he adored would fail him in the critical, desperate moment that it was needed.

Eleazaar looked up at Jayden who was sitting next to him and staring. Jayden pulled his fingers across his lips and nodded, as if to say "just keep those lips sealed." As always, it seemed he could count on his friend for little in the way of support. He thus resigned himself to the longest and most miserable ride of his life.

The wagon rumbled and bumped its way on down the dirt and rock road as the day continued to grow increasingly hotter. Eleazaar tried repeatedly blocking out the sun which was beginning to feel like it was roasting his brain. He at last dug out a rag from his belongings. He took a quick drink of water from his wineskin and then doused the rag, flopping it above him to cool his head. As the wagon passed a clump of trees to the right of the road about six hours into the ride, Yost had the driver bring them to a stop. Eleazaar looked around but could only see rolling fields of tall grass opposite of the trees. He thought a break from sitting on that hard board would be nice at least, if that was why they were stopping.

"Everybody take ten and stretch," Yost announced, confirming his desperate hope. "There is a nice little creek beyond the trees if anyone is interested, but do not be wandering off. We will be leaving again shortly and I am not waiting around for anyone."

The passengers slowly began to climb down from the back of the cart. Clearly it seemed no one was enjoying the ride much and Eleazaar puzzled as to why they were all not just riding horses there. Surely everyone would have been far more comfortable and would have arrived far less drained by the suns relentless heat. What he was not aware of was that the cart actually had been contracted for a dual purpose; it was not just there to transport them to Luitgarde, but also to carry bodies if the group were to recover any.

Depending on their condition and circumstances of course, the church desired to be able to inspect and evaluate them with local authorities as part of any investigation process without involving any third parties in the matter. Even the driver was not quite what he seemed to be. He had hauled many wagons full of bodies during the plague for the church and knew the best procedures for dealing with contaminated or otherwise potentially hazardous corpses.

"Kalise?" Yost called out as he stepped down from the driver's bench. "Would you do something for me while you are out?"

As she turned and walked toward him, Eleazaar headed into the clump of trees to find that creek. The idea of cool, running water sounded great to him and would probably be more refreshing than the sun-warmed water that was currently filling his wineskin. Unnoticed by him in his urgent quest was Jayden, who was following him into the woods not far behind.

As he emerged from the cover of the trees on the other side, the ground sloped downhill slightly to the creek which passed by not far ahead. He hurried down to it and knelt in the weeds next to the water. With his cupped hand, he scooped up the water to smell it for quality. Certain pollutants or toxic substances could be detected by smell if the person knew what they were doing and had the nose for it.

He could not smell anything that would give him pause, so he brought his hand to his mouth to taste it. As he did so, he heard the distinctive sound of a stream of water hitting the water there in the creek. He looked over to his right and saw Jayden standing on the bank nearby, urinating in the creek. Eleazaar was instantly furious at him and could not believe his friend was so disrespectful, despite how well he knew his penchant for such antics. He was not going to let it just pass either. He jumped up and went right to Jayden, shoving him hard with both hands and knocking him down to the ground in the weeds along the bank.

"Idiot!" Eleazaar angrily scolded him.

"What is wrong with you, mu'dak? Jayden shouted back at him. "You made me piss myself!"

"What, *really*?" Eleazaar said in angry sarcasm. "I mean, the woods is not big enough ... you have to do it in the water?"

"So, what?" Jayden replied smugly, indifferent to the criticism.

"For starters, some people drink that water, you jerk-weed!" Eleazaar continued to blast at him.

"Oooooo ...," Jayden observed, belligerent, "were you attempting to curse at me? Now hear this! I have been sworn at by a cleric!"

That was the last straw for Eleazaar. He had taken enough belittling from Yost and Barrister today; he was not going to take it from Jayden too. He was getting very tired of the endless cleric-bashing in particular.

He clenched his fist and took a rage-filled swing at his friend. Jayden had been looking for a fight though ever since he had gotten back, filled with cockiness from his recent fighter training. He ducked out of the way of the blow and punched Eleazaar in the gut. Then he grabbed the back of his head and kneed him right in the face. Eleazaar staggered back and paused to wipe the blood running from his nose, but Jayden was not done yet. He grabbed the collar of Eleazaar's armor and tried to punch him again.

This time Eleazaar was ready and done playing games with his friend. He batted his fist away to the side while grabbing the arm that held onto him. He twisted Jayden's arm and shoved him back away. Then he launched his foot and punted Jayden right in the onions. Jayden fell straight to the ground coughing. He rolled and moaned there in the weeds, probably thinking there was one more spot he should consider adding armor to.

Satisfied he had made his point and ready to move on, Eleazaar turned and started to walk away but Jayden had not gotten his fill quite yet. He rose, jumping onto Eleazaar's back and the two of them crashed to the ground. There they rolled and punched and wrestled until they heard the sound of someone clearing their throat.

"A-hem," Kalise sounded as she stood not far from them, watching.

Locked in each other's arms there on the ground, they stopped and looked up. Kalise stood there with her arms crossed and holding an empty pail. Yost had asked her to get some water for the horses before they continued on with their trip.

"Are you two lovebirds finished ... or should I just come back later?" She asked them smartly.

"What?" Eleazaar said with surprise, suddenly feeling awkward about the appearance of his relative position with Jayden.

"No ... we are done!" Jayden huffed in reply as he pushed Eleazaar off of him. "Thanks."

Jayden jumped up with a bloodied and foul look upon his face. He looked first at Kalise and then Eleazaar before spitting blood in the grass and stomping off in a snit, back up into the trees. Eleazaar watched him go as he leaned on one knee, and then looked up at Kalise. He was a little embarrassed, but less so after she offered him her hand to help him up to his feet.

"I can not believe him," Eleazaar said, perhaps as much to explan himself as it was anything.

"Forget about it ... I saw," she replied in a comforting way. "I was going to say something, but you took care of it."

"Something like that ... yeah," Eleazaar said, sheepishly. "Jay is a ... he is a little quicker than he used to be."

"Well, it is nice to know you are not some stiff like most of the clerics I have met," Kalise commended him. "You have a mind of your own ... and you really do give the derr'mo about people; about things like virtues. I like that. I thought it was very noble that you took in the dwarf."

"Grunda? Yeah," Eleazaar said. "She is a very interesting character for sure. I try not to judge people too much, unless I wish to be judged by the same standard. You can just never know how we all fit into the grand scheme of things; of life."

"I could not agree more ... Eleazaar," She replied, smiling at him.

"So what happened to all that ... opine about your own specialty ... stuff?" he asked her, trying hard not to blush in the shadow of her attention. "Oh," she nearly laughed, "that still stands for the most part. You are just gaining some credibility with me. I just thought I should, as your holy book would say, extend a *reed of ilum* to you."

"You have read the holy book?" Eleazaar asked, a little surprised though he did not know why.

"Some of it," Kalise revealed. "My mother was ..."

"Come on now, yous two," they heard Grunda call out, interjecting from the edge of the trees. "The carriage'il be leavin' wit out yous!"

"We will be right along shortly," Eleazaar said, waving to her.

Kalise quickly bent over and dipped the bucket in the water. As Eleazaar turned back to her, he saw her bent over in a revealing way and quickly looked away, uncomfortable to look at her, or rather *part* of her, in such a way. When she leaned back up, it seemed he was looking away in a strange, purposeful manner.

"Is something wrong?" Kalise asked him.

"No … no," Eleazaar explained. "I just did not want to be rude while you were … you know …"

"Bent over?" Kalise offered shrewdly, a wry smile emerging upon her face.

"Yeah, that," Eleazaar replied, uncomfortable in talking openly about it.

Kalise giggled at his timidity. He was really blushing now and she thought him to be quite the funny boy. He was not at all like most boys, or most men for that matter. Maybe that was what she liked most about the young cleric. He seemed really smart and concurrently very awkward; it was kind of funny and attractive to her at the same time.

"In all seriousness now," she began, still smiling at him, "you need to try to get along with Manny and that Barrister fellow. I know they are pretty shallow, ugly people, but they will likely need you far more than they realize before this is all over. We are all probably going to need you in the end."

"I am glad you think so," Eleazaar replied graciously, perhaps somewhat relieved that not everyone seemed to think he was useless. "It makes me feel better just to hear it from someone else, so thank you. Are you thinking we will be walking into some kind of serious trouble out there?"

"Ah … I do not know yet;" Kalise said, "but what I do absolutely know is that we should get back to the wagon now and rejoin the others. I think Manny would leave his own mother behind if it came to it."

"Yeah;" Eleazaar agreed enthusiastically, "he probably would."

Kalise gestured toward the road beyond the trees with her hand and Eleazaar turned and walked on ahead. She followed behind him with her pail of water and took the opportunity to look unfettered at *his* rear. She raised her eyebrows and smiled slyly as she hurried to catch up with him.

The two of them emerged from the woods where the others were waiting around the wagon. Kalise flashed Eleazaar a flighty look as she changed direction to take the water to the horses. Eleazaar looked back and away and then again at her. Was she actually flirting with him, or was he imagining it? He had to admit, he was extremely ignorant when it came to girls. Even so, there was no way he was going to consult Jayden on that subject. Maybe it would take him a little longer, but he was going to make understanding girls a priority and resolved to figure it all out himself.

Technically, Kalise was not still a girl; she was a woman. At twenty-one years old, she was four years older than he was. He knew even less about women as it were, but thus far he liked women a whole lot if they were anything like this Kalise. She walked to the front of the wagon and stopped, placing the pail down in front of the horses and stroking the neck of one as she watched Eleazaar climb up into the back of the wagon.

He sat down next to Jayden, but the two of them did not speak. Sometimes it took a while for one or both of them to get over one of their spats. Eleazaar was just glad half of the ride was already over with and he looked forward to getting out of the wagon for good. The wagon continued down the road with only minimal conversation among any of the passengers. It was a good indication to Eleazaar that this was not a cohesive group of people, at least not yet.

Even if everyone did not really like each other, he hoped they would at least try to communicate a little more when they went off into the forest. He feared it was a disaster waiting to happen if they did not find a way to work together. After hours of bumping along in the hot sun, the town of Luitgarde finally appeared in the distance. It grew minute by minute until at last they rolled up to the gate on the southeast side of the town. The driver stopped the wagon and Yost jumped down to talk to the guards who were standing at the closed gate.

"Are you the group from Warfall?" one of the guards asked, looking at the others in the back of the wagon.

"We are," Yost replied. "Nothing has changed?"

"No sir," The guard said as he handed Yost a roster to sign. "Not as far as we have been told anyway. The constable is waiting for you."

Yost handed the signed roster back to the guard. The guard then thumped on the gate with his fist and called to a guard on the other side to remove the locking bar. Once the locking bar had been lifted, the two guards then pushed the doors of the gate open for the wagon to pass through. After the disappearances had continued, the town had kept a roster of everyone entering or leaving the town as a matter of tracking and monitoring people.

If someone never arrived at the next town, or if missing persons coincided with the arrival of any individual or groups, the roster provided evidence for the local authorities to work with. In short, they still had no solid answers and were continuing to grasp at straws, even on the eve of the volunteer group's venture into Satoochie Forest.

As the wagon lurched forward once again, Yost grabbed the metal bar on the side and pulled himself up into it again. Resident activity was low as they rolled into town, as people were not going out unless they had to or really wanted to risk doing it. The people who *were* out-and-about stared at the group as they rolled by them.

"Why they be a starin' like that?" Grunda asked no one in particular as she stared back at them.

"A wagon full of people in armor." Eleazaar speculated indifferently, "they probably know why we are here."

"Me thinks the lot would be chuffed to bits," Grunda said. "Theys had some hard lines an all I guess. Theys behavin' as if theys all just been pinched."

"I suppose they have been," Eleazaar annotated under his breath. "In the worst possible of ways."

It was not long before the wagon rolled up in front of an old brick and mortar building and slowed to a stop. It was the second oldest building in town in fact, next to the St. Vicente church, but had been remodeled and expanded a few times to accommodate the growth of the town through the years. It was getting more use than usual as of late with the tragic events that had been ongoing.

"Alright people; everybody out," Yost declared over his shoulder as he started to climb down from the bench in front. "We will be meeting inside the town hall here with the constable for a briefing."

"A briefing?" Jayden said, trying to be funny. "It sounds like we are going in for a wedgie."

"Could that be some sort'a ruddy snack or somethin'?" Grunda asked, her growling stomach hopeful. "I's rather famished from'a ridin' alls the day."

"Heh heh heh heh … no, Grunda," Eleazaar replied, nearly beside himself at the thought. "A wedgie is *DEFINITELY* not a snack."

Eleazaar had to wipe a tear away because he was so tickled by her ignorance about such a simple but silly thing. Apparently wedgies were not a universal concept. He was pretty certain they would never become a popular food item either. Of course, the idea of what dwarven wedgies might be like was kind of scary, so he thought maybe it was better for everyone if dwarves did not learn about such things and he avoided elaborating on it to her. One by one, each of them dismounted the wagon and slowly headed inside the building. They were stiff from the ride and it showed in the way they walked. Like a bunch of hobbled old men, their strides seemed painful.

Yost pulled open the brass ring door and led them into a large room with walls covered by sheets of pressed and seemingly laminated wood. To the left was a counter where a clerk conducted town business with the locals and in the center of the room was a hallway that led deeper into the heart of the building. Constable Spillman was standing in the hallway when they entered and he immediately came up to greet Yost, who extended his hand to him in a formal manner.

"Mr. Yost, Lord Barrister;" the constable acknowledged them with relief. "I am so glad you are finally here."

"At your service," Yost said as a cordial gesture.

"Constable," Barrister acknowledged likewise.

"The ranger captain is waiting for us back in the conference room," the constable informed them. "If you would kindly follow me, we can get started right away."

"Certainly," Yost said warmly, eager to get things moving along. "Lead the way."

Constable Spillman escorted them down the hall to a door on their right. As he twisted the handle and they subsequently entered the room, they could see a long wooden table surrounded by chairs that had a map sprawled out across the middle of it. Sitting in one of the chairs was the captain of the ranger team and he stood up politely as they entered. He had graying hair and sun-darkened skin, with some scarring evident on his face. Yost recognized who the man was right away.

"Captain Jahko Silger," Yost said approvingly.
"Manny," the captain replied. "How the hell are you?"

Captain Silger reached out and shook Yost's hand in greeting. It seemed the two were well acquainted and apparently he was also acquainted to some degree with Barrister. In fact, they had adventured together back when they were younger.

"You remember Lord Barrister?" Yost asked him.
"I do indeed," the captain said. "How is the quiet life treating you, Stan?"
"The travails of running a chateau rival even that fracas on Pico's Mountain."
"Ha ha ha! the captain chuckled. "I am glad we could offer you a respite then! Come … sit, all of you … please."

The idea of sitting was not the ideal suggestion after the long ride, but at least they were not boiling in the sun this time. They all took seats around the table, but when Grunda sat down, her nose barely cleared the top of the table. Eleazaar just shook his head and turned away. At times it seemed to him that being a dwarf must have a lot of drawbacks.

"I am sure you are up to speed on the summary report we sent to you," the constable said presumptuously. "The captain here does have some additional information to add to that, so I will turn things over to him."

Jahko Silger had been a ranger for nearly thirty years. He had adventured across the land, fought in battles and helped hunt down enemies for hire. The situation at Luitgarde had provided more of a challenge than he had expected but his team had done all they had been contracted to do thus far. He was glad to finally turn over the operations to another team and hopefully see the matter concluded.

"If I can draw your attention to the map for a moment," Captain Silger said as he gestured to the map on the table, "this area here is the zone of particular interest. I sent the rest of my team out to scout for signs of our missing team member yesterday. Now, they did not find him or any evidence suggesting his fate unfortunately, but they did find his markers; small flags he had set up discreetly to mark his path."

"It seems," the ranger captain continued, "quite fortuitously for us, that he was concerned that something might happen to him and wanted to make certain that we could retrace his footsteps should he not return."

"And you are quite certain these markers were placed by your ranger," Barrister asked with concern, "and not some sort of trap set for us ... or to mislead us?"

"Quite sure, Stan," Captain Silger replied confidently. "Many of the rangers do this when they are operating alone in dangerous situations. In addition to that, I do also have confirmation from other team members that Ritter was carrying these particular markers in his pack."

"That was good thinking on his part," Yost said. "That will simplify the first problem a little too ... figuring out where we are going."

"A forest like that would be a nightmare," Barrister added in agreement.

"Where did the marked trail lead?" Eleazaar asked, curious.

"Well into Satoochie Forest," Captain Silger replied. "Exactly where, I can not say. The trail went beyond the perimeter of their permitted search area ... I placed a limit on how deep into the forest they could go. By the time they would have gotten approval to extend their radius ... well ... it would have been getting dark and around here that has not been such a good thing of late."

"What about biological signs or other evidence left behind?" Kalise chimed in with a question of her own. "Did they find anything new or more descript than in the previous searches?"

"I am afraid not...." Captain Silger said in reply, holding out for her name.

"Kalise," she finished for him.

"Kalise," Captain Silger repeated. "Your animal expertise will hopefully enable you to answer those questions that we could not. I apologize that we have not been able to give you all something more useful, but this is pretty much all I have for you."

"It is not much to go on," Yost said, "A marked path is huge though, so overall it is certainly better than nothing."

"I wish there was more, Manny, but we have done all we can do on our end," Captain Silger said apologetically. "Go get yourselves a good rest tonight. You will want to head out at dawn and get as much daylight over top you as you can."

"We have rooms for you at the inn in the center of town tonight;" the constable added. "on the town, of course. Just make sure you stay inside when the sun goes down. No one is being allowed outside after dark now."

"Where would we go?" Jayden whispered as he leaned over to Eleazaar. "The town is a lifeless dump."

"With good reason, probably," Eleazaar whispered back.

"The Duchess?" Yost asked the constable.

"That is the one," the constable said. affirming.

"I guess we will do that now, then" Yost said, considering that the day was waning. "Okay, if everyone would follow me on over, we will go get situated and settled in for the night."

"How is the food over there?" Barrister inquired, hungry as was everyone else. "I have a particular palate."

"It is alright; we tend to like it," the constable opined.

"It is acceptable, Stan," Captain Silger added. "The boys been eating there about every night and I have heard no complaints."

With that, everyone began rising from their chairs. They still had a little time before nightfall, but the thought of food was enough to make them hurry. Yost again shook hands with Constable Spillman and Captain Silger, exchanging pleasantries before leaving.

"Good hunting," the constable said, well-wishing them all.
"Thank you," Yost replied.
"Good luck; all of you," the ranger captain added. "We will see you again, bright and early."

Chapter Seven

Nature

As the group followed Yost out of the town hall into the streets of Luitgarde, they crossed over in front of the wagon to a street just on their left. The street was one of two running north-south in the center of town and most of the town's businesses were located there. Not far ahead of them, a sign hung from metal rungs on the front of a building that read: Duchess Inn and Pub.

"So, is we t'be gettin' a room t'each's own then?" Grunda asked, unclear by what limited details the constable had given.

"I do not think so, Grunda," Eleazaar said, unsure himself as well. "They will probably pair us up. That means you would be sharing a room with Kalise."

"If that is okay with you, Grunda." Kalise added, assuring her she was welcome to do so.

"Oh, that be still quite nice me thinks," Grunda replied graciously. "Anyways, been donkey years since me slept in a proper bed."

"It could conceivably be a while before any of us sleep in one again too," Eleazaar said, mostly to himself. "God only knows what we are getting into tomorrow."

The group arrived shortly at the inn and entered into the pub, which encompassed the whole of the ground floor. Yost went up to the bar counter and found the innkeeper cleaning up from the previous night. Some people had taken to drinking there all night, since there was little to do but drink around there and they were not allowed to walk home. Of late, the pub had become a messy place.

The innkeeper had set aside rooms for them and handed Yost a clump of iron keys for the doors upstairs. He pointed them to a narrow entrance at the edge of the room where stairs led to where they would be sleeping. As Yost started to lead them to the entrance, he offered a vague plan for the evening.

"Let us get a quick look at our rooms and unload our gear," He suggested. "We will come back down and get a drink afterward … maybe a bite to eat before the locals fill up the place."

That sounded pretty good to all of them. It had been a long, fairly unpleasant day but would probably pale in comparison to tomorrow. They could only imagine what things might be in store. The stairs were as narrow as they looked and the hallway between the rooms upstairs was not much better. Despite the name of the inn, no one was going to mistake the place for royal accommodations. Suffice to say it was a little run down from the heavy use of late. Jayden rattled the iron key in the lock of one of the doors and swung it open. He stood in the open doorway looking at the interior room as Eleazaar looked over his shoulder and Kalise and Grunda slipped past them. Eleazaar grabbed Kalise's arm as she passed him.

"Are you sure it is alright … sharing a room with her," he inquired in a soft voice.

"Do not worry," Kalise responded firmly. "We will be fine, right Grunda?"

"Chuffed to bits, love," Grunda replied matter-of-factly. "We ladies 'il be a right ace 'for you knows it."

The room Jayden and Eleazaar would be staying in left a lot to be desired. There were two small, stuffing mattresses laid across wooden boxes and they did not look particularly clean. Neither of them dared imagine what might have soiled them; it was often better not to know such things.

"Not exactly what I was expecting," Jayden said aloud to himself as he stood looking at the room before him. "I suppose it is better than the army barracks maybe ... or not."

"Quit whining already," Eleazaar snipped in reply as he nudged Jayden forward into the room.

"Whatever," Jayden said dismissively as he went to one of the beds. "I got dibs on this one."

Jayden plopped down on the bed to the left and it slipped off of the blocks at one of the corners. The bed subsequently tilted, sending him sliding down to the floor. He looked up at Eleazaar, aghast.

"You have got to be kidding me," he expressed with disgust.

Eleazaar looked down at him and smiled, humored. At least that was one humiliation he could now avoid. He carefully sat down on the other bed which held just fine and extended his hand to Jayden to help him off the floor.

Yost and Barrister opened the door to their room a few doors down. It was a little better than the one the boys were in, but not by much. Barrister, who was accustomed to a higher standard of living, was expectedly put out.

"Remind me not to come back here on purpose," he grumbled smartly.

"Do not knock it, Stan," Yost said. "We will likely be sleeping on the ground tomorrow."

After setting aside their gear in their rooms, they ventured downstairs, one by one. Being very conscience about the care and condition of his potions and other delicate gear, Eleazaar was a little slower getting there. Satisfied at last, he locked the room behind him and started downstairs to the pub. As he turned the corner to descend the narrow staircase, he ran right into Kalise, startling her as she was coming up.

"Oh!" Eleazaar immediately exclaimed with surprise. "I am … so sorry … are you alright?"
"Yeah … yeah I am fine, really," she said, a bit awkwardly. "I … just did not expect …"
"To come around the corner just then," he finished for her.
"Yeah," she agreed.

In that cramped space, they were squeezed very close to each other and it made them both feel a little anxious in the awkward silence that ensued. They could both feel the tension between them … a good kind of tension, but someone had to break the deadlock. Eleazaar was not real sure how to do that, so Kalise took it upon herself to get them past it.

"I was … just coming up to see if you were joining us," she said at last, studying him with her eyes.
"I was coming, I … just had things to … you know, put away … and stuff," he replied in short bursts; trying hard to read into her and the odd excitement that being so close to her was producing.
"We should probably join the others then," Kalise suggested.
"Right," Eleazaar agreed. "I was just … right."

She smiled at him and her eyes lingered as she started back down the steps to the pub. He was completely certain now that figuring out women was going to be a monumental task. He was pretty sure he had never had a feeling like the one he had just had, ever before. He did not know how to react, so he did not do anything in particular. Instead he just smiled back at her and tried to run the potential options in his head as he followed her down to the others.

Everyone else was relaxing in the pub and enjoying a drink while they waited on food to be served. If it was not already obvious before, a distinct divide between members of the group was readily apparent. Yost and Barrister sat alone at a table of their own while the others crowded together around a separate table.

"Kalise!" Barrister called to her as she and Eleazaar came to the table with the others. "Come on over here."

"I will be back," Kalise noted softly to the others as she turned away.

The locals were filtering in already and tended to stare and whisper a lot, but particularly at Grunda. Granted, besides being a diminutive dwarf, she was probably the first female they had ever seen with a beard. Shortly after Eleazaar sat down, a barmaid appeared with the others drinks.

"And can I get something for you, Mr. Cleric?" she asked in a spunky voice. "The first round is compliments of the house tonight."

"A pint will be fine," Eleazaar replied. "Something stout, if you have it."

"There is nothing better than free ale," Jayden proclaimed, before remembering there was indeed one thing he thought was better; a barmaid. "So, are you busy later?"

"I beg your pardon?" the barmaid said, a little caught off guard.

It was Jayden being Jayden, of course. Eleazaar knew this side of him and it always embarrassed him when his friend started his antics. He flashed a disturbed, mortified look at Jayden who predictably ignored him.

"Well," Jayden began, "we are about to embark on a perilous journey to save the town. Since no one can leave after dark, I thought maybe you and I could spend some time together. You know ... a hero's farewell."

Now the short, brown-haired barmaid was no little girl. Eleazaar would have guessed her somewhere around the age of thirty. Handsome as some might have considered Jayden to be, his cheap entreatment was not going to impress a woman anytime soon, least of all a barmaid who had probably heard it all a time or two.

"The drinks here at the Duchess are complimentary, little boy;" she said, trying her best to be pleasant, "not the barmaid."

"Ouch," Eleazaar whispered with a wince, before intervening to smooth over any potential bad feelings his words might have caused. "Thank you, Ma'am. We appreciate your hospitality."

The barmaid walked away and Eleazaar sighed with relief. There was one thing he did know about women at least; you do not get far talking to them like Jayden. He glared at him across the table in disgust.

"What is wrong with you?" Eleazaar inquired at last.

"What?" Jayden replied, indignant.

"Never gets nowheres chattin' up a lady like that now," Grunda said.

"Shut up!" Jayden snarled back at her. "Nobody asked you!"

"Do not yell at her like that!" Eleazaar chastised, wagging a finger at him. "That is *your* problem. You just do not have any respect for anyone, Jay. If you want to make an arse out of yourself, do it when we are not around!"

"Whatever," Jayden said dismissively, looking away.

Kalise was having a little problem of her own. It seemed Barrister had taken some sort of fancy to her and was making her uncomfortable. Chide remarks about her gender were one thing, but Barrister was starting to touch and entreat her now as he continued drinking. A pinch on the bottom was not an uncommon practice and most accepted it as culture between the sexes. But his hands were lingering and she was upset.

Finally she had/had enough and left them, walking briskly away. Eleazaar had watched her get up and bat Barrister's arm away, but he could not hear anything being said in the exchange. By the way she was walking back to his table though; he could tell she was upset, even shaken.

"Are you alright?" he asked her as she walked up and sat down next to Jayden.

"I hate men," came her truncated reply.

"Did they say something to you," he probed, looking over at the men who laughed and carried on indifferently.

"Do not bother to ask," she said. "I do not even want to go there."

"Best to get used to it, deary," Grunda said before catching herself and turning to Eleazaar apologetically. "Bunch a'blimey brutes men are … seps for yous, love."

"You have got to be kidding me," Jayden snorted as he rolled his eyes. "I am in hell."

A few hours later, the group began turning in for the night. Planning to rise before the dawn, no one wanted to be dragging or hung over when morning came. Yost and Barrister were the first to leave, letting the others know they should probably do the same. Kalise did not even want to look at Barrister as they passed by, and Eleazaar noticed. Whatever he had done, it must have been pretty offensive.

After they had passed by and started up the stairs, the rest of the group began to rise from their table. Jayden would have rather stuck around for a while to keep trying his luck, but Eleazaar and the rest of them convinced him to give up his fruitless pursuit. As they made their way up the stairs and entered their rooms, Kalise watched Eleazaar from the doorway as he was about to close his door.

"Goodnight, preacher boy," she offered, smiling at him in a way he thought odd.

"Goodnight, uh … druid girl," he replied sheepishly.

Kalise smiled and shook her head as she disappeared into her room and closed the door. Eleazaar put his hand on his forehead in disgust with himself. He wondered how someone so smart could simultaneously be so stupid sometimes.

"Druid girl, really?" he chastised himself under his breath. "Ungh ... stupid."

He shut the door and stood there for a moment, disgusted with himself for being so inept. He then turned and walked to the bed, where he sat down and removed his boots for the night. Tomorrow threatened to be the biggest day of his life and he was annoyed that most all he could think about was some girl. He laid down and rolled over onto his side.

"Problems talking to girls?" Jayden, who had listened to the exchange as he lay there, asked smartly.
"Shut up," Eleazaar retorted, closing his eyes.

Morning seemed to come quickly, or perhaps it was just the crummy beds that denied them a restful sleep. Regardless, they dragged themselves into their gear and gathered outside of the inn. Once everyone had arrived, they started on their long journey ahead. It was not a long walk to the edge of town where they would rendezvous with the team of rangers. The rangers were to escort them to the edge of the forest where they could pick up the trail that was left behind by their missing member. After that, they would monitor the area outside of the forest and await a signal from the team if they were needed.

As they approached the men, Yost shook hands with one of them and briefly exchanged pleasantries. Not wasting any time, they began to move out and the group of volunteers followed. It was mostly a quiet walk, as much of the group was half asleep still.

After a while, they came upon a short hilly trail with tall grass, wild flowers and a few small-leaf bushes growing sporadically. Just beyond the second hill, the imposing expanse of Satoochie Forest loomed menacingly. The trail lead straight into the forest and Eleazaar stopped at the top of the second rise to look back at the town of Luitgarde behind him in the distance, one last time.

"This is where we part ways, chief," one of the rangers informed Yost.

"Is this the end of your search radius?" Yost inquired of him.

"No sir," one of the other rangers interjected, "it goes in a'ways, but we are restricted from entering the forest … for now at least."

"Cap's orders," the first ranger said. "We are to patrol the perimeter by day, dawn to dusk, until we get a sign from you. If things go badly, we are authorized to help extract you from the area, but that is all."

"Hmmmm," Barrister replied. "That will not help much. You will never hear us if we get in a spot deep inside that godforsaken monstrosity."

"Sorry, Lord Barrister," the first ranger said, empathizing. "Orders are orders. We will give you whatever aid that we can. Cap does not want to risk losing any more of us until we know what we are up against."

"Or in other words," Eleazaar whispered as he leaned over to Jayden, "we are expendable."

One of the rangers immediately looked over at the two. Jayden was not sure if the man had heard Eleazaar or not, but he put on a big, dumb smile as if nothing had been said. Unlike his friend, Jayden was very image conscious around people he thought might be important to him somehow, either now or later.

"Shhhhh," He responded to Eleazaar out of the corner of his mouth.

"Okay everyone," Yost announced, "let us get this party started. Druid, cleric; guard the rear. Jayden, come up front here with me."

Jayden smiled arrogantly and slapped Eleazaar on the arm as he walked away. He loved looking like a big deal, because that was essentially how he viewed himself. He flashed Eleazaar a hand sign that, in some adolescent circles, meant "loser," before turning away and joining Yost.

"Whiffet," Eleazaar mumbled aloud in counter.

The trail before them ran directly into the forest and was apparently a common entry point for those who dared venture in. There was new growth at the forest's edge, but inside the trees grew large and tall. From the size and scope of the canopy they provided overhead, it was easy to imagine walking from one end to the other without getting any direct sunlight upon someone. For a small person like Grunda, it appeared even more imposing.

"Cor!" Grunda exclaimed aloud to no one in particular. "Me's never seen anythin' like this before. A dwarf'd have to be right barmy to go in there; well, by meself anyways."

"It is not that bad, once you get used to it," Kalise explained in response. "It is usually very peaceful, with plants and animals living in perfect symbiosis. A forest is a well-spring of life."

"So says a druid," Eleazaar said smartly with a chuckle.

"I thought you like nature, El? Kalise inquired, surprised. "Can I call you El?"

"Yeah, if you like;" he said, "and yes, I love nature. I just … um … I do not really like it *crawling* on me."

"You mean that you do not like bugs?" Kalise giggled.

"No," Eleazaar replied matter-of-factly. "I do not dislike them … I *hate* bugs."

"Cut the chatter back there," Yost called back to them.

The trail that ran inside the forest was a little rough at times and not well traveled. There was little doubt it had seen recent traffic, however. While there was no grass to speak of with little direct sunlight, the vegetation that was along the trail showed signs of being damaged or disturbed.

The sounds of birds, perhaps bugs and frogs too, and sometimes the odd animal noise echoed through the trees. The forest was alive with life, though much of it could not be seen amongst the foliage. The growth along the sides of the trail continued to encroach upon them as they pressed deeper into its humid depths.

As Jayden walked along and pushed a branch out of his way, he noticed something he thought seemed out of place with the environment. He bent over and pushed aside a leafy vine. There before him was a small, wooden peg with a little strip of red ribbon tied to it.

"Manny?" he called. "I have something."

Yost paused and looked back at him. Seeing Jayden bent over something on the ground, he walked back to have a look for himself. He knelt down and picked up the peg in his hand.

"A trail market left by the missing ranger," Yost noted. "Good eye, Jayden. It will be more important to find these as the trail disappears in the growth. Now we all know what to look for."

"I had scout training when I was at Kurg," Jayden revealed.

"That is good; we can use that," Yost nodded with approval. "Let us keep moving. We have a long way to go yet."

Yost also took note of a sizeable disturbance in the soil next to the marker. He reached down with his hand and traced the edges of it with his fingertip. He filed away a mental note and rose to his feet, moving on down the trail. Kalise watched him go and looked down at the disturbance herself. It was a print of some kind, but nothing that she had ever seen before. That fact and the size of the print gave her concern. If this was some unknown, upright walking predator of a roughly larger than man-sized dimension, they might have more trouble than they bargained for.

As they continued on, hours passed and increasingly there was less direct light squeezing through the trees. They were only walking, but the humidity was causing them all to sweat as profusely as if they were running. All of that growth compacted together could hold a lot of moisture in the air.

Yost was the next one to spot a marker and he used the opportunity as an excuse to stop briefly. Sweat was dripping from the end of his nose and he took out a cloth to wipe his face and forehead. He decided it was a good time for the group to take a break.

"Alright," he said. "We will hold up here and take ten. Get yourselves a drink of water if you have not already; rehydrate and sit for a minute."

There was probably no one more uncomfortable than Barrister was. The armor the others wore was undoubtedly hotter than his robe, but his recent years spent in luxury and comfort had made him less tolerant of such extreme conditions. Covered in sweat, he tugged as his robes which were sticking to him uncomfortably.

He reached into them and pulled out a fancy, personalized towel to blot his wet skin.

"It is hotter than a hot poker in a goblin's ass crack," he annotated colorfully to Yost.

"Good times, Stan," Yost replied. "Welcome back to the good life."

Grunda sat down quietly against a tree along the path while Kalise uncorked her wineskin and lifted it to drink. She was very careful not to try and drink too fast so she would not spill any. There were a few plants in every forest from which water could be extracted if they ran out, but finding them would take time and could cause other problems in the process.

Jayden took a knee and leaned his head against the hilt of his sword. Eleazaar, meanwhile, stopped and placed his hand on a long, spike-like growth coming out of the foliage. Feeling sluggish, he leaned against the spike to rest. As he did so, the spike jerked suddenly and moved forward.

Surprised and off balance, Eleazaar fell to the ground. As he looked up, mandibles emerged behind the spike. Phobic of big bugs even more than little ones, he leaped into the air from seemingly a prone position on his back, and somehow managed to come down on the opposite side of them. The mandibles belonged to a Rhinoceros Beetle; a full twelve feet of monster bug. Its exoskeleton was hard like iron and it was not a picky eater either. It would eat pretty much anything organic and had too little intelligence to comprehend fear.

Its mandibles and body were coal black, while the hard-shell that protected the wings on its back had touches of brown around the edges.

The mandibles were particularly fearsome looking; they were huge and were known to be able to crush bone. The beetle came straight for Eleazaar, of course, because he was the closest. Eleazaar instantly went into a hyper- panic and blindly steamrolled his friend Jayden in desperation to get away from it. He fell over him and was back on his feet so fast that he was almost a blur. The others stood in complete shock as they watched the event play out before them.

"Wha ... dude!" Jayden exclaimed, surprised and confused at first.
"Oh!" Grunda squeaked with a panic.

Suddenly realizing what had happened and what was coming at him now, he quickly scrambled out of its way. The beast ignored him and continued its pursuit of Eleazaar. Though he could have easily outrun it and been fine, his fear took over and he fled in a wild, blind flight into the forest. He ran straight into a spider's web and then became hysterical. Running blindly and flailing his arms to get it and any spiders that may have come with it off of him, he ran straight into a low branch. Nearly beheading him, he was slammed to the ground, stunned. Before the beast could get off into the forest after him, Yost and Jayden quickly attacked and tried in vain to kill it.

Their swords made a metallic-like thud when they hit it and bounced right off. It did, however, get the beast's attention and caused it to stop its pursuit to defend itself. The beetle swung its horn around and chomped at them with its mandibles. They continued in vain to hack at it, if for no other reason than to keep it busy until they could figure out a weakness. Barrister kept his distance, shielding himself behind Yost and Jayden. On the opposite side of the bug, Kalise unsheathed her scimitar.

"Its shell is too hard," she called to the others. "Strike the seams ... where it is most vulnerable."
"Tell me something I do not already know," Yost shouted back.
"Cor!" Grunda exclaimed, frightened and confused. "Whits do ah do!?"
"Just poke at it;" Kalise quickly advised, "but keep it at a distance."

In no uncertain terms, Grunda was terrified by the big bug. She was not bug-phobic like Eleazaar, but this particular bug was big enough that it could easily eat her. She took her cue from Kalise and tried to stab it in the side with her short sword while it was occupied with Yost and Jayden. The beetle spun around when she poked it with the sword and she quickly scurried away from it. After all, a short sword was called *short* for a reason, and there was not much distance between her and the bug at that point. She had to get pretty close to use it, so no one was going to slight her much for being timid.

When the beetle turned on Grunda, Yost and Jayden struck at its backside, trying to get under the shell. In response, the agitated bug lifted the hard-coated wings on its back and whipped them fast and furiously.

The fast rush of air from the wings knocked both of them off their feet and one of the wings hit Jayden's sword, knocking it away and out of his hands. The beetle spun around on them again and advanced with its mandibles snapping. Jayden scurried away quickly to retrieve his sword while Yost battled the mandibles with his own sword, trying to get up and stay out of its clamping range. It lunged forward repeatedly, swinging its horn back and forth, and snapping at his legs.

Bravely, Grunda crept up and stabbed at it again as hard as she could. Then, the beetle turned swiftly to her and she stabbed it again right in the head, reacting defensively out of fright. This time the beetle clamped onto her little sword and ripped it from her hands.

It immediately swung its horn around at her but she ducked out of the way as she began to retreat again. Kalise was not as fortunate. Stepping in to try and protect Grunda, the horn struck her and slapped her aside. She subsequently went tumbling through the air into the brush. That left an unarmed Grunda all alone on her side of the beast.

The beetle ignored the others and now took off after Grunda. She squealed in terror and took off into the forest in the direction Eleazaar had gone with the beetle clamping its mandible at her heels. Even with her short little legs she could outrun it, but there was no telling how long it would pursue her either. Barrister had seen enough though and at last intervened. He stepped forward past Yost and began waving his hands in the air.

"Like burning sulfur, a vaporous shroud;" he chanted in evocation, "the poisoned breath of a killer cloud."

A mottled, sickly yellowish vapor suddenly streamed from his fingertips. The streaming vapor expanded into a murky cloud that enveloped the beetle, moving with it as it chased Grunda. The smelly, pungent substance began to bubble and melt the hard shell, burning the bug like an acid. Grunda came upon Eleazaar in her flight, who was still lying stunned on the ground. As she ran, she slid next to him and began to shake him. The beetle was charging hard and fast down the incline towards them, trying to escape the burning cloud, which was beginning to dissipate.

"Get up, love! Get up!" she squealed desperately. "No time t'be a nappin', les you fancy lunchin' wit a beetle! Cor! Get UP ... NOW!"

Eleazaar shook his spinning head to try and get his bearings. Grunda fell away from him in fright as the beetle closed, directly at him now. Seeing her reaction, he rolled over quickly to see the monstrous bug nearly on him. Reacting instinctively with a gasp, he slung his long sword up in front of him. As fate would have it, the beetle charged right into the blade which plunged into the head. A stream of yellow goo sprayed out from the head all over Eleazaar, soaking him. The beetle collapsed on the spot and its mandibles twitched for a moment before they too moved no more. Shaken, Eleazaar crawled back away with wide eyes and a sick, shocked look on his face.

He sat there shaking, just looking at the thing. Grunda tugged at him until he finally looked away from it and slowly began rising back to his feet. He hesitantly grabbed his goo-covered sword from the beetle's head and dragged it along as Grunda tried to help him walk back up to the trail. He staggered and stumbled up the hill as he regained his senses. Just off the trail now before him, the others watched him approach.

"Come on, hero," Yost commented before turning away and returning to the trail.

"You alright, El?" Kalise asked, reaching out to grab him as he stumbled forward.

"I think … I am going to be sick," he replied sluggishly.

"That … was awesome!" Jayden exclaimed, thrilled at the experience.

"What?" Eleazaar asked as he looked over in disbelief at his friend. "Seriously?"

"Ha ha ha," Jayden laughed at him as he turned away to join Yost and Barrister back on the trail. "Hell yeah … that totally ruled!"

"For you maybe," Eleazaar mumbled back.

"Just ignore them," Kalise soothed as her and Grunda helped steady him to walk up to the trail. "Come on, El. Let me help you."

Chapter Eight

SECRETS REVEALED

As Kalise and Grunda got Eleazaar back up on the trail, she looked him over good. He had a knot on his head from the branch he ran into and was covered in bug-goo which had a light but unpleasant odor. If he had possessed any pride at all, he had lost it with the latest incident. He looked quite pitiful.

"Does your head hurt?" she asked as she touched the lump on his head.

"Aaaaahhh … YES!" He replied in a raised voice, looking at her in shock with wide eyes. "Particularly when someone pushes on it!"

"Sorry," Kalise said with a giggle at her own thoughtlessness. "We need to get this goo off of you."

She fiddled in her belt pack and removed a cloth. Then she dug into another and pulled out a small bag of sewn animal skin, which was filled with a medicinal balm. She began blotting and wiping away the goo from Eleazaar's face.

"It is ok, you do not have to do that," Eleazaar told her, feeling a little awkward that she was so close to him and touching him in such a gentle way.

"The ... blood ... of the Rhinoceros Beetle;" she began, explaining the importance of her actions to him, "has the chemical properties of an irritant. It is known to cause rashes or even skin lesions, so I need to spread a balm wherever it came into contact with your skin."

"I did not know that," Eleazaar revealed.

"Well, now you do," Kalise added.

"You know ... it is funny;" Eleazaar said as he watched her tending to him, "you sounded just like me ... just then ... for a moment."

A smile stretched across her face as she kept working on him without responding. He was still trying to figure out if she was flirting with him, but he still had no clue. This was all just too new to him. He felt kind of stupid because of it, but he hoped she was flirting. He was starting to like it, a lot.

"Well El;" Kalise said at last, "just because I am a girl does not mean I cannot be smart too."

"Awww, are not yous two just lovvly-jubbly now," Grunda observed as she stood off from them watching.

Grunda may not have been as well educated as the two of them were, but she had been around life for a while. Maybe Eleazaar was clueless and Kalise good at keeping things to herself, but she could see as plain as day what was going on. They liked each other.

"Wha ... no," Eleazaar backpeddled from the insinuation, his face suddenly flush with red.

"Ha ha ha," Kalise laughed at him, "you are blushing again, El."

"Fiddle," he said with a sigh, quite embarrassed.

"Eets be alright now, dears," Grunda said soothingly. "Nothin' t'be ashamed of. Me sees a mighty glows when yous together like that."

Yost and the others were already moving up the trail while Kalise tended to Eleazaar. He was not one to linger and did not want to waste daylight if he could help it. As their voices got farther away, Yost stopped begrudgingly and yelled at them to hurry up.

"Come on, people!" he shouted. "This is not a love-fest. Move it along!"

"Just go on, Manny," Kalise shouted back. "We will be along … we have the rear."

"Bunch of feckwits," Yost growled aloud to the others as he began walking again. "Come on."

The division between the two halves of the group seemed to be becoming more distinct over time rather than dissipating. Jayden was doing everything he could to impress the older men, and Kalise was clearly going the opposite direction. Something would have to give, sooner or later.

"There … that should do it," she said as she finished dabbing the balm on his face. "Now, let us go before they get too far ahead."

"Thanks … really," Eleazaar offered.

Kalise just smiled at him and turned to walk. Eleazaar continued walking next to her while Grunda walked several feet ahead of them. Seeing that things were starting to open up between them, Kalise probed him with questions to get to know the young cleric a little better.

"So," she began innocuously, "Do you have any brothers or sisters?"

"Twelve, actually," Eleazaar replied, completely serious.

"*What*!" Kalise exclaimed in disbelief. "Twelve? Really?"

"Yeah," he confirmed matter-of-factly. "Um … I have an older brother; a full-blooded human from my father's first wife … she died. Then he married my mother, Yita, the princess of the Elven Kingdom of Wendaria. I guess he really liked her … you know; she just kept bearing children. There are eight brothers and three sisters in all."

"Wow," Kalise said in response, amazed and trying to wrap her mind around it all. "Talk about a full house. I have never heard of this ... Wendaria ... is it?"

"Yeah," Eleazaar again confirmed.

"Is it like ... far away from here or something?" She continued to ask, before the magnitude of what he had just said finally hit her. "Wait! *You* are a prince? A cleric *prince*?"

"I know ... I get that reaction a lot, actually," he noted, realizing that now he would have to go and explain everything.

"*You* are a prince!" she continued, still not sure if he was toying with her. "No ... *really*?"

"Mmmm; really, or I was ... am ... I mean I will be;" he fumbled with it, a bit confused himself since he was tossed through time, "I mean ... it is complicated. That is one reason I do not like talking about it much. It is far away ... in a manner of speaking. It is hard to explain."

"Okay," Kalise then said, trying to make some sense of it all. "So let us just say for the moment that you *are* a prince. Why are you *here* then? Were you banished or something like that?"

"Oh no, nothing like that," Eleazaar clarified. "I was sent here ... by accident actually. My father was the king of a land called Pinnea. There was an evil land called DeGothia that we fought with frequently, and they launched a massive surprise attack that ripped through the land and sacked our capital city of Torkul. My father and mother were killed and the royal mage used the last of his magic to send us, the children, far away."

"Sounds terrible," Kalise commented, entranced by the story.

"It was ... I still see it in my sleep sometimes," he elaborated. "But uh ... something went wrong with the magic I guess ... I do not really know what, but we ended up scattered in different places somehow I think. It was supposed to be an inter-dimensional spell that would spread us out, probably to increase the chances of survival and that at least one of us would return to the throne. In my case ... it seems that I got sent through time somehow. I was thirteen years of age then."

"Just a boy," Kalise observed. "What about your older brother? Was he killed in the fight too or was he sent away like the rest of you?"

"He was not there when it happened," Eleazaar clarified. "I think he was always angry that my father remarried and they were not getting along, so when he turned seventeen he apprenticed to a sorcerer and went off somewhere. He is probably king by now; at least I hope he is."

"Did you get along with him then?" Kalise continued probing. "I mean, did he not resent you like I guess he did your father?"

"It was kind of different, really," Eleazaar answered her, searching his memories. "I was the first born of the others and kind of a novelty at first maybe. He never really took to the others much, but as we grew up we spent time together and talked and stuff. His resentment of my father really came about as he was getting older. The two of us were pretty close really ... until he left. He could be a good king, I think. Anyway, I ended up here ... the church took me in and I became a cleric.

"That is quite a story," Kalise said finally, her head almost spinning. "It is way much more colorful than mine, I assure you."

"Oh, I doubt that," Eleazaar suggested. "Just a lot of drama in my life, but every life is a worthy story. The meaning of it all is nothing more than someone else's interpretation of it, I think anyway."

"Hmmmmm ... well, *my* father was a furrier," Kalise began, offering up her own story. "I always hated what he did as a little girl. I thought it was cruel to do the things he did to those beautiful animals, but then everything he did after a while was cruel. My parents were religious and strict, which was fine. You remember I told you about reading the holy book ... that is why."

"Oh, I see," Eleazaar affirmed as he listened to her tale.

"Anyway," Kalise continued, "something happened with my father over time; I am not sure *what* really. We were pretty poor and times were hard a lot. He started drinking all the time and would come home drunk like a fool. When he did there was always a fight. He would take out his ... whatever it was in life ... on me and my sister, then on my mother. He nearly killed her one time and that is when I started running away."

"That is really horrible," Eleazaar tried to empathize. "I cannot really imagine what that must have been like ... for all of you."

"Well ... El," she replied. "Now you see that you are not the only one with a little drama in their lives."

"Indeed," Eleazaar agreed. "So does it still *bother* you? You know, like do you think about it still?"

"No, I have kind of made peace with it over the years," she said. "It was a long time ago and in some ways, I think it made me a stronger person, maybe."

"Hmmm. So, is that what made you want to work with animals then?" He asked, reflecting on her story. "Become a druid?"

"That played a part in it, I am sure," she said. "The thing is, I just like that animals are always just what they are. They never do anything half- heartedly like people do."

"I guess I cannot really argue with that," Eleazaar replied, thinking. "So, if you could be any animal; any one at all, what would you be?"

"Please ... that is easy," Kalise said with a twinkle in her eye. "I would most definitely be a wolf."

"Really?" Eleazaar asked with surprise, though he was not sure why. "You seem pretty sure about that. Why a wolf?"

"Graceful, powerful, independent animals ... free," she answered him. "What is there not to like?"

As Eleazaar was digesting that thought, he happened to notice something on the ground. He put his arm out to stop Kalise and squatted down for a closer look. There was another very distinct impression, the print of some creature, there in the soil.

"What is it?" Kalise asked before noticing the print herself.

"Look at this," he said. "What makes an impression like this? A really big bird?"

"I do not think so," she replied. "I have seen a few of these on the trail already and there were several more before we entered the forest. It is of the Reptilia class; that I am fairly certain of."

"An upright-walking reptile then?" Eleazaar continued to query.

"It is not anything common if it is, and I do not think it is a resurgent dino-lizard species either," Kalise speculated. "It is actually the other, less noticeable impressions near it that are interesting."

Looking around for an example, to illustrate to him what she meant, she found one close; just behind the other print, and knelt down to it. She took her finger and outlined the disturbance in the soil so he could see it more clearly. It was an unspectacular tube-like drag across the dirt.

"Look here," Kalise directed him. "You see this?"

"Yeah," Eleazaar affirmed. "That tubular drag mark in the soil?"

"Precisely," she acknowledged approvingly. "Not really like a snake, but more like a tail would drag. The giant lizards of antiquity held their tails up as they walked or ran, but not this creature. It is odd too though, because it is not a straight mark, but seems to swish as it drags. It is a heavier push on the ground with more texture, like the creature uses it more for stability and push than normal. It makes me think that whatever creature made this, is from the Serpentes suborder of Squamata."

"Whoa … wait a minute," Eleazaar said with a chill in his spine. "Are you saying this is a snake … with legs?"

"I do not know what it is, El," Kalise conceded gravely. "I just know what it looks like."

By late afternoon they had penetrated miles into the forest. It was beginning to seem more understandable as to why the rangers stopped when they did; the trail seemed to have no end in sight. Yost stopped to wipe sweat from his brow as Barrister walked up next to him.

"This humidity is insufferable," Barrister lamented.

"Yeah, and it may not be the worst problem we have before the day is out," Yost added.

"If we do not find something soon, we have to start thinking about making a base camp for the night."

"Oh, goodie," Barrister remarked.

Indeed, it would be hard for them to set up a camp if darkness set in. Thus, keeping an eye out for some suitable site now became a consideration. They still had significant daylight ahead of them, but if they could not find a site in the area before darkness fell, it could be a serious problem. Jayden then emerged behind them.

"Are we stopping again?" Jayden inquired.
"Just for a bit," Yost said. "Go on and scout ahead of if you like, but do not go out too far."
"Gotcha," Jayden answered him, eager to do anything to impress.
"And do not go and do anything stupid either," Yost added. "If you see something, come back and tell us about it. Do not get too curious about anything."
"Right," Jayden said as he moved past them to the trail ahead.

Barrister watched the kid go and frowned. Digging into his things, he extracted a leather wrapping from a bag and sat down. As he began to eat, he let his thoughts be known to Yost.

"The kid will get himself killed;" he said, "the lot of them will; you watch. Probably us too … damn kids."
"Maybe," Yost replied in kind. "Or, maybe they buy us enough time to finish the job and get home. You need to look at the big picture, Stan."

They cut off their conversation as Grunda came up the trail to them. She made eye contact with Yost, who always seemed to be scowling, and quickly looked away. She thought of him as akin to something like a dangerous dog; much safer not to look him in the eyes.
She sat down and stretched out her stubby legs. Unlike taller folk, she had to work much harder to get anywhere on short legs; almost twice the walk for her compared to them. Seeing Barrister eating, she pulled out an unleavened cracker she had saved from the shelter and took a nibble.
Kalise and Eleazaar appeared soon thereafter and gladly embraced the pause from walking with the others. They refreshed themselves with water and likewise found something to eat in their packs. Kalise had continued contemplating the particulars of the tracks her and Eleazaar had discussed and wanted to run her thoughts by Yost.

"I do not know if you have noticed or not, Manny;" she began, "but the tracks we keep finding along this trail look a lot like a bipedal reptile."

"I do not really know, or care what it is," Yost replied succinctly. "I just want to find it, before it finds *us* ... and kill it."

"Well, therein lies the problem," she added with a touch of aggravation evident in her voice.

"We are not seeing anything by day. If it is nocturnal, which all evidentiary indications suggest and particularly if it is related to the order of snakes, it will likely have infravision and see us better than we see it."

"Well then;" Barrister chimed in, "when we make camp, we just have to set up wards and watch in shifts then, will we not?"

"Yes;" Kalise hesitantly agreed as he was missing the point she was trying to make, "but it could strike very quickly if it is a bipedal life form."

"What do you want me to do?" Yost growled at her, the cracks in his temperament starting to appear. "I am a soldier ... not some damn tree-hugger! And, we do not even know what this is for sure. I cannot do a damn thing about what it may or may not do. We just need to find it, kill it and get the hell out of here. That is what I do."

"Would anyone else like to share some ideas?" Kalise asked, frustrated at the perceived lack of cooperation she was getting.

"Me sees real good in the dark, miss," Grunda offered.

"That is right," Eleazaar quickly agreed. "Grunda is a dwarf, so she has infravision too, albeit limited."

"That would be great;" Kalise countered, "but it will not do us any good if the creature is cold blooded. It would have to have a body temperature greater than the environment around it."

Eleazaar shrugged. It was a good point and one he had clearly overlooked. Reptiles were cold blooded, so the advantage would clearly belong to the creature in that case. There was, however unlikely, one other possibility to consider.

"Maybe it is warm blooded," he said, just throwing the idea out there.

"That is not a good bet," Kalise replied, skeptical. "A warm-blooded reptile? I do not think so; there is no such thing."

"I know what it sounds like," Eleazaar agreed. "Just think about the pattern of disappearances for a moment. People were being taken for weeks with no one seeing anything and little evidence. It is not just some kind of eating machine, as far as we know. It could be highly intelligent and that is most common with warm blooded animals."

"That is a huge stretch," Kalise noted.

"And very unlikely, I know," Eleazaar again conceded. "But, nature mixes her handiwork up sometimes ... I am just saying. Wait a minute ... where is Jayden?"

"I let him go on ahead to scout," Yost explained, unconcerned.

Eleazaar was instantly angry and rolled his head in disgust as he pushed past Yost in a huff. It was not like him to act in such a way, but he felt like Jayden was being reckless in his desire to impress them and the men were taking advantage of that for their own benefit. Jayden had a knack for finding trouble, and no one knew that better than Eleazaar did.

"Alright," Yost said with a disgruntled sigh. "Our rest is over it seems. We are losing daylight anyway; come on."

"Stupid boy," Barrister grumbled quietly. "Let us hope that is all we are losing."

The rest of the group picked up their belongings and slowly started down the trail again. As Eleazaar moved quickly up the trail searching for Jayden, the growth grew thicker and thicker in an ever tighter squeeze of the path. Here, plants grew across the path and in the middle of it, impeding easy walking.

A ways ahead of him, Jayden was knelt down beside a bush where he found a tattered strip of clothing. Curious, he pushed the leaves and branches aside, looking for anything else that might be of interest to show the others. As he pulled the bottom branches of a thorny, leafy bush-type plant aside, he spotted another wooden peg with a red ribbon.

As he continued searching for a second ribbon, since there were always two markers to show direction, he did not find one where he expected to. Instantly realizing the ranger's path may have changed direction here, he searched frantically through the foliage to find the second marker. It took some unsavory searching, but he finally found the second marker to the right of the trail like the first one.

The ranger, it appeared, had left the trail altogether here and went off into the dense forest. He figured that meant they were getting closer to something, or at least he hoped that was the case. It also probably meant that finding more markers would be much harder now and losing the path of the ranger would be much easier. He arose and started back to inform Yost when he heard Eleazaar's voice calling to him.

"Jayden?" Eleazaar called loudly ahead as he searched and listened for a response. "Jayden?"

"Will you shut up!" Jayden growled at him as he hurried back to meet him. "What is the matter with you?"

"With me?" Eleazaar said, astonished. "Are you out of your mind, going off by yourself like that?"

As the boys argued, Yost could hear them plainly as their voices echoed through the forest. Agitated, he hurried through the thick growth to get to them. Right behind him, Barrister and the others hurried along to catch up.

"Pipe it down!" he growled angrily at them. "You sound like a goddamn trumpet brigade out here."

"I found something, Manny," Jayden quickly remembered. "Show me," Yost acknowledged, quickly moving on to important things.

Jayden lead him on ahead to the place where he had found the markers. He showed him the tatter of cloth and pulled back the branches to reveal the change of direction the ranger had made. Yost was quite impressed with the boy.

"I found these," Jayden said. "Looks like our ranger made a right turn into the forest here."

"Nice job, kid," Yost commended. "This is very important and a good sign, I think. Excellent work."

"Just putting all that training to good use," Jayden noted, admiring himself as the others joined them.

"You might want to stay here, little cleric," Barrister sneered as he walked off to follow Yost and Jayden into the forest. "There is probably a lot of nasty little bugs this way … I would not want you to soil yourself."

"Don' yous-a listen to him none, love," Grunda consoled him. "That bloody arsehole hid behind everyones he did."

"And that was a pretty big bug," Kalise said. "I would have run too if it was chasing me."

"I know what you are trying to do," Eleazaar replied, "and I appreciate it … I really do, but …"

"Look," Kalise said, cutting him off. "He is just trying to beat you down, El … because that is what he does."

"Right she is," Grunda agreed. "Dinnea need t'be gutted on his accounts."

"I know," Eleazaar said. "Thanks … both of you … really."

Eleazaar put his hand on Grunda's shoulder appreciatively as she started off into the forest. As he was turning back to Kalise, he noticed the tatter of clothing lying on the ground that Jayden had previously found. He picked it up and rubbed it between his fingers, then put it up to his nose. His face crinkled unpleasantly.

"Grunda!" he called to her, waving her to come back.

"What is it, El?" Kalise asked, curious.

"A tear from a workman's shirt, I think," he replied. "Tell me what you smell, Grunda."

"Eewww," Grunda grimaced. "Smells like some chap was good'n bladdered up it does."

"Yes," Eleazaar agreed. "That is what I thought as well. It cannot be that old if the smell is still distinct like this."

"That be a long ways out in the forest for a chap on the piss," she added.

"And that could only mean that whatever it is that has taken people from the town;" Kalise speculated, "has dragged them all the way out here. It is definitely not typical of a reptile."

"None that we have ever seen, at least," Eleazaar corrected her.

Kalise just nodded her agreement in response. It seemed most of what she thought she knew was upended by this creature. Every possibility was on the table now; even Eleazaar's wild suggestion of it being warm blooded. Normally discovering something new would be exciting, but in this case it was getting a bit scary.

Eleazaar tossed the cloth aside and continued on together with Kalise and Grunda into the forest. They walked on through the dense forest for what seemed like hours with no sign of markers to be found. With dusk finally creeping up on them, they stopped momentarily near an unusual hill to make a decision on what to do next. As Barrister stood there next to Yost, he swatted away gnat-like bugs from his sweaty face.

"Do we have any idea where we are or where we are going?" he asked, disgruntled with the conditions as much as anything.

"Uh … no, not exactly," Yost said. "We have not seen a marker in a couple of hours and it is too late to double back … the sun is going down."

"We had better find a place to set up camp then," Barrister replied. "We cannot wait or it will get too dark."

"Just what I was thinking," Yost agreed as he looked up at the strange hill. "Let us check out that high point over there. It may give us a more defensible position if we come under attack."

"I think that is a wise choice," Barrister said as he started up the hill.

"Alright everyone," Yost announced to the rest of the group, "we are going to look for a spot to make camp while it is still light. Up the hill … come on."

"This is not a good idea," Kalise mumbled aloud.

"Me hopes there be a nice, tall tree up there," Grunda said. "Sure dinnea fancy me sleepin' on the ground tonights."

"That is an understatement," Eleazaar added in agreement. "Shilud only knows what would be crawling on you."

"I think we might be in luck, Manny," Barrister called back to him as he stood atop the hill looking around. "The growth up here is more thinned out and it appears to be pretty flat."

"Good," Yost said as he came up from behind. "It is probably as good as we will find in this hellhole."

The others arrived at the top one by one and looked around. If they were going to set up a camp, it was indeed probably the only reasonable location they would find. They set down their packs and gear, and then began searching and clearing the area for a shelter.

"Ok, people;" Yost declared. "Take out your canvas rolls and bring them to me."

"One big tent?" Barrister inquired.

"No, I was thinking canopy," Yost elaborated. "We will sleep in shifts tonight, and we will need 360 degree visibility if we are going to have any chance at defending ourselves ... from whatever."

"Better have us on the late shift then," Barrister cautioned. "You will forgive me if I do not trust these kids to watch while we are sleeping."

Grunda was tired from the long walk and her legs were sore from fighting through growth that, at times, was bigger than she was. The puffy, padded armor she had to wear was quite hot, like walking around in a blanket that grew heavier through the day as she sweat. Already it had developed tears in it too, from the thorny plants and sharp branches. She eagerly sat down beneath a tree there to relax from the long day. Jayden, meanwhile took off his backpack and was beginning to untie his canvas roll when something red caught his eye.

"Wait!" he said, excited and surprised. "There is a flag here, guys."

Yost and Barrister leaned over to look as Jayden reached under a bushy plant and retrieved the marker. It was a huge stroke of luck and made them feel much better to know they were not lost. Now they just needed to find the second marker so they would know which direction they would be heading in the morning. Grunda looked over to her right and suddenly gasped. Right next to her, between two roots of the tree, was the second marker.

"Cor!" she exclaimed. "I gots another flag … right here next to me leg!"

"It appears we have a little luck after all," Yost noted. "Thank the fates for small favors," Barrister agreed.

"Good job, Grunda," Kalise praised her with a big smile, proud for her that she was contributing.

Eleazaar, who had just been standing by watching, walked toward Grunda to congratulate her and inspect the flag. He was thinking of getting a look at the line-of-sight for their trek tomorrow, when his boot made a strange thud beneath him. He looked down right away, but did not see anything there that could have made it. Kalise heard it too and looked toward the ground where he stood, then at him.

"What is it, El?" Kalise asked.

"Not sure," he said, before a strange notion hit him. "I think … I am standing on a trap door."

"That is ridiculous," Barrister immediately dismissed. "You are delirious."

"A secret passage?" Grunda asked with wonder.

Eleazaar tapped his boot on the ground and the same sound continued to rise. Kalise crawled closer to him and began to pull at the moss which covesed the ground in that area. To her amazement, her hands discovered a hard, wooden edge and she looked up at Yost.

"It sure could be," Yost said to her.

Eleazaar stepped carefully away and got down on his knees. Along with Kalise and Yost, he probed the ground to locate all of the edges. Finding the edges and pulling away the moss revealed a cut, wooden construction of twine-bound saplings about four feet wide and six feet long.

"Looks like that camp may not be necessary after all," Yost said, pleased. "Get your gear ready, people."

Kalise pulled her dagger from her belt and slipped it under the edge of the wood to pry it up. Yost and Eleazaar both eased a hand underneath as it lifted and raised the trap door up, exposing an opening into darkness underneath. The others crowded around to look into the black unknown before them.

"Oooooh," Grunda gasped. "A might dark down there it be!"
"It will get just as dark out here soon," Jayden said before moving to go into the hole. "We should check it out."
"Just hold up there a minute," Yost ordered, grabbing him to hold him back. "One person to check things out first. Hand me a torch out of my bag, Stan."
"I will do this," Eleazaar volunteered to Yost's surprise, even though he was the only one who had all of his gear still packed. "You all just get your things ready."
"You ... okay," Yost said, relenting. "Just do not go in too far. Just see if it is safe for the rest of us to enter."

Eleazaar nodded that he understood and a reached a hand into the armor covering his chest. He pulled out his holy symbol and held it firmly before him. Closing his eyes, he summoned the divine power of Youja Shilud.

"Illuma et mak symbasa," he declared.

The symbol began to glow brightly, casting its light into the darkness below. He eased forward, careful of where he was stepping and entered the hole.

Chapter Nine

THE HOLE

Eleazaar descended slowly as he panned the light from his holy symbol before him. The first few steps down were tiered soil, which had been cut out and packed tight. Then the soil beneath his feet gave way to cut stone, and the walls of the hole became giant stone blocks. He came shortly to a bottom, and the opening now turned to his left into some kind of larger room. He carefully eased himself to the entryway to look inside, unsure of what he might find lurking there.

As his light beamed in and filled the room, it became immediately clear to him that this was far from just some hole in the ground; it actually appeared to be some ancient kind of stone structure that could be of an enormous size. The room that lay before him was empty, but there were roots that had squeezed their way through the cracks between a number of the stone blocks. As he looked across the room, he could see that there was also some kind of opening in the floor; potentially a set of stairs leading down even deeper into the structure, he surmised. He pursed his lips in thought and, deciding the room presented no immediate threats, he thusly crept back up to the opening to tell the others it was safe to enter.

"There is a sizeable stone structure down here of some kind," he said as he emerged and knelt on the top step. "It might even be a lost temple or something. There is a room there and some kind of opening in the floor; possibly for an entrance to a lower level."

"No activity at all?" Yost asked.

"The room was bare ... completely empty;" Eleazaar replied, "for the moment at least. I wanted to get the rest of you before checking out the opening."

"Good decision," Yost said. "We are safer together,"

"It must be an ancient pyramid of some sort that got buried over the centuries;" Kalise speculated, "though I have never heard of any that were found this far north before. Those civilizations that built them were typically located in the tropics."

"Many think the world had a hotter climate at one time," Eleazaar said in response. "Maybe this area was a tropical climate when the structure was built?"

"That could be, I suppose," Kalise replied.

"We had better think about this, Manny," Barrister cautioned. "Who knows what could be down there. There may be a good reason that ranger disappeared."

"This is what we signed up for, Stan," Yost countered. "I do not see that there is much to think about. Would you rather spend the night up here ... exposed in this ... jungle?"

Barrister just shook his head, indicating that spending the night on the hill was not something he actually thought was preferable. Maybe he was just exercising a cautious conscience for the group, or maybe he was averse to being underground; Eleazaar was not certain, but it seemed out of character for the heroic figure he had read about. Certainly, a time away from this kind of life could take your nerve, or at least make you second guess it. It did not matter though, because they were all going down into that mysterious place, whether they really wanted to or not.

"Jayden?" Yost called out.

"Yes sir," Jayden replied.

"Go on down there and secure the room," Yost instructed him. "Make sure nothing comes up through the opening that the cleric here described."

"On it," Jayden replied as he moved past Eleazaar into the hole. "The rest of you, make sure you have all of your gear together and meet me at the bottom," Yost then said as he took out a torch from his kit to light it. "Are there any questions?"

Seeing there was none, Yost secured and adjusted his pack and set his torch ablaze. Eleazaar ducked back into the hole, where he followed Jayden back down into the strange room and illuminated the way for him. Yost then descended behind them after a few moments as the others were picking up their things.

"There had better be a treasure trove down there," Barrister said aloud, airing his thoughts. "That is all I have to say."

As the rest of the group at last entered the hole, one by one, Jayden and Eleazaar looked around in the room below. As Jayden eased ahead toward the opening in the floor, Eleazaar squatted down and took notice of the layer of dust that had settled upon the floor over countless time. The dust had been disturbed by foot traffic recently that was neither his nor Jayden's, and the boot marks of a human were clearly identifiable.

"Look here, Jay," Eleazaar said, pointing at the prints. "The ranger came this way."

"Right over to the stairs … you were right," Jayden agreed. "You know, this place reminds me of the time we explored those ruins near Anticost."

"I remember the bugbear," Eleazaar recalled smartly. "You uh … wet yourself."

"Oh … yeah," Jayden said, "I forgot about that part."

"I figured you did," Eleazaar said under his breath.

Eleazaar chuckled softly to himself, reflecting on the day seemingly so long ago. He had largely forgotten about the incident too, until

Jayden brought it up, but now he thought he might bring it up again the next time his friend got to sling his huge ego around. The others finally emerged from the entryway at the stairs to join them and they too began looking around at the strange new structure they had discovered.

"Ooooohhhhh;" Grunda said, "this must a'been a grand temple once upon a day. Some fine stonework it is … even fer'a dwarf, me thinks."

"Look at this, El," Kalise said as she too knelt to study the disturbances in the mucky dust of the floor. "You see this right here?"

"See what?" Eleazaar replied

"Here," Kalise said, pointing. "This is serpentine, not bipedal."

"I see the same toed prints," Eleazaar said in counter.

"No no;" Kalise continued, "there are three types of prints here. One I am sure is the ranger's, but this other one here has a distinct slither while the second set does not. It does not make any sense unless there are two variations of the creature."

"Polymorph," Eleazaar said matter-of-factly.

"Oh, my God," Kalise gasped. "You mean like some kind of cult?"

"Maybe;" Eleazaar said with a shrug, "if it is a snake cult."

"What the hell does *that* mean?" Jayden asked.

"You meaning these … beastly things a-bein' controlled by some rubbish cultists?" Grunda interjected.

"No, Grunda;" Kalise said, "if El is right, the creatures themselves *are* the cult … human."

"Warm blooded reptile," Eleazaar added.

"We may have a problem, Manny," Kalise advised.

"Now there is a surprise," Barrister said smartly.

"With two distinctly different sets of tracks here, one serpentine and one bipedal," Kalise began, "it could be that we are dealing with …"

"Absolutely nothing," Barrister finished for her. "It has been obvious from the start that we are dealing with an intelligent creature and, as such, it has likely made some sort of alliance with one or more other creatures. Humph! Or, maybe it has a pet?"

"Ever heard of something called ritual polymorph?" Eleazaar said, turning to Yost.

"No," Yost replied in short, his face looking troubled. "Transhuman creatures?"

"That is utterly ridiculous," Barrister snapped condescendingly. "Polymorph only lasts for a short time and that includes lycanthropic, despite the fact that it is recurring."

"Wrong!" Eleazaar snapped right back. "It is actually similar to the disease in some respects, yes, but a ritual transformation is a religious-based process where the transformation is gradual and permanent. It is not *at all* like the magic process as you understand it."

"Bah!" Barrister snorted. "You are not going to listen to this rubbish, are you Manny?"

"They could be a right swarm of beasties down there then," Grunda said in astonishment as she looked up a Kalise.

"That is right, Grunda," Kalise agreed. "There very well could be, indeed."

Yost put his face on his wrist and scratched it with his stubble as he stood thinking. Being a veteran military man, he at least had to consider all potential scenarios which they might face, regardless of how strange or unlikely they might seem. The prospect of a much more numerous enemy was certainly one of those situations which could at least alter the plan of attack.

The real question on his mind and, the only relevant one to him, was did this finding change their mission in coming here. An argument could have been made that, faced with a clearly superior force which they could not subdue or eradicate, they should return and report the finding while gathering adequate reinforcements to finish the mission. The only thing they had, however, was speculative indications that something far more dangerous lay ahead of them, not established facts. Thus, he made the obvious decision before him.

"An interesting development, but I do not see that it changes anything," Yost said at last. "We have a job to do either way, so that is what we are going to do, unless something changes. We will just need to be mindful not to get in this over our heads. Jayden? Is the opening clear going down?"

"All clear, sir," Jayden replied. "As far down as I can see at least."

Eleazaar walked over to Jayden and cast the light of his holy symbol down into the opening. The light illuminated the length of the stairs and revealed the bottom, which appeared clear of any movement in the light's radius. Jayden gave Yost an affirmative nod that the area was clear at the landing too.

"Go on down and secure the landing," Yost ordered Jayden. "Let us keep moving along until we find something."

"Come with me, Grunda," Eleazaar said as he prepared to descend the stairs behind Jayden.

"Right behind yous, love," Grunda replied.

Jayden descended the cut stone stairs and stepped down onto the stone floor below. Quickly, he scanned the room around him as Eleazaar arrived right behind him and his light chased the shadows into the corners of the room. The room appeared to be roughly twenty feet by thirty feet with open entryways to either side of it and some kind of passage or corridor at the other end. Just offset left from the center, three smooth-cut granite pillars, about three feet wide and a good half foot or more wider at the base, lined the middle of the room about seven feet apart from each other.

This new area was different than the one above, in that there was more moisture evident all around them and the area had debris littered about. It seemed from that debris that the entryways most likely had wooden doors of some kind at one time, which now were just rotten remnants in pieces. There was also a sweet, but foul odor choking the air about them.

"It does not look like anyone has been here for hundreds of years, does it?" Jayden said aloud to no one in particular as the last of the group finally joined him there from above. "The place is trashed."

"Well, it is a buried temple," Yost said. "I doubt that whoever built it intended it to be that way.

"I am surprised it is still standing," Barrister said. "You would think it would have collapsed."

"Which reminds me," Yost added, "we need to keep an eye out for slippage of any kind in the stone. With an ancient structure like this; moisture and decay accumulating between the blocks … a cave-in is always a distinct possibility."

"That strong smell is mold too, Manny," Kalise said. "It is very thick here. We probably should not linger for too long; breathing it in for an extended period could make us sick."

"Quite right," Yost agreed. "We will check the rooms here really quickly and then move on down that corridor ahead. Jayden … you take the one on the left. The little … dwarf here … can check the one on the right."

"Right chief," Jayden replied as he took out a torch of his own to light his way.

"Grunda will not be going anywhere by herself," Eleazaar protested. "She is *my* hireling and only I will say where she goes or she does not go."

"Humph!" Barrister snorted in his disdain. "Send them both then."

"Fine kid," Yost said in reply. "You can just go on in with her then … if that is how you prefer it."

"Quite right," Barrister agreed in his usual condescending way. "It will be a good chance for both of you to be useful … for once."

Eleazaar gave Barrister a long frown, though he already knew by now that a man like that would be indifferent to the simple respect normally afforded others and wholly unapologetic for himself. He was who he was and the chances of that changing were not very good in the short term. It was rarely easy holding the moral high ground when it came to people like that, but holding it was what separated him from so many others. There were a number of things he would have liked to have said, but none of them benefitted him in saying them. Regardless of how good speaking his mind might have felt in the moment, he knew that stooping to the level of such a person as Barrister was always a poor reflection of himself. He turned away and started walking toward the entryway to the left.

"Come on, Grunda," he said. "Let us go make ourselves useful, for once."

"M'feels like the ruddy maid around here, ordered abouts an all," Grunda said to Eleazaar as they reached the doorway, making sure she was loud enough for Barrister to hear. "Would'n work for that cheeky twit for a hundred quid."

Barrister made a sour face, somehow imagining him to be the one who was the victim of an insult. After all, how dare a filthy little miscreant like Grunda speak to a man of high social position in such a way? On the reverse side, Eleazaar was quite amused and actually a little proud of her for speaking her mind, even if it did stoop to Barrister's level. He saw her behavior as an indication that her sense of self-worth was improving at least.

Jayden, meanwhile, entered into the room to their left, eager to stay out of the others' drama. Aside from that, he hoped to find something important so he could further make a good impression on the older men. The first thing he found was far from that, however.

"It smells like something died in here," he said, largely to himself.

The room before him had roots coming through the seams in the stone that seemed like mostly dead and rotting leftovers from ages past. They glistened with moisture and fungus had grown on both them and in the plant debris that collected in the creases of the surrounding stone and upon the floor. In the center of the room, an oval of stone blocks, each about a foot high, was arranged on the floor. He thought, perhaps, it was where ancient people had sat and prayed or meditated for their rituals long ago.

He unsheathed his sword as he eased slowly in. It was not so much that he felt threatened; there was really nowhere for anything to suddenly jump out at him from. But, there could be something smaller, and he really did not want to touch any of the muck with his hands either. With the tip of his sword, he poked at the rotting organic matter, looking for anything of interest.

There was a steady dripping sound where water seeped through the stone and fell in drops into a small pool that had collected upon the floor. The muck proved to be just that; muck, and Jayden was not all that patient or committed to muck-digging. The thick and putrid-smelling air was overwhelming him, so he abandoned any further search and decided to return quickly to the others.

In the room on the opposite side, Eleazaar and Grunda had entered a place vaguely similar to that which Jayden had seen, with a minor difference. This room appeared to have a stone altar of some sort, over five feet long and maybe two feet wide. It seemed that it had been damaged sometime over the years, with one of the corners now broken off.

He could see pieces from it as it must have crumbled and shattered when it hit the floor. There was no arrangement of stone blocks to be found here, but plenty of rot stinking up the place. Plant matter and what he thought might have been old wood had collected in wet clumps in several places upon the floor.

"Be very careful," Eleazaar advised as the probed through the room. "There might be something in this gunk that bites."

"Dinnea haves to tell me, love," Grunda said confidently. "Learned a thing or two 'bout beastly places livin' on the streets. Got meself in a mess wit ants once; fell right asleep on theys bloody nest. Cor! Dropped me a clanger that time! Had ants in me pants all that night I did!"

"Heh heh heh," Eleazaar chuckled. "Oh … I can just see it. You are lucky they were not poisonous, or the burning ants."

"Gave me a fair spot'a aggro n'any case," Grunda agreed. "Itched meself for days."

"Well," Eleazaar continued in thought, "better not make that mistake here, Grunda. We would probably never get them all out of that padding you are wearing. You go poke around at that … goop on the floor, but be careful about it. I want to get a closer look at this … altar thingy."

So, the two of them moved in different directions; Grunda cautiously poked at the decay and moved it aside as Eleazaar inspected the old altar closely. The rectangular altar had a groove smoothed into it that ran from one end to the other and was stained darkly; even more than the darkening that had likely occurred from moisture collecting over countless years. The groove was also cut in a crossing pattern to each side, so that it ran to each of its four edges.

"Sacrificial ... by the look of it," Eleazaar said under his breath. "Stained dark in the grooves.... the grooves were probably for the draining of the blood. The only question is: why and what did they sacrifice?"

Back in the main area with the pillars, Kalise stood by, guarding the stairs against any intrusion from above them. Yost had walked to the other end of the room and was gazing into the corridor leading out of the area as he placed his hand against the stone wall at its entrance. Barrister, casting a light from a ring on his finger, quietly reviewed his spell book while eyeing Kalise's figure. Emboldened by his self-admiration, he closed his book and walked over to her. She looked at him as he stood before her, weary of his intent.

"I think you would look much more appropriate in satin and silks," Barrister said as he stroked her hair to the side with his fingertips. "Perhaps when this nasty business is over with, you could come visit me at my chateau for a time ... hmm? Be my little pet? Oooooomph!"

Barrister made an unpleasant, distorted face. He looked down and saw Kalise had a knife pressed menacingly against his groin. She stared him down with little emotion evident, for everything she felt was conveyed clearly by her knife. That did not stop her from speaking her peace, however.

"Touch me like that again, and I will cut your balls off," she said firmly. "Got it?"

"Yes," Barrister answered her, careful with his words. "Understood clearly."

"Good," Kalise said. "Now back off."

As Eleazaar studied the altar closely, he noticed some kind of coloration on the wall behind it. He could still make out faint pictographs on the altar, but they were too compromised to have any hope of making some sense of them. He thought perhaps the wall might have some that were more clearly identifiable.

He arose and went to the wall, digging away the crud. While there was some chipping and certainly fading, he could make out these drawings much more clearly. It appeared to be ritual scenes and then, there it was; the head of a snake inside an oval. That was significant, as ancient artists often used an oval behind something to characterize radiance of their rulers or gods. The drawings, or glyphs, were something he could reasonably understand as he had seen similar depictions in his studying of ancient lore.

"Cut the sacrifice and drain the blood into clay pots," he said under his breath as he tried to read the glyphs. "An offering of blood to the snake god for his own life-giving blood. The blood makes us whole in the image of him. Snake god ... possibly Heptmuz from the look of it."

"Nothin' in heres but filth and pieces of dead animals," Grunda said from the corner of the room. "Oh, look ... found me a copper!"

It was the pieces of animals that grabbed Eleazaar's attention. As the words sunk in, an alarm went off inside of him. The only way there would be pieces of anything lying there is if something had been eating animals and leaving those things behind. He rose quickly and turned to her.

He froze for a moment and his eyes grew wide. From out of a dark, broken nook that had eroded away between two of the stone blocks, a coal black, multi-segmented creature with many legs, squeezed out onto the wall. Its body kept winding out like a ribbon behind Grunda as she looked at Eleazaar strangely. A good five feet and a million little legs later, it reared up as if to spring and strike Grunda from behind.

Meanwhile, in the main room, Jayden returned to the others to report. He stopped and looked at Kalise, who was still holding her knife and seemed to have an unfriendly disposition. He was not even going to ask; even he knew better than that. Seeing him return, Yost left the corridor and came over to him.

"Anything?" Yost asked.

"Nothing but putrid, rotten stink," Jayden said, disappointed. "Can we just go already? This place is making me g ..."

"Run away!" they suddenly heard Eleazaar yell out from the next room.

Grunda's whole body jerked in surprise, startled by his panic-filled yell. Immediately frightened, recognizing only a few things caused such a reaction in Eleazaar, she instinctively turned around to look behind her. Eleazaar leaped over the altar, running desperately toward her with his sword drawn.

To the surprise of them both, a rogue blade blasted forth and met the springing meglopede in the air as it struck at her, impaling it. The meglopede whipped and undulated on the blade wildly, trying to free itself, or perhaps continue its attack. The blade, it seemed, came from Grunda's own hand but *this* blade was long and not the short sword she was carrying.

Eleazaar grabbed her by the shoulder and yanked her back, away from the creature. As he did so, the blade retracted and disappeared ... the blade was her own arm! He pulled her behind him and squared off against the frighteningly ugly bug, putting himself between her and it. Just then, the others rushed into the entryway to see what was happening, led by Kalise, as Eleazaar swatted at it to keep it at bay.

"Keep it away from you," Eleazaar instructed Grunda as the bug undulated around, looking for a vulnerable point to strike. "This one is poisonous.

"Canna say a'fancy havin' it for tea," Grunda declared in reply.

The meglopede seemed to be more interested in Grunda than Eleazaar, and tried to work its way around him to strike at her. It scurried to the left side and tried to spring at her, but Eleazaar swung in an upward motion from the ground and caught it, lifting it high in the air. As it fell back to the floor along the wall, he timed its fall with his boot and stomped its head against the wall. It made an ugly cracking sound as he crushed it, and the meglopede dropped to the floor, twitching. Kalise immediately ran over to take a closer look while Yost and the others looked on idly.

"Meglopede ... deadly poisonous," she said, looking at Eleazaar with surprise at his actions. "It is a good thing you did not miss. You were very lucky."

"I will take lucky over good, any day," Eleazaar replied, a little surprised at himself also. "Ugly thing."

"Show is over," Yost said. "Let us move on, people."

"Come on, bug boy," Jayden added, amused.

Eleazaar was getting a little tired of the bug cracks, and he looked forward to the time when someone else would have to deal with one instead of him. For whatever reason, he seemed to be like a magnet for them of late. In any case, he offered Jayden his appreciation with a three-fingered salute and then leaned down to Grunda, whispering.

"Now, you want to tell me how you did that whole ... thingy thing ... with your arm?" he asked, confounded.

"Bugger if me knows, love," Grunda said with a shrug, unsure herself. "Was jus' jammy, me thinks. Dinnea really thinks 'bout such things when theys happen, so me canna proly say, rightly."

"Hmmm," Eleazaar said, thinking. "Well I will say this: if you ever learn to control that ... that thing that you do ... I have a feeling you are going to be one dangerous little dwarf."

"What thing?" Kalise asked, unaware of their little secret. "Did I miss something?"

"Oh yeah," Eleazaar chuckled, "but we can talk about that later when we have some time ... it will take some explaining, I think;

probably a lot of explaining. For now, let us just get out of this sewer before something else starts crawling out."

"Are you alright, EL?" Kalise asked, curious.

"Yeah, of course … why?" Eleazaar said.

"I am not sure … first you are volunteering to lead the way in the hole, then the big meglopede and all," Kalise said in reply. "You seemed to handle it really well."

"I guess I was more scared for Grunda than I was for myself … maybe?" Eleazaar said with a shrug. "It was really after her more than it was me. I just reacted and did not think about it, I guess."

"That is great … I am proud of you, really," Kalise commended. "I just wanted to be sure you did not feel like you had to prove anything to anyone because of what happened earlier."

"It was nothing like that … I promise," Eleazaar said. "It was just a different situation; that is all."

"Came in likes a white knight, he did," Grunda said appreciatively. "Ruddy thing was abouts t'eat me up, it was."

"It depends on how long it would have taken to get through your fluffies," Eleazaar mused.

"Come on, people!" Yost snarled at them from the entryway. "This is not some damn social event; time to go!"

The three looked at each other and started walking to the entryway. The excursion so far had certainly been adventurous for them already and they, at least, had seemingly built a strong bond between the three of them. They could only imagine what the adventure had in store for them next.

Back at Luitgarde, the sun had gone down, but the rangers still stood monitoring the perimeter of the entry path into Satoochie Forest. They stuck together in groups of two as they watched and listened for any activity or signs from the group. Captain Silger arrived, emerging from the darkness behind them.

"Any sign of the party?" he asked one of the rangers.

"No, cap;" Ranger Bo said. "Nothing so far."

Captain Silger nodded and sighed as he gazed out at the dark and foreboding forest before them. He was not really an optimist by trade; he felt it was above his pay grade and dangerous to be so. The job was always important, but never more important to him than the men under his command. Given that, he made a judgment call to err on the side of caution.

"I want you boys to pull back to the edge of town," he said.

"Cap?" Ranger Bo asked, surprised.

"Maintain your watch from there for about two hours, then I want everybody to bunk for the night," he continued. "You can return here to check for them again at first light."

"We would never hear them from town, cap," Ranger Bo said in protest. "They might need our help."

"No one is going into that forest at night," Captain Silger replied. "If they need help now, there is not much hope for them. I do not care what you hear. They are on their own until morning, or unless they come out of the woods ... that is an order."

"Yes, sir," Ranger Bo said, morally conflicted but obedient.

"I will come out myself in the morning after I report to the constable," Captain Silger added as he turned and started back toward town. "We are pulling back, guys!" Ranger Bo called out to the others.

"Back to where?" Ranger Stack called back, in disbelief.

"Luitgarde," Ranger Bo said. "Cap's orders ... move out."

Ranger Stack looked back at the forest, frustrated. Like most of the others, the thought of abandoning the group in the forest did not sit well. The danger to themselves did not matter so much to them, given what they felt the others might be enduring. It felt a little like a betrayal. He turned away at last and headed for town.

"Good luck guys," he said under his breath.

Chapter Ten

ASCH-KUR

Eleazaar, Kalise and Grunda re-entered the main room where the others were waiting for them. Though the divide between the group's members was clear to all of them, no one seemed willing to broach the issue and resolve it. Instead, it continued to boil under the facade of their professionalism, waiting for the right moment to explode.

The corridor ahead of them went a few dozen feet and then split left and right to areas unknown. Now that everyone was here, they were ready to resume their search and advancing down the corridor was the next objective. Yost thus issued one final order before moving on.

"The corridor ahead is a confined space and obviously we do not know where it leads or how far, so we will need to make sure everyone has space to move and fight in, should we run into anything. Kalise ... you guard the rear. The dwarf ahead of you, the cleric and Stan will be in the middle so they can do what they do without any problems. Then it will be me, and Jayden ... you can lead the way."

"Awesome," Jayden said as he jogged ahead proudly to the end where the corridor split. "I got this."

"What? No!" Eleazaar protested, snapping angrily. "*You* are supposed to be the experienced one here, remember?

"Hey!" Yost growled back at him. "I am not ..."

"You are not going to use him for fodder so you and fancy-pants here can lay back and play it safe!" Eleazaar ranted, cutting him off.

"*You* have got a lot of nerve, kid," Yost snarled, taking an aggressive step toward him, "and the last time I checked, *I* was in charge here. If you do not like the rules here, then you can *walk your little ass* right back to town."

"Just *shut up*, El," Jayden added, sick of his friend meddling in his affairs. "Everyone is sick of your know-it-all attitude and no one cares what you have to say. Oh! Look at me! I am a big book geek and I know everything! Well, you know what? I got thi ..."

While Jayden was distracted by making light of his friend and quite possibly showing off, instead of watching out for danger, something else was closing on him. Before he could finish his rant, something grabbed him from around the corner. A snake-like humanoid held Jayden immobile with a long, curved blade at his throat. Kalise, who was looking right at Jayden when it happened, was shaken by sudden terror.

"Jayden!" she screamed.

The creature holding Jayden had arms with three clawed fingers and an opposable thumb. It was scaly like a snake and had no legs. Rather, it perched itself up on a thick and flexible tail. From around the corner, a second one then appeared. Unlike the first, this one had two scaly legs that were otherwise very human-looking, as well as arms like the first. Their heads were very snake-like and they rose from the torso on a thick neck that was equally like that of a traditional snake's body.

"Discard your weapons," the first one, known in antiquity as a Yuan-ti, said in an odd voice that seemed to hiss, "or this one *dies!*"

It was terrible timing for everyone, but for none more than Eleazaar. He was already worked up and boiling over before the creatures appeared. Now, he added panic to anger and his logic fled away from him, leaving him to explode.

"No!" Eleazaar screamed at the creature. "You will release him *right now* ... or I will bleed the both of you from your asses to your eye slits!"

He meant every word of his threat too in that fraction of a moment. He drew his sword and took an aggressive pose, shaking with anger. Everyone else seemed frozen in time, paralyzed by the sudden shift of events, perhaps. It all had happened so quickly, there was little time for anyone to think. Before Yost could intervene and calm the situation, events quickly spun beyond their control.

The bluff called, the result was inevitable. The Yuan-ti made a series of gutteral, popping and chirping-like sounds. Like a sequence in slow motion, Eleazaar watched in horror as it ripped its blade through Jayden's throat.

Jayden's eyes opened wide and his body went limp as Blood spewed in streams from his throat. The Yuan-ti then released him and he dropped like a rock to the stone floor.

Eleazaar launched himself at the two creatures, attacking them wildly in his shock and sudden despair. He hacked down with his sword from left to right at the legged Yuan-ti who stepped up to meet him, but it met his sword with its own. The other one struck at his exposed side, but he withdrew enough of his sword back to the left in time to push the strike aside.

At that moment, logic returned and he realized he had put himself in a pretty bad position. He began to back up and withdrew slowly to the others behind him as he parried subsequent attacks from the Yuan-ti. Kalise immediately drew her bow and fired off an arrow. It was an excellent shot, hitting the legged Yuan-ti in the neck, but it had nearly hit Eleazaar instead as he moved.

As Yost moved to position himself in the fight up front, Barrister reacted quickly. He reached into his robes and dug around, pulling out a dart, and two pouches. He sprinkled powder from one bag onto the dart in his other hand, and removed a small, dried-up organ of a small animal from the other. He crushed the organ into a powder with the other items and began a series of gestures as he spoke.

"Burn like the adder, fly like the sparrow;" he chanted, "strike down the serpent, my acid arrow."

He hurled the powder-covered dart at the Yuan-ti who had held Jayden, and it became an arrow as it left his hand. The magical arrow curved around Eleazaar as it flew and struck the creature in the jaw on the side of its head. The Yuan-ti flailed in pain as the arrow burned its flesh and grabbed at it. Eleazaar blocked the attack from the other Yuan-ti and, seeing the first one exposed, he gave it a quick kick in the midsection to knock it back from the fight.

That allowed Yost to step in, and he engaged while Eleazaar moved to the side to fight the creature Barrister had injured. Yost uppercut the legged Yuan-ti's sword and slashed back across its midsection, cutting it open. The creature let out an odd, painful sound as blood streamed down from the cut. But, it was hardly dissuaded and quickly recovered, counterattacking him with punishing force. It swatted aggressively with amazing strength at Yost, who could do nothing but commit to blocking.

As Kalise fired off another arrow, finding it hard to target in the small space with so much movement by everyone, Grunda stood watching helplessly. She had no ranged weapon to help them and she could not come up and do anything either in such a small space. Kalise's arrow only grazed one of the creatures this time, bouncing harmlessly off of the stone wall behind them.

"Oh, dear," Grunda said. "Ah must do somethin'."

Finding nothing else in the moment she could think of, she picked up a small piece of rubble; the equivalent of a pebble, and hurled it at one of the creatures. As fate would have it, she actually hit her target, but the little rock bounced off harmlessly, scarcely noticed in the heat of battle. Then Kalise let loose another arrow.

This arrow was intercepted by Eleazaar's moving sword and glanced off. The arrow shifted in flight and caught the sword arm of Eleazaar's opponent. It was merely a flesh wound, but the strike caused the Yuan-ti's attacking sword to shift wide. Instead of simply blocking the strike, Eleazaar knocked the strike away, opening the opponent to attack. He quickly slashed back from the left and his blade caught the Yuan-ti in the side, cutting into its torso.

The wounded Yuan-ti leaned back, spinning away and whipped its tail at Eleazaar to keep him at bay. The snapping tail was powerful to stun or even break bones, but Eleazaar saw it coming and luckily ducked underneath it, bending backward out of its path. Thinking quickly, Eleazaar grabbed the creature's tail to prevent it fleeing the fight or repositioning itself. But, the Yuan-ti was much stronger than he imagined. To free itself from his grasp, it mustered its amazing strength and whipped its tail to the side, lifting Eleazaar off the ground and hurling him into the wall of the corridor with a thud.

Next to him, Yost and the other Yuan-ti repeatedly clanged their swords together, locked in a stalemate. The creatures were strong and fast, so it was difficult to best them in a straight fight. Barrister was not much help in this situation, but did what he could to help. He grabbed a tiny, miniature arrow from his robes and gestured again in the air.

"La magie survient," he said. "Fly forth and strike; you cannot fail. Pierce the enemy through its hard scale."

The magic arrow, this time the product of a magic missile spell, never misses its target so it easily struck the Yuan-ti engaged with Yost. While not inflicting a whole lot of damage, it was sufficient to disrupt the creature's pounding attacks. Allowing Yost the opportunity to become the aggressor, he lunged forward, slashing at creature with every ounce of angry fury within him.

As Eleazaar crashed into the wall, he smartly took his sword in his left hand and stabbed the blade into the tail of his opponent. The creature angrily made a sound like a roar and turned itself back around to attack Eleazaar. With his sword stuck in the tail, he reached across his body and grabbed his mace with the other hand.

He hurled the mace around to meet the Yuan-ti as it came at him, but he missed and it slammed with a thud against the corridor wall. The Yuan-ti thrust its sword out and the blade hit the seam in Eleazaar's armor, slipping through and plunging into his shoulder. The sudden, searing pain caused Eleazaar to drop his mace. Having no other weapon he could think of at the moment, he twisted his body and punched the Yuan-ti in the head with his fist. It created enough of a jolt that he was able to grab and pull his sword free from the creature's tail.

Despite Yost's aggression, his opponent was very skilled and recovered quickly. It let Yost drive him back, then slipped to the side and slashed him with its sword across the thigh, catching the thin covering on the side of his leg. Cut by the blade and driving forward, Yost stumbled.

As the creature drew its sword high to strike down upon him, Kalise got the opening she was waiting for. She quickly let her arrow fly and it struck the creature in the chest, knocking it back and cutting off its attack. As Yost quickly rose, he steadied himself again and took a step back. Barrister then stepped up from behind him and thrust his staff at the creature to protect Yost's withdrawal.

Grunda was still determined to do something and edged closer to the fighting as she looked to find some kind of opportunity. With all the action so fiercely going on in front of her, she saw a brief gap between the combatants. Staying low to the ground, she scurried through the action unnoticed and emerged on the other side of the creatures. Thrilled at first that she had actually made it through, she suddenly realized she did not have a plan for what to do once she had gotten there.

Before her, Eleazaar and the wounded Yuan-ti were locked together in a desperate close-quarters fight. The creature grabbed hold of him and hurled him against the hard stone wall repeatedly, trying to weaken him so it could finish him with its sword. Frustrated by her own indecision and fear. Grunda stiffened her jaw determinedly and drew her short sword at last.

"Oh, bollocks," she said as she mustered her courage.

She scrunched up her face and charged at the Yuan-ti with her sword raised. She drove her sword straight into the creature's back. Surprised, it immediately straightened its body up, whipping its head back in forth as it roared in pain. Eleazaar, a little stunned, began swinging wildly at it with his sword as he stumbled forward awkwardly. As his blade heaved up, it struck the creature across its neck. Then, as the blade fell, he pushed its sword arm aside and thrust his blade up into the creature's abdomen.

The Yuan-ti tried biting at him, but he held its arm fast and was able to avoid its fangs as he lunged with his sword repeatedly, ripping up through its flesh with his blade as its blood sprayed out upon him. At last the creature collapsed and he kicked it for good measure as it hit the floor.

Seeing his comrade now fallen, the other Yuan-ti suddenly lunged sideways at Eleazaar, blindsiding him and hurling him into the wall of the corridor again. He clanged against the stone and fell to the floor, separated from his weapons. The Yuan-ti could not capitalize on his vulnerability, however, because he was still engaged with Yost.

"El!" Kalise screamed as she watched him fall.

This Yuan-ti in particular was a very good fighter and was aware of his disposition. While keeping Yost occupied with his weapon, he lashed out with his tail at Grunda too. He snapped it against the side of her head and knocked her off of her feet, cart-wheeling her end over end.

Kalise fired another arrow and struck it in the shoulder. As it twisted away in pain, Yost struck at it, but the creature recovered quickly yet again, blocking his sword away as before. Then Barrister stepped up and thrust his staff at it, but the creature blocked that too as it brought its own sword back across its body. It slapped the end of his staff against the corridor wall and, with its free hand, lashed Barrister across the face. Barrister stumbled away, crashing into the wall and dropping his staff.

Eleazaar got up on his knees and recovered his mace, which was closest to him. He then struggled to his feet, using it for support. After seeing the others fail so much in striking the Yuan-ti in close combat, he decided it was time to simplify the situation.

He raised his mace to strike the Yuan-ti and as the creature went to block it, he dropped down to his knees and drove the mace under its weapon, striking the Yuan-ti on one of its over-sized feet.

The tremendous and unanticipated pain from the strike opened up the creature's defenses, which allowed Yost to plunge his sword into its abdomen.

Not ready to quit even then, the Yuan-ti snapped its tongue out, lashing Yost in the eyes. Yost let go of his sword and the creature reached out and grabbed him by the throat. Opening its maw and leaning forward as if to bite him in the head, Eleazaar quickly grabbed his sword off of the floor and heaved it at the back of the Yuan-ti's neck.

His blade sliced into the Yuan-ti's spine and it fell forward, crashing to the floor and taking Yost down with it as it landed atop him.

As Yost struggled up to his feet, pushing the creature's body off of him, Eleazaar staggered over the corpse of the other as he rushed to Jayden's limp body. Jayden lay there shivering, his eyes wide open and barely clinging to life. Though he seemed to try, he could not speak. He was choking on his own blood which had been filling his lungs and depriving him of breath. Desperately, but hopelessly, Eleazaar tried to seal the cut and save his friend. He thought maybe if he could just stop the bleeding, he could use his healing powers to mend the wound sufficiently enough and heal it completely, but Jayden had lost too much blood already.

"I am sorry," Eleazaar said, tears welling in his eyes, "I am sorry ... please do not die ... I am so sorry."

Jayden's hand began to move, slowly edging its way to Eleazaar. It at last touched his boot before falling limp. His eyes remained open, but the shaking had abruptly stopped. Eleazaar checked for a pulse, but Jayden was dead. Eleazaar began to shake visibly and tears streamed down his face. He raised his blood-covered hand and manually closed Jayden's eyes.

"Proud of yourself now, hot shot," Yost said.

"Stupid boy!" Barrister growled. "I told you they would get someone killed, Manny."

"He did not get anyone killed!" Kalise fired back in his defense as she scowled at both Yost and Barrister.

"It was *you*, Manny ... both of you!"

"Oh.... ho ... ho ... ho," Barrister said smartly. "Look at little miss buttercups ... rushing to his defense; precious."

"And THAT!" Kalise exploded at them. "I am sick of that derogatory bullshit too! We are supposed to be a team, but all you do is talk shit to the rest of us. The deeper we get into this quest, the more the two of you hide behind others like the *cowards* you are!"

At that, Yost had reached his snapping point and he grabbed Kalise by the neck of her armor. He started to raise his fist, but held back as he conflicted internally about whether he would use it or not. He was not going to take such an insult from anyone.

"You just shut your dirty pie-hole!" he snarled through his teeth.

"Ho ho hold on now, Manny" Barrister cautioned, as much concerned about his own safety on the quest as for Kalise or anyone else. "Let us just think about this for a moment, okay?"

"You say something like that again;" he warned her, largely ignoring Barrister, "and I can tell you who the next one that will not be walking out of here will be."

Kalise jerked away from him defiantly, but did not press the issue. She had said exactly what she meant to say and she was not going to be apologetic for it. Regardless of the task's importance, she was quite willing to walk away as things stood currently.

Yost took a few steps back away from her and turned, walking off to the end of the corridor. He purposely hit Eleazaar with his leg as he walked past. Seeing a short dead end to the left, he turned right and walked on ahead down the adjoining corridor. Grunda had propped herself up against the wall at the end of the corridor, watching in disbelief, She got up and stayed well out of the way of Barrister who hesitantly followed after Yost. Once he had passed by, she scurried over to Eleazaar as he remained kneeling at Jayden's side.

"Twere not yous fault, love" Grunda said, empathetic to the deep despair emanating from him.
"Do not ... please," Eleazaar said in reply, grief stricken.
"God ... EL ... are you ...?" Kalise asked as he approached him; tears welling in her own eyes.
"I am okay ... I am okay," he reassured them. "I just cannot leave ... him here. I have to take his body back ho ..."
"We cannot," she cut him off, her voice starting to tremble. "He is *gone*, El, and we are in trouble. We still have to get *ourselves* out of here alive."

Eleazaar turned to look at her. His face was red and his nose was stuffy. All he could think about was Jayden's family and how they would feel about him leaving his body behind; how they would look at him for letting their son die.

"We will ... we will pick his body up on the way back; I promise," she offered. "Let us take whatever he has that we can use ... and try to make sure that *we* make it back."

Eleazaar reluctantly agreed with a nod. He did not like it at all, but he thought she was right under the circumstances at hand. Kalise motioned for Grunda to help him rummage Jayden's belonging and she knelt down beside him. Grunda immediately picked up Jayden's sword, which lay on the floor next to her.

"NO ... no," Eleazaar protested. "Give that to me."
"Sures, love," Grunda said softly, handing it to him.

He took the sword from her and held it in his hands, looking upon it with an empty stare. He quickly undid Jayden's belt and removed the sheath, adding it to his own belt. Then he slipped it in on his side. He did not know why he felt the need to carry it; he was carrying two weapons and the scythe already. He just felt like he should be carrying it.

Kalise was feeling his hurt like it was her own, though she did not quite know why. She did not really care for Jayden, but it was obvious how much Eleazaar did. She slowly knelt down beside him and placed her hands on his shoulders. Then she touched his face and held it in her hands.

"Stay with me, El," she said to him. "We need you; *I* need you."

"I am okay," he reassured her.

"You are bleeding," she noted, seeing the wound in his shoulder.

"It is not bad, but yeah," he said. "I will put something on it … wrap it later. We had better catch up with the others before something else happens."

They finished rummaging through Jayden's things and Kalise helped Eleazaar to stand up. He was shaken, extremely bruised and had that deep cut in his shoulder, but he was well otherwise. Then the three of them headed off together up the corridor after Yost.

Meanwhile, deep inside the temple and well below them in a cavern at its deepest part, three legless Yuan-ti crowded around a crystal skull they had been using to scry on areas familiar to them, particularly within the temple.

A bit like peering into a window through space to somewhere else, it was essentially a method of magical surveillance they used to guard their temple. One of the three, Verin, waved a clawed hand over the crystal skull as she made odd clicking and chirping-like sounds. Soon thereafter, a beam of light projected images out of it and onto the smooth rock wall behind them. They turned and watched the image of the group there on the wall as they continued on their quest down the next corridor at the temple's second level.

"It seems we have more visitors, my sisters" Verin said.

"We should dispatch them immediately," the second one, Gresil, said. "It appears they are strong, they could threaten us."

"No!" Verin sharply disagreed. "Let them come. We will defeat them and give them to Ixtacle Heptmuz."

"But one of them is a sorcerer," the third Yuan-ti, Sonnillon, pointed out. "He is surely quite powerful."

"As ... are ... we," Verin hissed in reply. "We possess the advantage down here with the clan at our behest. We will trap them; overpower and capture them. Then Heptmuz can feed on their flesh and be appeased."

"And what if they are stronger than we anticipate, Verin?" Gresil asked.

"They have already killed two of the strongest warriors of our clan," Sonnillon added.

"They were fortunate ... once;" Verin sneered, "but they are careless and divided. We will be better prepared for them now that we know they are coming. Once we have them were we want them, we will blot out this threat ... permanently."

The three Yuan-ti sisters continued observing the group with interest as they pressed forward, deeper into the temple. Eleazaar, Grunda and Kalise walked behind the others, distinctly keeping their distance. After the last blow-up between them all, they felt it best to create some space in the short term to let things calm down. It also seemed like a good time for Eleazaar to fill his friends in on some important details he had uncovered.

"Back in the room with the meglopede;" Eleazaar began, "there were markings in a very ancient glyphic style on the altar and walls."

"Could you decipher any of it?" Kalise asked, curious.

"More or less ... yes," Eleazaar replied. "Some of the glyphs were similar to those I have seen before in ancient pottery shards ... and others I recognize from my ancient lore studies. Distinctly, there was one which I believe represents the serpent god, Heptmuz."

"Was that not the god of darkness worshipped by some of the ancients?" Kalise returned.

"Gluttony, conquest ... and a lot of other things I am sure," Eleazaar confirmed. "He was a dominant force in their pantheon. There were signs of blood sacrifice on the specially designed altar; there were dark stains in the grooves for bloodletting."

"Oh, god," Kalise said. "That cannot be good."

"No, but it just confirms what we already suspected," Eleazaar said. "According to legend, the followers of Heptmuz would offer a sacrifice of human blood to Heptmuz ... pouring it into the mouth of some statue, I think, or something like that ... and then they collected the blood as it ran back out. This collected blood was supposed to be the blood of Heptmuz and they would ritually drink it in some special mixture of herbs or something. Over time, supposedly, this would transform them into the likeness of their god; make them serpents too."

"Cor!" Grunda gasped. "You meanin' those things back there was people who became snakes?"

"I am afraid so, Grunda," Eleazar returned. "My best guess ... is that this is the lost temple of Asch-Kur, which was mentioned briefly in ancient writings but had never been found."

"If it is ... then God help us, El" Kalise said.

"One of them is smart," Sonnillon noted to the others as they watched from afar through the scrying device.

"Too smart, Sonnillon," Gresil agreed. "Is this one a sorcerer as well?"

"No," Verin advised. "He was trying to heal the one who died and wears a symbol about his neck."

"He is a cleric!" Gresil said, greatly alarmed. "We must destroy him quickly before he can invoke his god's power to harm us!"

"He poses no threat to us, Gresil," Verin countered calmly. "He is but a boy and his god is nothing before Heptmuz; he is not powerful like the sorcerer. That is the one we must concern ourselves with first."

"Are you so certain, Verin?" Sonnillon asked, skeptical. "Quite certain," Verin said confidently. "Come ... let us assemble some warriors together and prepare a surprise for them. We will take steps to eliminate their strongest member and ensure our victory."

The three Yuan-ti sisters disengaged the scrying device and headed off into the tunnels at one end of their cavern sanctuary. As they left, they passed by a wide, deep pit where two other Yuan-ti tossed a limp, human body over its edge. Back in the corridor somewhere above, Yost stopped for a moment and looked behind him at the others. Exhausted, Barrister took the opportunity to make a prudent suggestion.

"We have got to stop and rest somewhere, Manny," Barrister said. "We are all tired … you are bleeding. We cannot possibly even think about entering a major fight like this without any rest."

"You are right," Yost relented. "The question is … where?"

Yost looked ahead and could see that the main corridor branched off to the right. He walked on ahead and looked around the corner. Before him was a short passage with a dead-end, but there was an opening to a room on the left side. He walked ahead and stuck his torch inside the room to have a look. The room was barren and dirty, but it had only one entrance to guard so he figured it would be the best place to rest they would likely find. As the others arrived from the corridor at the intersection with the passage, he turned to them.

"We need to rest and heal up," Yost said to them. "This room is clear and defensible, so we will stop here and recover for a while."

There was not really any argument to be found amongst the others. They had all been awake since before the sunrise, traversed a steamy, sub- tropical forest and had been in two fights already. They were all largely spent and both Yost and Eleazaar were wounded. As the group quietly passed Yost and entered the room, he put his hand on Barrister's shoulder.

"You take the first watch, Stan," Yost said. "I want someone I can trust."

"That will not be necessary … sir," Eleazaar interjected as he held up a large metal flask. "*This* will keep them away from us."

"I am afraid your holy water will not be much of a help, boy," Barrister said, annoyed.

"No, it would not," Eleazaar agreed, "but this is not holy water. It is a concentrated chemical solution called ammonium hydroxide. We use it a lot at seminary ... to clean the floors mostly. It has a strong odor that is particularly unpleasant to creatures with a strong sense of smell. We have used it to keep snakes away as well, so these creatures will definitely avoid it."

"Hmmm." Barrister replied as he turned to Yost, devoid of any good argument against it and actually welcoming of an idea for a change. "Well?"

"Alright, kid" Yost said at last, "if you are sure about this."

"Believe me," Eleazaar assured him, "nothing will go near the spot for hours."

"Get some rest, Stan," Yost said.

Eleazaar stepped out into the passage and returned to the intersection. He studied the floor, not wanting to pour it out where it might just drain away somewhere. He sprinkled the liquid all around the intersection, and then poured most of it in the middle where some of it could pool in small pockets that pocked the old stone. He then returned to the entrance of the room where Yost waited for him.

"My leg is still bleeding and it is getting more painful," Yost said.

"Sounds like infection," Eleazaar said in reply.

"Can you fix it so I can fight?" Yost asked.

"Of course, and probably even better," Eleazaar replied. "You will need to sit down somewhere and I can work on it."

Chapter Eleven

Know Your Enemy

The group spread out around the room to rest and let their wounds heal, unloading their gear. While they ate and drank, stretching their aching muscles and preparing mats for rest, Eleazaar followed Yost to a place along the back wall. Yost grimaced as he eased himself down to the hard floor and leaned back against the wall. Eleazaar knelt down before him and began to rummage his gear for the healing supplies he would use to treat Yost's leg. He laid out bandage wrapping, a small leather container and a metal vial.

"I am not going to lie to you," Eleazaar said bluntly as he picked up the metal vial. "This is going to hurt a little ... just so you know."

"What is it?" Yost asked, still a little distrustful of the boy.

"Hydrochloric acid," Eleazaar replied. "It is a weaker acid that will burn out the wound and kill any infection so that it heals quickly."

"Do not screw with me, kid," Yost said, clearly unsure about his methods.

"I am the healer here, okay?" Eleazaar reassured him. "In a week or so, maybe less, there will not even be a scar."

Yost just nodded reluctantly, giving him the okay to proceed with the treatment. He did not take his eyes off of Eleazaar though as the liquid dripped out of the vial along the length of the wound. Yost remained silent as the acid burned, but he jerked once from the pain. He swung his arm around as if to strike Eleazaar, but the cleric caught it and held it firmly while he waited for the acid to work.

Yost shivered and gritted his teeth as he managed the sting to an already painful wound, until Eleazaar finally took out his wineskin. He poured water over the wound to wash away the acid and then blotted it gently with a cloth. It still bled slightly but the bleeding was slowing at least and had almost stopped.

Cleaned out and dried, Eleazaar then wrapped the wound snugly with the cotton bandages, securing them with a small hemp weave with ties. He reached into his belt and removed a clear vial with a light blue liquid. He offered it to Yost as he prepared to pray healing upon him.

"Now drink this," he advised him. "It will restore your vitality and help you heal quickly."

Yost said nothing, but acknowledged him as he took the vial. He smelled it first, still a little unsure perhaps, and looked at the cleric as he tipped it up to drink. Then Eleazaar placed his hands around the wound and began a short healing prayer.

"Deus qui ut digni efficiamur;" he began, "curato et iniuria et in hora gratia. Blessed be your servants to fulfill your will."

The flesh of his hands seemed to almost become transparent as he prayed, as if a light were passing through them. When he removed his hands from the wound, it seemed as if it had already begun to heal shut. There was no more bleeding and the gash had closed. He nodded to Yost as he rose and retreated to the far wall where Kalise rested to treat his own wound finally.

Sitting down against the wall, he began to repeat the same procedure upon himself. With the help of Kalise, he removed the splint mail with some difficulty. The shoulder was stiffening on him and becoming more painful.

"Do you want me to ...?" Kalise asked.
"No ... I need to do this," he reassured her.

She grimaced empathetically as she watched him pour the acid onto the wound and shiver. Unlike with Yost, he felt because of the range of motion required in the short term, it would be best to stitch the wound shut as well before healing. He flushed the acid away with water and took out a needle and thread.

He worked slowly with the needle, managing his pain as he went. He closed his eyes and grit his teeth together as the needle broke through the flesh and he opened them again as he pulled the thread through. He had a numbing balm he could have used to ease the process, but he had decided to save it for someone else who might need it more later on. Fortunately, only six stitches were needed. When he was finished, he gently rubbed a healing balm on the wound to protect the exposed flesh and Kalise helped him wrap the shoulder with bandages.

"Concedo sancta Domine, curato et iniuria ... sustenden ut servo laus et via," he prayed as he laid his hands upon the wound.

Kalise could see the bones in his hand as they glowed with light beneath them. When he pulled them away, the wound had already begun to heal shut; as if it had been left to heal for days. His skill was impressive for such a young cleric, she thought.

"His servant brings him much glory, I think" she said.
"I dare not cloud the mind with such thoughts," Eleazaar replied. "The mind is cloudy enough the way it is."

Kalise, who was sitting at the corner of the room, leaned back against the other wall and began tugging on her boots. A pained look swept across her face as she removed each one. She tossed the boots aside and plopped her feet across Eleazaar's legs.

"Rub my feet?" Kalise asked assertively as she tossed a small pouch into his lap.

"What ... really?" Eleazaar said, a little caught off guard.

"They are killing me, please," she replied.

"What is this?" he asked as he picked up the pouch.

"It is a balm made from plant extracts ... good for the feet," she explained.

"Alright;" he said after a moment, "but first I have to perform a small ritual."

"A ritual?" she asked, a little confused. "There is a ritual for foot healing?"

"Ha ha ... no, not really," he replied. "This is a little different ... it is a very old and important one I was taught by Father Mannesh, my mentor."

He took out the metal pan he used for meals and poured water into it. After setting it under her feet, he took out a very small vial filled with a fragrant, oily liquid and sprinkled the contents onto her feet. Cupping water with his hands repeatedly, he dripped it over the length of her feet for several minutes. He gently caressed the water over her feet at last and then loosened his hair, letting it fall long. He let his hair fall across her feet and began to blot them dry with it.

"Aaah! What are you doing? she said with a giggle. "Stop that ... it is gross ... and it tickles."

"To wash the feet of another and dry it with your hair is the greatest display of humility and respect," he replied. "It used to be practiced regularly ... when the world was still humble."

"Okay, okay ... I get it ... still gross though," she said smiling as she lifted a foot back up to him. "Rub, preacher boy ... please."

Eleazaar raised an eyebrow, curled his lips in a crooked smile and took her foot in his hands. He picked up the tightly closed pouch and loosened the tie. He stuck two fingers inside and when he pulled them out, they were covered with a thick, greenish-white cream. He wiped the cream onto her foot and began massaging it into the skin.

"Ow ... ow ow!" Kalise exclaimed. "Easy there ... it is tender and I am a girl ... not an orc."

"I noticed," Eleazaar replied, smiling as he softened his touch.

"Ow ... uuuuuttttthhh," she continued as he rubbed.

"I am sorry," Eleazaar assured her.

"I know." she said, pulling up closer to him to grab her feet.

"Will you two quiet down, for Chislev's sake?" Barrister grumbled from across the room.

They both looked over at him briefly, then at each other. It suddenly hit both of them that they were very awkwardly close to one another. Their eyes met and for a moment, they both seemed to forget what they were doing.

Eleazaar's hands left her foot and began kneading her calf, then moved to her knees. His breath became short and hers quickened. His lips felt so dry and he drew them in to moisten them with his tongue. Something had to give.

"You need better boots;" Eleazaar said, never taking his eyes off of her, "if..... if you are going to be walking a lot."

"Shut up," she said in frustration as she quickly pressed her lips to his.

She bit down on her lip as she pulled away. She was not usually the aggressive type, but it was obvious to her that she would be waiting a long time if she did not take matters into her own hands. Afterwards, she was not quite convinced he was such an amateur at this sort of thing.

"How many girls have you kissed?" she asked him, suspicious.

"Uh ... including you?" Eleazaar said. "Just one, actually."

"You are such a liar!" she said, a smile stretching across her face. "Nobody kisses like that."

With that, he grabbed hold of her and kissed her again, this time much longer. He ran a hand through her hair and pressed her close against him. When he finally stopped to breathe, he leaned his forehead against hers. "I never lie," he said.

Looking him in the eyes, she suddenly shoved him against the wall. She rose to her knees and straddled his lap, putting her hands in his. Then she kissed him again.

"So what happens now?" he asked her, uncertain about this new territory he suddenly found himself in.

"I am not sure," she said, smiling awkwardly. "I feel kind of lightheaded."

She laid her head against his chest and he wrapped his arms around her. Barrister, shifting uncomfortably on the hard floor, turned his head around and looked at them. A bitter frown arose on his face and he sat up, leaning back against the wall. He opened his spell book and began to read quietly as he tried to get comfortable.

Yost had fallen asleep already, still sitting there against the back wall where Eleazaar had treated his leg. His head shifted to one side as he breathed slow and deep in his rest. Grunda, curled up in a fetal position on the floor, opened her eyes briefly and scanned the room as she lay there still. Satisfied all was well and safe, she closed them again. It was not long before the room fell deathly still, as everyone had finally either gotten reasonably comfortable or too exhausted to care if they were or not. Eleazaar and Kalise had slumped over together; her arm still across his waist as she lay next to him. Her head lay on his arm as they slept.

Back in the corridor where they had battled the Yuan-ti, Jayden's body lay cold and still on the floor where they had left him. Suddenly, his body jerked and began sliding along the floor. Something was dragging him away.

His armor grated against the stone as he was drug down into the pillared room. Then his body was dragged into the room with the altar and disappeared into a hole. The stone altar then shifted on the floor and covered the hole back up again.

Down the corridor beyond, not far from where the group rested, three pairs of red eyes appeared in the darkness. Three Yuan-ti made their way toward them, planning to surprise and attack them in their sleep. With the intent to kill Barrister before fleeing, they hoped to weaken the group and lead the remainder deeper into the temple to be killed.

One of the Yuan-ti tasted the air with his snake-like tongue and sniffed with his nose slits. He made a foul expression and shook his head from side to side. The other two did likewise with the same result. Putting a clawed hand to their nostrils, they turned to each other in fearful surprise.

"They have set powerful magic against us!" one of them exclaimed. "They must know we are coming. Let us flee and warn the others"

The three Yuan-ti quickly reversed course, turning away in a panic. They fled back into the depths of the temple, certain they were in grave danger from attack. Meanwhile, the group rested peacefully in the room, unaware the Yuan-ti had even come for them; all because of a chemical used to clean the floors at the seminary.

Later, deep inside the temple, the three Yuan-ti who had turned and fled emerged into the cavern below that was the heart of the cult's daily activity. Verin was quite surprised to see the warriors she sent returning so quickly. She had planned to scry and check on their situation soon, but it seemed that would not be necessary now. As the three approached her and her sisters, two other Yuan-ti tossed a limp human body, still in armor, into the large, cylindrical pit nearby.

"What is *this*?" Verin demanded with surprise. "Why do you return empty handed to us without even the wounds of battle? Speak!"

"They had powerful magics, great one," one of the Yuan-ti replied. "They burn the nose and eyes!"

"You see?" Gresil retorted smugly to Verin. "I told you they were powerful."

"Their puny magic will not avail them," Verin hissed angrily. "There are three of us and they have only one with magic. Besides, we have Puktah to aid us in defeating them."

Verin extended her arm, pointing as a clan member carried a goat to a spot on the cavern floor. The goat was bound so it could stand, but not walk away. The Yuan-ti then stepped well away.

Not far from them, at the rear of the cavern, there was a ledge up above where the cavern extended back even farther. There, a very large spider-like creature with bony plates like armor and an odd, long snout crept up to the ledge. It stopped there for a moment looking at the goat with its multi-segmented eyes.

Suddenly, a long, cord-like appendage erupted from the snout of the creature like a harpoon at lightning speed. The harpoon of Puktah, more formally known as a *cave fisher*, struck the goat and it blasted right through its flesh. The end of its appendage then produced short, claw hooks that curled out of the end of it like a grapple. Similar to a fisherman hooking his catch, it hooked the goat and reeled it in, yanking it high up into the air.

The goat was pulled up over the edge as the cave fisher backed away with its catch. The squealing, panicked and injured goat was quickly drawn to creature's mouth. Then there was a crunching sound and the squealing stopped as the goat was ripped apart and devoured by the thing's odd, bony maw. Verin looked over at her sisters with a satisfied, wicked gleam in her eyes.

"But ... they will be rested now and much stronger," Sonnillon said, still concerned about the group's potential threat. "We should still try to weaken them before they arrive here at the cavern."

"Yessssss," Gresil hissed gleefully. "We *shall* weaken them ... and, I know just how we will do it ... sisters!"

Meanwhile, Kalise and Eleazaar sat on a hilltop amongst wild flowers overlooking the valley of the Uradie. It was a wonderful afternoon, cloudy and cool as the breeze danced though the valley and tossed the tall grasses to and fro. They laughed as they told stories about their adventures there growing up with friends and he described a battle that had taken place on that very hill long ago. Finishing his tale, Eleazaar reached down and collected a cluster of wild flowers and gave them to her.

"Here," he said. "For you."

"You know;" she began in reply as she put her face into them and inhaled deeply, "wild flowers are my favorite of all."

"Really?" he said. "Is it one of those ... growing wild ... nature ... druidy things or something?"

"No!" she retorted with a playful shove. "They are more fragrant than the cultivated flowers they sell in town. I just think they are beautiful."

"I think you are beautiful," he said.

They looked at each other for a moment and she leaned over to kiss him. Just then, they heard an angry snarl right behind them. As they looked up, a Yuan-ti raised his blade and slashed it down upon them.

Eleazaar awoke from his sleep with a jolt. Realizing it was just a dream, he let out a relieved sigh. Hours had passed since they had fallen asleep and Kalise still lay there at his side. As he looked all around the room, he did not see Grunda anywhere. She had been curled up on the floor when he had fallen asleep, but was no longer there or seemingly anywhere else in the room. Immediately becoming panicked, he gently pushed Kalise aside and jumped up to his feet.

"Wake up," he said, reaching down and shaking her awake as he looked frantically about.

Kalise was groggy and struggled with her balance as she pulled herself up from the floor. She grabbed her boots and fumbled to get them on her feet. She looked around confused as others began to awaken also.

"What is going on?" she said.

"Where is Grunda? Eleazaar asked. "She is gone."

"Wha ..." she said, looking for her. "She is not ... *Grunda!*"

If there was any lingering sleep left in Barrister or Yost, it disappeared when Kalise called out for Grunda. The two were jolted wide awake and Yost quickly grabbed his weapon, initially fearing that they might be under attack. Eleazaar turned around and started to run out of the room in search of Grunda, but stopped as Grunda waddled in.

"What are you doing, Grunda?" Eleazaar demanded. "You cannot just go off alone all by yourself."

"A lady gots to take the mick from time t'time," she replied, not understanding what all the fuss was about. "Me cannot ruddy well do it 'round heres … front'sta everyones and all."

"Beans," Eleazaar said with relief. "Just tell someone next time before you go … please."

"You scared us, Grunda," Kalise said. "We thought something happened to you."

"Hmmm," Barrister interjected smartly with less concern. "Perhaps some of us were worried."

"Canna rightly see whit the fuss be abouts," Grunda said to Eleazaar with a shrug. "Not likes me was'a off gallivantin' wit some dwarvish rumpy-pumpy now, love."

"Oh … I get you," Eleazaar said, empathizing. "Just please, keep that in mind for future reference."

"Aye, love," Grunda agreed. "If'n you says so."

"How's the leg feeling, Mr. Yost?" Eleazaar then asked, turning his attention elsewhere. "Better?"

"Yeah," he replied in a deep, tired voice. "It feels surprisingly good, kid. You did alright. It is hard to believe that it is healing already."

"A little God and a little science," Eleazaar said. "It will keep getting better, I assure you."

"Get your stuff together, Stan," Yost said, turning to Barrister. "We need to get the hell out of here and finish what we came here for."

"I suppose taking the day off is out of the question," Barrister grumbled under his breath.

Barrister reluctantly nodded and rubbed his tired eyes. He collected up his things and put away his spell book into a leather holster around his waist under his robe. His eyes narrowed and he pursed his lips as he watched Kalise wrap her arms around Eleazaar and lay her head against his shoulder. But bitterness aside, he decided he was over the matter and just wanted to move on. He turned his head away and rolled up his sleeping mat as he continued gathering his things.

Yost wedged his right arm and used the wall as a crutch, wincing as he eased himself up onto his feet. His leg might have been feeling better, but he was stiff from sleeping on the stone floor and he had plenty of deep bruises and tissue damage that still hurt plenty. After everyone had collected and packed up all of their gear, Yost lit a fresh torch and headed toward the corridor outside of the room. Eleazaar quickly took his holy symbol in his hand and illuminated it as well.

"Illuma et mak symbasa," he commanded.

As always, the symbol began to glow brightly and cast radiant light all about the room. He ushered Kalise and Grunda to the corridor and they all followed Yost and Barrister to the intersection. The ammonia that he had poured out there hours before had largely dried up or trickled away.

"I can still smell that stuff you dumped here," Yost noted. "It must have worked. What was it called again?"

"Ammonium Hydroxide," Eleazaar said in reply.

"I will remember that for future reference," Yost said. "It looks like the corridor turns again here, right up ahead."

"It circles around to more stairs going down, I am sure," Barrister speculated. "It is not uncommon for old temples; still pretty common, actually."

"I hope you brought plenty of that good healing stuff, kid," Yost said as he began to walk on ahead. "I got a feeling we will be treating a lot of wounds before the day is finished."

At that prospect, Eleazaar looked down in thought. He was pretty sure Yost was right about that and he just hoped he would be ready when the time came. His failure to save Jayden was still weighing on his mind. As Yost and Barrister both walked on ahead of them, Eleazaar knelt down and closed his eyes as he placed his hand on the stone floor.

"El?" Kalise said, thinking perhaps there might be something wrong.

"Un spreken de stonen," he commanded.

A whirlwind formed in his mind as he drew up the absorbed energy from the stone around him. An image began to emerge from the whirlwind revealing three Yuan-ti coming up the corridor toward where he knelt currently. Two of them spoke before the third tasted the air with his tongue, followed by the others. Then they began shaking their heads violently.

"Let us kill them *all* now," the one said. "Then we will be great warriors before the clan."

"No," the second Yuan-ti corrected. "We are only to destroy the sorcerer for now ... and retreat to the sanctuaire. We are only to weaken them and finish them later."

"What be that smell?" the third asked. "It bad ... hurt smell."

"It burns!" said the first Yuan-ti.

"They have set powerful magics against us!" the second one said. "They must know we are coming. Let us flee and warn the others."

Eleazaar took a deep breath and opened his eyes. If he had any previous notion that they would be walking into a trap, it was now confirmed completely. He lifted his hand from the floor as he stared down the corridor ahead at Barrister.

"Helloooo ... El?" Kalise continued as she and Grunda looked down oddly at him.

"There be somethin' wrong, love?" Grunda asked.

"The cultists came to attack us while we slept," he informed them. "They were going to kill numb nuts there ... Barrister."

"What?" Kalise asked, surprised. "How do you know that?"

"Stone reading ... just something the order teaches us," he answered dismissively as tried to focus on the details of what he had seen. "They know he is a sorcerer ... which means we are being watched."

"Why do they want to kill him so bad?" Kalise then asked.

"Cor!" Grunda interjected. "They hafta get in line behind me, they does."

"And how are they watching us?" Kalise added.

"Well, that would mean there are more sorcerers around this place than just Barrister," Eleazaar speculated aloud. "They must have some kind of device they can see through; a scrying device that bridges distance and time. As I understand it, it lets them look in and view places that are familiar to them."

"Proly even watchin' me do me business," Grunda said.

"Ugh ... ewww," Eleazaar grunted, quickly trying to erase that image from his mind. "They must figure Barrister presents the strongest threat to them, so they want to weaken us by killing him. In any case, we are walking right into a trap."

"Like a trapper sets the bait and draws the animal in for the kill," Kalise noted.

"That is pretty much the idea, I think," Eleazaar agreed. "They only wanted to weaken us, not stop us from coming. With Barrister's magic out of the way, they must believe that clearly shifts the balance of power in a conflict to their favor."

"We should tell Manny then, El. Should we not?" Kalise asked.

"Not yet," Eleazaar replied at last after a moment of thinking. "I do not know how ready he is to hear any suggestions from me, any of us just yet really. Let us give it some time and see what happens in the short term. The important thing is that *we* know."

"And what about Barrister then? she continued. "He really deserves to know, arsehole or not."

"Yes he does," Eleazaar agreed, "but he would not listen. "He would trip over his own arrogance first. As much as it pains me, we just need to make sure that nothing happens to him. I have got a feeling that whatever wants him dead is far more unpleasant than he is."

Up ahead of them, Yost and Barrister stopped at the turn in the corridor. Yost looked back and saw the others still standing near the entrance. Eleazaar rose and the three walked on until they had rejoined together at the turn.

"What the hell was the hold up?" Yost asked.

"Nothing," Eleazaar replied, flashing a quick glance at Kalise. "Something came loose and I just had to get it readjusted."

"Well, let us know if it happens again," Yost informed him. "We need to stick together from now on."

"I will do that, of course," Eleazaar said.

"I thought you said you never lie," Kalise whispered from the side of her mouth as the group walked on.

"I do not," Eleazaar whispered back. "That was a tactical lie and they do not count."

"In whose opinion?" she whispered, dismayed. "We have categories of lying now?"

Eleazaar made a gesture of disbelief, inasmuch to suggest he could not believe they were having this conversation under the circumstances. Kalise glared at him and shook her head, thinking he must surely be in denial or something. Lying was lying in her opinion, regardless of how tactical it may be. Grunda watched them as they exchanged silent, argumentative gestures.

"Like watchin' two ruddy mimes havin' a go at it," Grunda giggled under her breath.

As the group neared the end of the corridor where another turn to the right awaited them, there was an opening to another room. Yost held out his hand to signal the others to stop as he approached the opening quietly for a look. He drew his sword and leaned forward with his torch to peer into the room. It seemed nearly identical to the room they had rested in earlier. It was pretty much just bare stone and did not appear to have been used for anything in the recent past. He stepped inside and illuminated the room, but there was nothing to see, except for one thing.

As he turned around to leave again, something caught his eye on the floor near the entrance. He knelt down with his light and picked it up in his hand. It was a little wooden peg with a red ribbon attached.

"The ranger," he said under his breath as he looked off in thought; "always thinking ahead."

As the ranger had penetrated into the temple, he had stopped to rest here for a short while and rummage his gear. Thinking ahead to his own possible disappearance, he had left the flag lying just out of sight around the edge of the entryway. Yost rose and stepped back out into the corridor, still holding the flag.

"Our ranger made it this far," Yost informed them as he held up the little marker flag. "Leading us with a trail of bread crumbs."

"To what?" Barrister said. "He did not make it back out, remember?"

"That … I do not know," Yost admitted. "I bet we find out sooner than later, though."

"No signs of a fight anywhere," Eleazaar observed. "He may have gotten deep inside."

"That is the advantage of single person over a party, kid," Yost said as he looked down the corridor ahead of them. "It is much easier to slip in quietly when you are alone. Rangers are pretty damn sneaky to begin with. Let us order ourselves for combat, just in case. We could get attacked at any time and we should be ready."

"Are you getting the sense we are in some kind of danger, Manny?" Kalise asked.

"Maybe," Yost replied. "Just want to be prepared … that is all."

"Weapons check," Eleazaar said.

Everyone who had not already done so drew their weapons and affirmed that they were good to go for combat. Yost placed the flag back inside of the room where had found it, just in case they too failed to return. None of them really had anything similar to leave behind or else he might have left their own marker there too.

"I will go first, the cleric will follow me, then Stan in the middle," Yost began as he assigned their marching order moving forward. "Kalise … you guard Stan's back and little dwarf … you guard our rear from surprise attacks.

Yost turned to look at Eleazaar, perhaps as much to convey a truce on his part from the way things were earlier, as anything else. Yost was not easy to read though, so few assumed to know his intentions. Eleazaar simply nodded his approval. He was not really worried so much about Grunda as he had been when the trip began. She had seemed to come into her own a little as the adventure unfolded. He thus felt fairly confident that she would guard their rear well. It was one of the few things he felt confident about at the moment.

Chapter Twelve

CLAY

Yost lead the way as the group moved down the corridor to the next corner. He eased his head around for a quick look before continuing on. About eighty feet down the corridor, there was indeed another set of stairs just like Barrister had predicted.

"Well Stan, you called it," Yost said. "How far to the bottom do you think?"

"We have to be getting close now," Barrister advised as he walked up and stood by Yost. "Might be another level, but I do not think the temple is large enough for more than that."

"Mmmm ... right," Yost said, agreeing. "You know what worries me?" said.

"What is that?" Barrister asked.

"They ... these cultists ... surely know we are here by now," Yost said.

"Probably," Barrister agreed.

"Why have they not made a stronger effort ... much of any really ... to stop us from coming?" Yost said, airing his thoughts. "They might not be aware yet," Barrister countered.

"Suppose they are," Yost said, pushing the senario.

"Then they probably want us to come," Barrister replied, "which means we are walking into a trap. You really believe that?"

"Call it a gut feeling," Yost said as he leaned over to look ahead down the stairs.

"You just keep that spell book handy, Stan."

"Are we going to go down, guys, or should we call for a round table discussion?" Kalise asked smartly.

"In a hurry to die, are we?" Barrister retorted.

"Are you?" Kalise snapped back.

Eleazaar gently put his hand on Kalise. They did not need this and he was afraid if the snippety bickering continued, something would happen to them again like when Jayden was killed earlier. Yost too could sense that things really needed to change quickly. He started down the long flight of stairs with the notion that, if things were going to change for the group, then the change needed to start with him as their leader.

One by one, the others descended the stairs following Yost. These stairs were far different than the others they had gone down before. These flared out at the bottom onto a small platform and then two steps descended from the platform to the floor. It seemed indicative that they might finally be getting close to a central area.

Below them, the stairs ended at a roughly sixty foot by eighty foot room with two actual, in-tact doors. The first door, to their right about halfway down, was a single door made of iron-reinforced wood. It swung on an iron hinge, but the fact that it was in-tact and seemed to be in good condition was surprising. It was the first working door they had encountered since they had entered the temple. They were all but certain now that they were getting close.

The second door was actually a set of double doors located on the far end of the room. They were large at ten feet in height, but the arched ceiling was a good fifteen feet above them at least. The doors were a rust color and Eleazaar was not sure at this distance if that was because they really were rusty or if they had been painted that way; not that it really mattered. By the look of them though, he figured they were metal; likely cast iron doors.

The room itself was largely devoid of anything. There were no constructs of any kind, nor was there anything that would suggest a use other than connecting one place to another. There was to be found, however, a considerable collection of pictographs or symbolic glyphs covering the walls.

"These are the same kind of glyphs that I saw in the altar room up above," Eleazaar said, to no one in particular.

"You did not say anything about glyphs before," Yost said.

"No," Eleazaar replied. "I did not figure anyone would be interested, I guess,"

"Perhaps not," Yost said. "I suppose that is on me. Can you interpret any of it?"

"A little ... bits and pieces of it," Eleazaar admitted. "I did not really specialize in lore or anything. Above us, it described ritual sacrifice and the exchange of blood with Heptmuz, their snake god. Here, it seems to be more like stories ... a pictorial history of the clan, cult or what-ever."

"Nothing useful of course," Barrister snipped.

"That depends on what you consider useful," Eleazaar retorted. "If we had a few hours, we could learn quite a bit about them probably; maybe even tidbits on how best to fight them."

"But, we do not have time for that," Yost clarified. "If we stick around here, we would get discovered and swarmed by the whole nest of them."

"I do not disagree with you," Eleazaar said. "It is what it is, Mr. Yost."

"So, you think this is the base of the temple?" Kalise asked, looking at Yost.

"In the proper sense ... yes, I think," Yost speculated. "They do not have a whole clan stashed around here anywhere close though. I am betting this goes subterranean somewhere."

"In-tact doors here ... none above us," Barrister noted. "Someone must be maintaining them. Surely, their sanctum cannot be too far."

"We will soon see," Yost said. "So what do you think, Stan ... door number one or door number two?"

"I do not know Manny," Barrister replied. "One is as good as the next. The big double doors are probably the way we want to go, at least in my experience. If there is an inner sanctum to be found, that would be the way to go."

While Barrister and Yost discussed what to do, Eleazaar scoured the glyphs on the wall for any knowledge that might be useful to them. He stroked them with his fingers to wipe away dust that had collected so that he could read them better. In some cases, they had worn down or deteriorated over time and were not so clear. As Barrister spoke about the doors, Grunda tugged on Kalise's arm and whispered to her.

"There proly be double doors at the gates of hell too," she said with conviction. "He gonna be walkin' through thems one day. You watch, love."

"Cleric?" Yost said, inquisitively.

"Hmmm ... what?" Eleazaar replied, distracted by the glyphs.

"What do you think we should do?" Yost asked.

"What ... you are asking me?" Eleazaar said in disbelief.

"Seeing no other clerics around at the moment ...," Yost mused, "yes, I am asking you."

"Oh, yeah.... well," Eleazaar began, completely caught off guard. "A set of double doors usually means a main chamber of some sort lies beyond, or a central passage or series of areas that form the heart of a complex structure. There could be anything behind the smaller door, which is always what concerns me the most. If we do not check and clear that area before we move on, there is always a chance we pay hell for a price later. That is just my thoughts, in general."

"It is a good point," Barrister agreed reluctantly. "I cannot argue with that."

"I agree, too. I think you are right," Yost said. "We will clear the area behind the small door first then."

"Am I imagining things, or did they all just agree on something?" Kalise whispered as she leaned down to Grunda.

"No, I heard it meself love," Grunda whispered back. "Someone has bewitched the lot of them, methinks."

"Okay folks, here is how this is going to go," Yost explained. "The cleric and I are going to go by ourselves first, just in case there are any immediate threats. We can retreat quickly here in that case without a pile up at the door. And you … Grunda, is it?"

"Ya means the stinkin' little prat? Grunda replied smartly. "That be me alrights. What it be t'yous now?"

Yost knew he probably had that coming. As leader, it was his responsibility to bring the group together and make them a team for the mission. He let his personal feelings about the members he was given for that team get in the way of that important duty. Now was the time to fix it, if he still could, while they still had time. He took a deep breath and pursed his lips as he took the plunge.

"Look, all of you;" he began, "I have said a lot of things I should not have said that has made this trip a lot more difficult than it should have been."

"Go on," Eleazaar encouraged, sensing some soulful progress was being made.

"There are probably some very bad things ahead for us," he continued, looking around at all of them. "The fact and the reality is that none of us have much of a chance of getting out of here alive if we do not work together. Like it or not, here we all are and we need each other."

Grunda raised a curious eyebrow as she listened to him. She was a bit skeptical since he had treated her the worst by far, but she was willing to hear him out. Kalise and Eleazaar looked at each other, a little surprised, but pleasantly so. It was a quite unexpected change of attitude, though one that was sorely needed. Barrister, by contrast, was less welcoming of change. He would do his part like a good soldier and try to limit his snippets at the others, but he would not lower himself to get all friendly with stupid kids or grubby peasants. That was too much for him.

"So with that Grunda," Yost proceeded in his new approach, "would you please go quietly to the door and tell me if you hear anything moving around or making noises in the area that lies beyond?"

"Well … alrights then," Grunda said after a moment. "Ah dinnea mind doin' anythins if ya speaks nicely to mes and all."

Yost just nodded to her. He was not one to get all bubbly apologetic on anyone, but it was sufficient nonetheless for everyone. Grunda eased over to the door and put her ear to it, listening while the others looked on curiously. She turned back toward the others after a few moments and shrugged, before walking back to them.

"Ah canna hears nothin'," she said.
"Okay then … in we go," Yost declared.
"Wait!" Eleazaar said quickly. "Let me do something first."

Eleazaar held up his hand to caution them to stay back as he walked over to the wall next to the door. As he knelt down, Barrister cocked his head slightly as he watched, trying to figure out what the boy was up to. He closed his eyes and placed his hand on the stone of the wall.

"The living spirit in all things," he whispered. "Un spreken de stonen."

Slowly, a whirlwind began to take form in his mind. It howled and shook with immense power, and a cluttering of countless voices echoed from within it. It was possible that these stones had absorbed the energy of the life that transpired around them for hundreds or maybe even thousands of years. He could not be sure, but the stones were full of memories over a great deal of time.

Why the stones before had not created this effect, he was not sure. Perhaps it was many years of little activity, he thought. Then again, a corridor was a route of passing and not an emotional epicenter of activity as this area likely had been.

He concentrated harder, forcing his will on the swirling vortex in his mind. Then there was a sudden blast in the vortex, like crashing through a wall. He plunged into a vision of being out in the middle of the main room as a man eased carefully down the flight of stairs. The man looked around before going to the door where Eleazaar knelt. He listened at the door briefly, before prying it gently open.

Then Eleazaar was suddenly transported inside of the room as the door slowly and quietly opened. The man slipped inside the room taking great care to be stealthy. He seemed to be about thirty years old, with a chiseled jaw and a nearly shaven head. It could only be Ritter, the missing ranger. He held up a stone that glowed to light his way; a moonstone, and held a dagger in his other hand.

The ranger gazed about inside the room quickly, before sticking his head back out and scanning the main room as he closed the door behind him. He seemed to be doing exactly what they were doing right now; checking his environment and trying to eliminate threats that could compromise him later. The room seemed to be segmented.

There was a main area where he was now and a door in the back, left hand corner to somewhere else. He figured the Ranger wanted to check behind the door in the back before moving on.

It was standard tactics they were teaching now in the provincial armies. Many rangers had served in one of the armies previously and many still did on a part-time basis. Ritter looked a lot like a soldier and, from what Eleazaar knew about the team he was a part of, he was pretty sure both conditions applied to this ranger.

The room itself was not particularly interesting. It had a wooden table and two wooden chairs. One of the chairs was broken and they looked rather old anyway. What was interesting was a massive statue of some kind of ancient warrior, he guessed, all seemingly dressed in the formal garb of his long forgotten culture.

The statue stood a good eight feet high and there was no base to it. It did stand on a pedestal, but the pedestal was clearly made from something else and not part of the statue. Broad, powerful-looking feet of the figure served as the only proper base supporting it. Eleazaar could not imagine that it was still standing after what was likely such a long time.

It seemed so precarious without a strong, broad base as part of the statue beneath to support it. He could not imagine what it was made of that would be so enduring and stable to keep it intact.

It was towering and a little intimidating standing there in the center of the room. The ranger was drawn to it also and he looked it over with a profound curiosity. It seemed too profound, in fact. The ranger examined it with an almost suspicious flair in his body language.

"What is he doing?" Yost asked no one in particular as he looked on, watching Eleazaar turn his head periodically with a strained face.

"He called it stone reading, Manny," Kalise said in reply. "Somehow he can see events captured in the stones or something."

"Religious mumbo jumbo," Barrister interjected, prompting a look from Yost. "Sorry."

The members of the group were not the only ones watching, however. In the cavern beyond and below that served as the hub of clan activity, the three Yuan-ti sisters were watching as well. They were also quite troubled by what they were seeing and becoming impatient. As their crystal scrying ball projected the image of the young cleric knelt by the wall for an extended time, they worried that their secret might get exposed before they could use it.

"What is the boy doing?" Sonnillon asked nervously. "Why do they not enter?"

"The cleric must sense something," Gresil replied, speculating. "He waits there too long. We cannot wait any longer, sisters. We must activate it now before they discover it."

"Agreed," Verin chimed in. "We must strike quickly before we lose the element of surprise."

Reaching down, Verin picked up a dusty scroll tied with a small piece of twine. She slipped off the twine and unrolled the scroll, holding it before her. She then began reading aloud into the crystal ball, ancient words that were written on the scroll in a commanding voice. As Eleazaar watched, the ranger stroked the statue with his fingers and brought them to his nose, smelling them.

"Clay," the ranger said softly. "Surely not."

"Cannot be," Eleazaar said to himself in his mind. "Clay would never survive such a long time with the weight and design … unless …"

Suddenly, the arm of the statue began to move. The ranger caught the movement out of the corner of his eye and immediately turned his head to look. As he did, the statue clubbed him in the face, sending the surprised ranger tumbling across the room.

"Oh, fiddle," Eleazaar thought. "This is so not good."

The statue became fully animated with complete motion ability in the head, arms and legs. It stepped down off of the pedestal with a thunderous thud. Easily weighing in at six hundred pounds, it was a serious, solid chunk of pure, merciless crushing power. The sisters had unleashed a clay golem upon the ranger.

The ranger first tried to scramble to the exit, but the golem was closer and blocked off his escape. Then, the ranger grabbed his sword and hurled it upon the golem as it advanced mindlessly at him, but it merely clanged and bounced off. The golem did not need a weapon as it was the weapon. When it hit the ranger, the only thing bouncing off was the ranger himself. The blows were crushing and fast. But, the ranger fought vigorously with everything he had, even if it was pointless and desperate. He stabbed at it and in the end beat his fists bloody against it trying to save his own life, but he could not. The golem pounded its heavy, magic-hardened clay fists into the ranger until his bones were broken and his skull crushed.

The golem had no soul, and so its cruelty was soulless. It was the thing Eleazaar hated most about sorcery and to an extent, many of its practitioners; it was a soulless exercise unbounded by moral restraint. A feeling of grief for the poor ranger swept through him.

"No one deserves to die like that," he thought to himself.

Then, remembering suddenly where he was, the grief was replaced by fear. He was concentrating in the stone reading so hard, that blood began to drip from his nose. He jolted out of the vision and jumped up to the surprise of everyone, who stood looking wide-eyed at him. He turned to them with urgency in his voice.

"Does anyone have enchanted weapons?" Eleazaar asked.
"No … why? Yost returned slowly, looking strangely at the young cleric.
"Because … that is exactly what we will need in about ten seconds," Eleazaar said in reply.
"Just what in the nine hells is that supposed to mean?" Yost probed further, confused. "Are you alright, kid?"
"Not sure really … actually," Eleazaar replied, anxious about what he knew was to come.
"But, what I am sure of is that a golem is about to come crashing through that door and it takes an enchanted weapon to harm it. With the exception of Barrister and his staff, the rest of you need to start running … right now."
"What … and you have an enchanted weapon?" Yost asked, skeptical.

Eleazaar fumbled nervously as he reached for a weapon on his belt. He was almost shaking and Kalise had noticed. She watched him closely, quite concerned and especially so after seeing the blood drip from his nose. Eleazaar pulled out his mace and held it up.

"Mace of Disruption," he said almost sheepishly. "Father Mannesh gave it to me for my seventeenth birthday. It is supposed to be wicked on zombies … I just hope it works well on golems too."

As if on cue, there was a thunderous stomp that seemed to come from the room beyond the door. A surprised expression came over Yost's face and he looked at the cleric in disbelief. He was especially unhappy that the young cleric was right this time.

"I told you," Eleazaar said, a little dismayed that everyone seemed frozen in place. "Go on, Mr. Yost. Take Kalise up the stairs and cover our backs. Grunda, hide in the shadows ... quickly!"

"Right, love," Grunda replied.

"We cannot just leave you," Yost protested.

"Yes you can ... no choice," Eleazaar said urgently, trying hard to hurry them away.

"I am staying El," Kalise pleaded. "I can help you."

"NO ... Kalise," he shouted, almost desperate now. "Not this time. Please go now."

Reluctantly, Yost grabbed Kalise's arm and pulled her toward the stairs. He did not know anything about golems and he did not like the way they were doing this, but the desperation in Eleazaar's eyes convinced him to comply. Kalise, on the other hand, was feeling very afraid because of that same look.

She knew of golems through stories, though she had never encountered one before. The stories were all fearsome and savage tales of great destruction and loss of life. In her heart, she felt like she was leaving him behind to die.

The two of them ascended to the top of the stairs and stretched to look down into the room below. Eleazaar stretched his neck out and pulled his mace up into a combat-ready stance. Then, a sudden silence came over the room.

"You got a plan, kid?" Barrister said as he stood there with his staff trying not to seem nervous.

"Yeah," Eleazaar replied. "If it chases you, then run like hell. If it does not ... it will be chasing me ... so *hit* it."

The single door exploded into the room around them, shattering into splinters as it was ripped from its foundings. The massive golem came through without so much as a flinch, completely indifferent and immune to any semblance of pain. It stopped and scanned, identifying Barrister.

"Oh, it is definitely looking at you," Eleazaar concluded. "I hope you brought clean britches."

"Shit," Barrister said, now realizing what a big pile of it he was in.

"Yep," Eleazaar agreed.

The golem took off, stomping straight for Barrister. The evoker's whole body jerked in surprise and panic as he took off running from the thing. Eleazaar jumped in front of the golem and heaved his mace into its hard chest.

The mace made a deep thud, like a metal sledge hitting rock. The golem scarcely even budged from the blow, even though he had swung his mace around with a lot of force. It did, however, bust away shards of clay from the impact point.

To the golem though, Eleazaar was nothing more than an irrelevant obstacle like the door it had crashed through. It stomped ahead right into him and swung its big arms around at him. Like being slapped by a tree trunk, Eleazaar was knocked away to the side and crashed into the wall near the stairs.

"El!" Kalise yelled down at him as she saw him crash below her.

"I am fine ... I think," he said with a cough as he tried to assure her and himself as well.

Eleazaar got up slowly and felt a sharp pain. As he looked up, however, he could see Barrister running in circles for his life and quickly forgot about it. He rushed in to try and intercept the golem with his mace again, if nothing else than to get Barrister some separation and buy time.

Back down below them in the cavern, the three Yuan-ti witches watched as the golem chased Barrister. They were troubled, however, and debated among themselves about a change of plan. They did not anticipate anyone having a weapon that could hurt their prized golem.

"Impossible," Verin lamented angrily. "It cannot be. The boy has damaged our golem."

"I told you the cleric was dangerous," Gresil hissed. "You never listen to me, Verin."

"His mace must have an enchantment upon it," Sonnillon said.

"Of course it is enchanted, idiot!" Verin snapped. "Shut up, both of you. I cannot think."

"We must destroy the cleric first Verin," Gresil suggested. "If we do not, we may fail to kill the sorcerer."

Verin looked at her sisters for a moment. Time was of the essence and a decision had to be made. Considering everything, Verin resolved that Gresil was correct and eliminating the cleric first was the only sensible strategy. She nodded to Gresil and leaned down to the crystal scrying ball.

"Golem," she said, commanded it. "Kill the cleric."

"Ow," Eleazaar moaned as he rotated his shoulder.

Every time he hit the golem, his mace bounced away hard and reverberated. At times, it seemed like it was hurting him as much as he was hurting it. He did not exactly have any better or even other options at his disposal though.

Then the situation changed suddenly. The golem stopped chasing Barrister and pivoted, turning toward Eleazaar. It began stomping toward him with a stiff gait and Eleazaar readied his weapon in a fighting stance.

"Oh ... well now," he said aloud to himself. "Finally someone appreciates my talents."

As the golem stomped mindlessly at him, Eleazaar tried to duck under its arm to the left and spin away from it. He swung his mace at it as he did, trying to hit it in the exposed back. The golem was totally locked onto him, however, its fist grazed his back as he ducked, causing him to hit the golem awkwardly and stumble. It turned on a dime after him and Eleazaar quickly rolled back up to his feet.

There was no pause to its pursuit, so it was upon him quickly again. With only a fraction of time to think of what to do, he did the first thing that came to mind: run. It was not that large of a room, when you are being chased by a golem at least, so he ran in long circles to keep out of its reach.

For a big, chiseled block of clay, it was deceptively fast. Despite his every effort, the thing stayed right on his heels. It could keep that pace up all the day and night too, unlike Eleazaar or anyone else.

"Feel free to hit this thing, Barrister," Eleazaar said breathlessly as he ran, a little perturbed at the lack of help he was getting. "You know ... anytime you get a moment. Now, would be nice."

Barrister steeled himself and whacked the golem as it passed by, hot on Eleazaar's heels. It did not do much. The staff bounced right off and reverberated in Barrister's hands.

"It did not do anything," Barrister called to him as he streaked across the other side of the room.

"Well, try hitting it again!" Eleazaar shouted back. "A little harder maybe."

At the top of the stairs, Yost was getting anxious as he and Kalise listened to them battling the golem below them. It did not sound like they were doing well at all. He started to go down the stairs to help, but Kalise grabbed his arm and held him back.

"I have got to go help them," Yost reasoned with her. "It is going to kill them both."

"No Manny," Kalise replied firmly. "We cannot help them. We have to let El fight this battle."

"Well, why in the hell is Stan not using his magic?" he asked in frustration.

"Maybe the golem is immune to spells," Kalise said, offering her best guess. "Like it is to non-magical weapons maybe."

"Hmm," Yost said, a little dismayed. "That is *damn* inconvenient."

Barrister hit the Golem again and again as it passed by, but his staff had little effect on it. It seemed he could do little more than scratch its hard clay. Eleazaar was getting winded too and he knew he would eventually slow down and be caught if he did not do something, even if it might be a little stupid.

"I am going to try something Barrister," Eleazaar shouted. "I just need you to help me out a little, okay?"

"What do you want me to do?" Barrister replied. "My magic stick does not seem to be helping much."

"Noticed!" Eleazaar called back to him as he raced around breathlessly. "I just need you to hit it a couple of times real good and buy me a second or two. Give it everything that you have got … okay?"

"Sure, kid," Barrister said, before uttering under his breath. "It is your life."

Eleazaar swung wide in his flight to the edge of the wall and then veered hard to his right. As he swung around again and passed Barrister, he ran straight at the back wall as hard as he could run. Barrister reared back with his staff and swung it as hard as he could at the golem, putting his whole body into it.

The staff struck the golem across the neck with enough force that it arched back slightly and slowed. It also did a number on Barrister. The backlash of force spun him around and he fell to the ground.

With just a little extra space as the golem stomped after him, Eleazaar grabbed his mace, leaped and took two steps right up the wall. Pushing off, he did a backwards sommersault, and swung his mace at the back of the golem's head. As improbable and ill-fated as the idea actually working might have been, his mace struck the thing in the back of its head as if guided by angels.

He hit it so squarely, in fact, that the hard-charging golem's momentum sent it crashing right into the wall. When it did, a chunk of the head fell off. An airborne Eleazaar then fell unceremoniously to the hard floor with a thud, on his face.

His mace popped out of his hand and slid across the floor away from him.

The golem stood motionless for a moment, and then it stepped back away from the wall. It looked odd with a chunk of its head missing, but there seemed that something else was different about it now; something more savage than even before. Eleazaar fumbled to his feet and sensed it right away as he looked upon it standing there.

"Oh ... fffffffffffiddle," he said, very concerned about the sudden change.

He had read enough about golems in books to have an idea of what unexpected things can happen sometimes with magic-animated constructs. Rarely, if ever, were they good things. If he was sure of anything, he was sure that what was about to happen was probably not a really good thing.

Chapter Thirteen

ROKKA UND TRAMUTA

Something was indeed wrong with the golem and the three Yuan-ti sisters were trying to figure out what had happened as well. It was still active, but had stopped and was not responding to Verin's commands. It was something that had never happened with the golem before.

"What?" Verin said angrily. "It is not responding."
"What is happening?" Sonnillon asked. "What have you done, Verin?"
"I have done nothing," Verin replied defiantly.
"You have lost control of it!" Gresil hissed, panicked. "Get it back!"
"I am trying, idiot," Verin snapped.
"This is not good," Sonnillon said. "Not good at all. Keep trying, Verin. I will go summon our warriors and ready them for battle."
"Golem," Verin called to it through the crystal scrying ball, trying to regain control. "Golem!"

Back in the room, the golem took a step toward them and Eleazaar turned quickly to run away. Barrister, however, just stood there confused, looking at it strangely. He swatted it once with his staff and hit it, for whatever good it did. The golem took a second step toward him and Barrister swatted his staff at it again.

This time, the golem knocked the staff away and swung back at Barrister, who barely ducked away from it in time. He still stood there, backing away slowly and seemed indecisive as to what he should do.

Eleazaar stopped running, reached back and grabbed Barrister by his robes. He pulled him back away from the golem and started running again.

"It has broken free from their control," Eleazaar said with urgency.
"What?" Barrister asked, confused.
"It is going to go berserk," he said even more urgently now. "Run, you fool."

Barrister came to his senses and started running away from it. When it came to danger and self-preservation, he did not usually need to be told twice. The golem began stomping forward again, chasing after Barrister at first.

Then, it unexpectedly changed direction and targeted Eleazaar. The surprise move caught Eleazaar flat-footed and the golem caught him, clubbing him with its huge fist in the back as he turned to escape it. The blow lifted Eleazaar off of his feet and sent him careening across the floor. He slid into the wall and came to an abrupt stop.

All the while they had been battling with the golem, Grunda had been largely forgotten as she stood quietly in the corner watching, hidden by the shadows. Suddenly, Eleazaar's mace appeared from below the golem and struck it squarely in the groin. The blow busted out a chunk where a person's privates would have been.

Grunda had picked up Eleazaar's mace as it came to rest near her and struck at the most opportune of times. Had the golem gotten to Eleazaar, he would have likely been dead. As fate would have it, however, Grunda slid right into and collided with its legs. She was kicked away, but the combination of her impact and that of the mace caused the golem to stumble.

Carried by its momentum, the golem fell forward and crashed onto the floor. Eleazaar picked up his legs and pulled them out of the way as it came down just short of him. Spinning around and rolling away, he quickly rose back up to his feet. He staggered with stinging pain for a moment as he looked around and spied Grunda.

"The mace, Grunda!" Eleazaar called to her. "Quickly."
"Right," she replied as she scanned the floor for it. "Ah gots it."

Grunda struggled up from the floor and raced to the mace which lay nearby. As the golem rose to its feet once again, she hurled the mace with all her strength through the air at Eleazaar. Leaning back as he gauged the spinning weapon coming at him, his hands exploded outward and grabbed the handle out of the air as it flew by.

He let the momentum of the weapon drive him as he spun to his left and brought the mace around. He stepped out as he swung and leaned into the force as he struck the golem in front of him. A burst of clay erupted from the chest of the golem as the mace pounded into it; so hard in fact that the golem was knocked back a step.

Then, from seemingly out of nowhere, Barrister came leaping through air. His staff crashed down upon the side of the golem's head, powerfully enough that it chipped off its ear. Barrister had not really thought about what to do after the strike though.

He came down right into the golem's arms. With nowhere to evade, he was an easy target. The golem slung its huge arm around and clobbered Barrister, knocking him off his feet to the side and into the air. Instantly dazed, he crashed into the wall and fell to the floor unconscious.

A little late to react, Eleazaar swung his mace around trying to protect Barrister. He hit the Golem's arm as it tossed Barrister away. The golem slung its extended arm back around at Eleazaar, who narrowly ducked away from it. Ducking put his shoulder in range, however, and the mighty fist pounded into it, sending Eleazaar spinning away and in crippling pain. His shoulder had been dislocated.

The golem immediately stomped after him for the kill. Eleazaar could barely orient himself as the thing swept upon him. Off balance, he fell and swung his mace up at the golem with his good arm as he was going to the floor. The mace struck the side of the golem's chest, but not with any great force. He fell hard enough on his back though that his shoulder popped back into place.

The golem tried to deal a crushing blow down on his head, but Eleazaar whipped it to the side in time. The fist pounded against the stone floor with a loud thunk that was almost deafening. Grunda, trying desperately to save Eleazaar, leaped into the air and planted both of her feet into the golem, hoping to knock it over, but a (less than) one hundred pound dwarf had little hope of dislodging a six hundred pound golem.

Her feet pounded against the golem, but she still hit it with a thud and fell straight to the floor. What it did do, however, was get the golem's attention. Stunned for only a moment as it turned toward her and struck down with a crushing blow, she quickly scrambled out of its path and rolled away.

Having a moment to act, Eleazaar swung his mace back up at it again and hit it in the side of its already battered head. As more clay burst away, the golem seemed disoriented for a moment. Eleazaar scooted from beneath it and stumbled up to his feet again.

With all the remaining strength he could muster, he slung his mace over the top and plunged it down into the golem's head. The mace plowed into the magically hardened clay and shattered it; the entire head collapsing into shards upon the floor. The golem was not finished though. Headless, it stumbled around swinging its arms wildly.

Eleazaar quickly dug into his pack and removed a scroll. It was a magical scroll with a clerical incantation that was intended to return a person to flesh after they had been turned to stone by some creature. It did have other secondary uses, however. Eleazaar unraveled the scroll and quickly began reading:

"Per Deus et totus res ego precor;" he began as he first tossed holy water, then silica upon the golem, "ut exsisto macto per officina suus vernula! Akor amet el rokka und tramuta, et epiderma!"

The scroll instantly disintegrated in his hands as he finished reading. The golem staggered in short, choppy motions and then began to shudder. The golem burst into muddy clumps of clay that dropped to the floor in goopy pile.

Eleazaar dropped to the floor and rolled over onto his back. His breath was short and strained; he felt like he had just been run over by a rock avalanche. He could barely move his left arm it hurt so badly.

Yost immediately came racing down the stairs with Kalise following on his heels. As he hit the bottom, he looked at Eleazaar and Grunda lying on the floor before spotting a motionless Barrister against the opposite wall. Seeing that the others were moving at least, he ran over to Barrister to check on him. Kalise ran to Eleazaar as Grunda rose to her feet, seemingly okay. She lifted his head in her hands and looked him over for injuries.

"El!" she shouted as she dropped down to him. "You okay? You hurt? Where does it hurt?"

"Beans,' he said weakly. "It hurts everywhere … ah. Ever been hit by a six hundred pound boulder?"

"Anything broken?" she continued to query him.

"Left shoulder … it dislocated, briefly," he moaned. "Maybe a couple of ribs are broken, I do not know. It hurts though, a lot."

"You may have a bone fracture in the shoulder, El," she said. "At the very least, probably a bone bruise."

"Could have been worse," Eleazaar said weakly. "How is Barrister?"

"Let us worry about you first," Kalise said assertively as she placed her hands on his shoulder. "Gott der Natur und aller lebenden sachen. Von der erde, fleisch heilung!"

There was a flash of a warm, yellow light like sunshine that burst from beneath her hands and spread briefly across his shoulder. Druids, of course, were healers too. They just drew upon the same holy energies a little differently than clerics did.

"Any change?" Kalise asked him.

"It is a little better, yeah," Eleazaar replied as he moved and tried to rotate his shoulder. "Still sore, but it is better. I had always heard that druids were capable healers. Never actually had one heal me before though."

"Now you have, hmm?" Kalise said, smiling at him. "Now let me have a look at your ribcage."

"That was a bang-up job you did, Grunda," Eleazaar then said as he noticed the dwarf standing not far behind Kalise. "You probably saved my ham hocks, if not everybody's."

"Cor!" Grunda exclaimed, reflecting on it all. "Nasty thing that was. Gots'im right in the goolies and he still widnea go down."

"If I forget, just remind me not to brass you off," Eleazaar mused at her, smiling up at Kalise. "You did great, Grunda."

At the same time, below in the depths of the cavern, Gresil and Verin fought among themselves. With the golem destroyed and both the evoker and cleric still alive, there was a sense of panic. Wounded or not, the group had clearly proved more dangerous than Verin had calculated.

"Incapable hatchling!" Gresil snarled.

"Do not speak to me in such a …," Verin said in retort.

"I speak the truth!" Gresil continued. "Had you targeted the boy first as I said, we could have been rid of them both."

"The golem malfunctioned!" Verin hissed back. "The boy was lucky, nothing more."

"You lost control of it," Gresil replied contemptuously.

"I did no such thing!" Verin said. "The magic failed … there is a difference."

"Your magic failed, not mine," Gresil quipped back.

Sonnillon heard her sisters arguing as she returned and rushed up to them. She had gone into the lair; the tunnels and smaller caves where the Yuan-ti lived and slept. She had returned to report that the whole clan had amassed and were ready to attack the intruders when they arrived at the cavern.

"Sisters!" Sonnillon howled at them. "The clan is ready for battle. Stop your petty squabbling and let us focus."

"Grrrrrraaaah," Gresil growled in frustration.

"They will be here in no time," Verin said. "Get the warriors into position, Sonnillon. We will finish them, right here."

"Or they will finish us," Gresil snarled under her breath.

Back up in the room, on the opposite side near the wall, Yost had turned Barrister onto his back and was trying to wake him up. A nasty blow to the head had nearly done the evoker in. His face was bloody and swollen and, he was slow to respond. Kalise tossed a pouch over to Yost and he removed a piece of a small plant from it. Breaking it open so the juices inside would be exposed, he rubbed it under Barrister's nose. Barrister shook his head slightly and then more vigorously as he opened his eyes at last.

"Get that foul thing away from me," Barrister grumbled groggily.

"How are you feeling?" Yost asked him. "You okay, Stan?"

"I have been better," Barrister replied. "He nearly got me killed."

"He is the only reason you are alive," Yost said, correcting him. "It would have killed all of us. Come on now, let us get you back on your feet and see if everything is still working. The show is not over yet."

"And that goes for you too, Barrister," Eleazaar called from across the room. "You were a big help at the right time. I appreciate that."

"All is well that ends well ... I suppose," Barrister said, begrudgingly.

That was as close to gratitude as anyone was likely to get from Barrister. It just was not his thing and he likely saw such offerings as a sign of weakness. In any case, Kalise went across to help Yost get Barrister to his feet and heal him as Eleazaar sat up and looked around.

Eleazaar then noticed a faint glow coming from the room where the golem had been. He looked over at the others helping Barrister, then got to his feet and hobbled over slowly to find the source. He cautiously stepped into the room and saw the source of the glow lying near the base of the pedestal that the golem had stood upon.

Kalise finished her healing on Barrister and looked back over her shoulder. Seeing Eleazaar step into the other room, she left Barrister and followed after him. Eleazaar walked to the pedestal and bent over, picking the glowing item up.

"What is it, El?" she said as she emerged behind him in the doorway.

"Moonstone," he replied. "There is an internal anomaly in the rock which causes it to glow. Here … you hang onto it. It can be very useful." "You do not want it?" she asked.

"I have no need of it," he replied. "I have God to light my path and my way."

Eleazaar walked ahead to the door in the back corner of the room. He listened at the door briefly and then slowly wedged it open for a peek inside. It was pitch dark beyond, so he moved his holy symbol so as to cast its light into the darkness.

The light cast shadows eerily into a hall with several rooms that exited its length. It seemed very still and lifeless beyond, but he knew looks could be quite deceiving.

"Get Grunda," Eleazaar whispered to Kalise.

Kalise nodded and returned to the doorway leading to the main room. Yost was supporting Barrister as he walked around and testing him to make sure all of his marbles were still working right. Then she saw Grunda standing off to the side watching.

"Swyyyt." she whistled to get her attention. "Grunda."

Grunda turned her head to look and Kalise waved her over to follow her. Grunda turned and followed after her as Kalise disappeared into the secondary room again. Yost also saw them going and turned Barrister that way also.

"Come on, Stan." he said. "Let us see what they are up to."

Kalise returned to Eleazaar and together they waited for Grunda. Grunda stopped at the doorway and peered in at them as they stood by the far door. Eleazaar motioned for her to hurry to them and Grunda began scuttling toward them.

"It used to be that men always wanted to get *me* into a dark room," Kalise whispered as she put her hand around his back.

"Maybe later." Eleazaar said sheepishly. "When nothing is trying to kill us."

"Whit we be whisperin' abouts?" Grunda asked in a whisper of her own.

"There is a really dark hall beyond the door," Eleazaar said. "You can move quietly in the shadows, so I want you to sneak in and see what is there."

"Aw by meself?" Grunda whispered emphatically in reply.

"Do not worry," Eleazaar reassured her. "I will go in too and stay just inside the door. I will cover your back. I just want us to have a look before we move on."

"Well, alrights," she agreed reluctantly. "Whit if me gets into troubles?"

"I will be right there. I promise," he said.

He eased the door open for her and followed her through into the dark hallway. He tucked his glowing holy symbol inside of his armor and shirt to hide its light and allow their eyes to adjust to the darkness. Eleazaar took a knee in the center of the hall just outside the door and tapped on Grunda's shoulder, pointing for her to go on ahead.

Her Dwarven infravision was of some help to her, if there happened to be anything alive to see, but dwarves spent plenty of time in dark places anyway and had very good eyes for the dark. She crept on ahead while Eleazaar trained his keen ears for any sounds. Kalise stood at the door peering out into the darkness and listening for any signs of trouble. Behind her, Yost and Barrister hobbled up to the doorway from the main room and saw her.

"What is going on?" Yost asked.

"Shhhhhh," she replied, pointing beyond.

"Off doing something stupid," Barrister quipped.

"Just take it easy Stan," Yost cautioned him. "How about we sit you down over here?"

Yost led Barrister to the single, unbroken chair that remained in the room. He tested it first to make sure it was stable, and then eased Barrister down to it where he could relax a bit after his harrowing ordeal. Then, he started over to join Kalise.

"Just hang out here for a bit," he told Barrister.

In the dark hallway, Grunda found it hard not to kick rubble as she went forward. The ceiling seemed to be getting lower as she moved forward also. Indeed, as she looked around and passed door-less rooms to either side, the amount of rubble and the height of the rooms all seemed to changing. Being naturally geologically-aware creatures, she spotted something amiss with the structure right away.

As much out of curiosity as anything, she entered one of the rooms to try and understand why this was the case. There was a rather sooty smell in the air and when she touched one of the walls, a blackish substance came off on her hands.

A fire had burned here at some time, though she could not imagine what could have burned so greatly inside a stone temple. The slant in the ceiling above her was sharp and odd though, as if some cataclysmic event had taken place here. She thought perhaps an earthquake had hit, but then why the fire? Volcanic activity would have surely done worse than this and there were no indications of a volcano ever being in this area anyway.

There was a thick cluster of rubble near one end of the room and she felt her way into it, since what she could see was limited. Feeling through it with her hands, which were getting very dirty from everything she touched, she came across something that felt very odd and brittle. She probed around with her stubby fingers before realizing what it was she was touching.

"Gaaa!" she said aloud, jerking away from it.

Eleazaar heard her and, as promised, took out his glowing symbol and charged after her. Kalise threw open the door and Yost came and stood in the doorway, keeping an eye on both them and Barrister. Eleazaar nearly slipped on the small rubble that was strewn across the stone floors as he ran. He spied her in one of the rooms and entered. She turned to look at him as he approached and he saw the pile of rubble and dark, charcoaled material amongst it.

"You alright?" he said quickly.
"Mes be fine, love." she replied. "Ah dinnea thinks this'n be though."

Eleazaar eased up to the clump and his eyes followed across it. There, in the midst of it all, was what was left of a person or Yuan-ti, melted and turned to charcoal right into everything else. Eleazaar cast his light all around, looking at the odd shape of the room.

"Some kind of collapse," he said as he looked around.
"Me thoughts an earth shake, but the fire be a strange thin' down here," she added.
"What is going on?" Kalise said as she entered behind them.
"We have a dead ... something here ... cooked well," he said smartly. "Maybe a Yuan-ti or maybe not, hard to tell now."
"Ugh," she replied.
"What kind of earthquake-like effect could burn a place up like this?" he asked her.
"Well, some earthquakes open fissures with hot fires from below," Kalise said, "but there does not seem to be any evidence of that."
"A ruddy ol' dragon could do it," Grunda interjected.
"No sign of that either," Eleazaar countered. "It would have a hard time fitting in here and the place would be busted open in that case. A baby dragon could maybe, but it would not have the fire to do this kind of damage."

"You know, I have heard of strange explosions in the swamps before," Kalise said. "Someone walking with a torch near their camp got burned badly one time I guess. The air around them just blew up."

"Some kind of gas trapped underground maybe?" Eleazaar suggested. "If it escapes in a rush and hits flame, that could possibly be huge."

"Aye," Grunda agreed. "When the ground shakes, aw kinds of things be comin' up from below yous."

"It could have collected before igniting," Eleazaar went on. "That would explain a lot. The whole place seems to have been crushed on one end by a mighty force."

Eleazaar stepped back into the hallway and looked ahead. The hall was almost completely crushed down together at the other end, which would mean the event took place somewhere ahead in the direction they were to be going. While such events destroy, he figured they must also create. If such an event did take place, there was surely some kind of pocket in the ground where the explosive gas was contained.

"These were most likely living quarters for some of the cult long ago." he said, thinking aloud to the others. "Before whatever happened here happened. So … they do not repair the living area and they do not live outside of the temple … even as the population increases; where do they go?"

"Below the ground … beneath the temple," Kalise suggested.

"Into a new area created by the same event that destroyed their home," Eleazaar said, completing her thought.

"There must be a pocket or a cavern below us then," Kalise said.

"I am sure it was a much larger space too," Eleazaar said. "It should have been easily big enough to house their whole society."

"Cor!" Grunda exclaimed. "Couldst be thousands down there, could be."

"Cheery thought," Eleazaar said. "Let us get out of here. This place could still collapse at any time."

The three of them returned back to the room where Yost and Barrister waited. Eleazaar explained what they had found and his thoughts about what it meant for them going forward. Yost likewise concurred with his findings.

"That would explain the general disuse of the temple except as an access point to the world above," Yost agreed. "A larger, even more secure space for them to grow, you can bet this will not be a pastry walk."

"You know, no one would blame you if you decided this was too big for us," Kalise offered. "We could always go back and get help."

"I would blame me," Yost said. "It was hard enough to find the few of who did come. By the time we gathered a small army to come back down here, they would have had time to change their strategy and they would still know we are coming and be lying in wait. They could kill a lot more people between now and then."

"So, they know we are coming?" Barrister said disgustedly. "That is great."

"I think it is a foregone conclusion, is it not?" Yost returned. "The golem was evidence enough of that."

"They sent a party to kill Barrister while we rested Mr. Yost," Eleazaar at last revealed. "I was reading the stones back in the corridor.... the ammonium chased them away."

"Pbbbtttt!" Barrister scoffed. "And, you were going to tell me when, exactly?"

"When you felt it necessary to listen to a kid, Mr. Barrister," Eleazaar said firmly in response. "They have been watching us for a while, apparently."

"Which also means we are walking into a trap," Yost continued.

"Well then, why are we doing it, for Chislev's sake?" Barrister snapped.

"Firstly, because we do not have better options," Yost said.

"I have better options," Barrister grumbled under his breath.

"Secondly, because we have to put a stop to what they are doing," Yost continued. "The first rule in avoiding a trap is in knowing it is there. We do know it now. That means we have to put ourselves in the best position to defeat them, knowing what we know."

"Maybe easier said than done Manny," Kalise said.

"We seem to have a smart group of people here," Yost said. "Let us make it count for something."

"A nice way of saying ... do not get killed," Barrister quipped.

"We all signed up for this," Yost replied. "Anyone here like to take their chances, turn tail and go home? Now is the time."

Everyone looked around at each other. All of them, at one time or another, had thought about just going back for different reasons. The idea of going back and explaining how they left their companions to die did not seem to have much appeal now. Not even Barrister wanted to carry that shame.

"No?" Yost asked. "Then, let us go kick some serpent tail."

Yost led the way back out into the main room. Barrister rose slowly from his chair, walking like a decrepit old man through the doorway after him. He straightened up and stretched his back, readying himself for whatever may be yet to come.

"You gonna be alright, Stan?" Yost asked.

"I just need to move around a little," he replied. "I was getting stiff."

"Good," Yost said. "We need you."

They all gathered together before the double doors at the far end of the room. Yost made certain everyone was ready for anything that might be beyond them before they went in. Satisfied at last they were ready; he grabbed hold of both doors and pulled them open.

The iron hinges whined as they slowly swung open. The room beyond was lighted by torches in sconces along the walls to either side and they could see everything clearly. A room with rows of pillars, each a few feet from the wall to either side, lined the room from end to end.

This room also was a good eighty feet in length, with a high, arched ceiling. Each wall was draped with a velvet-looking fabric of red and gold. There was a sparkle to them also, which seemed to possibly come from precious stones woven into the material.

"I did not realize ancient peoples could work so eloquently with fabrics," Kalise observed.

"Give any group of people a few hundred years, maybe a thousand, their skills evolve like most any other group," Eleazaar said in reply.

"Them stones be quite valuable, methinks," Grunda added.

"We are not treasure hunting, folks." Yost said.

Down the center of the room, there were three long tables. They were lined end-to-end down the length of the room, but there were no chairs evident. Considering the physical changes of the polymorph process that turned humans into the Yuan-ti, it was not surprising and an indication that the room was probably still used to some degree.

"Looks like a meeting … or dining hall," Kalise said.

"No chairs," Yost added. "It must be close enough to their main area that they still use it."

"They are planning a feast in our honor, perhaps?" Eleazaar sported smartly.

"Hmmm," Barrister said. "Only if we are to be the main course."

"Speak for y'self nancy boy," Grunda quipped. "Y'not be findin' any ruddy apples in my mouth today!"

Barrister turned and scowled at her while Eleazaar and Kalise looked away, trying not to laugh. The more assertive Grunda became, the funnier she seemed to get. As far as they were concerned, he had it coming anyway.

A second set of double doors loomed ahead of them at the other end of the room. They seemed to be colored a brighter shade of red and had been painted with glyphic symbols in a white color. Clearly they seemed to be something more new to the temple than anything they had seen before.

They began walking toward the doors, weaving in and out of the pillars as they scanned all around them. The pillars had been carved with the images of serpents, which wound around them from bottom to top. At the top of the pillars, a serpent's head with fangs protruding from an open mouth looked down upon the center of the room. They moved ahead slowly out of caution, not sure what to expect. Despite the room seeming empty of any life but them, they could not be certain if any Yuan-ti would suddenly pop out through some cleverly hidden secret door to attack them. They were already beat up from the golem and down one member; no one was taking anything for granted.

At last, they had crossed the room and reached the double doors on the other side. There they stopped, perhaps apprehensive about what the future held beyond them. Yost looked at the glyphic writing on the doors and turned to Eleazaar.

"Any idea what these say, cleric?" Yost asked him.

"Welcome all visitors," Eleazaar began, intending to be funny. "Nice to eat you."

Chapter Fourteen

NICE TO EAT YOU

Yost frowned at him. Apparently, he did not feel humor was appropriate at the time or was not in the mood for it in any case. Eleazaar, chagrinned, just threw his hands up.

"I really have no idea what it says," he admitted. "The style has changed from the ancient glyphs we saw earlier. New language variations means the doors were added or replaced at some time in the near past; I presume replaced after their written language had changed. It could be connected to whatever crushed the old living area of the temple."

"Well, we can bet it does not offer tourist information," Barrister said smartly.

"No," Yost agreed. "We will just find out the hard way then, I guess."

Yost reached down and grabbed a handle on one of the doors. Eleazaar stepped forward and quickly grabbed the other as he looked over at Yost. Yost nodded to him and the two together yanked the doors open.

"Holy mother of hell-holes," Yost said as he looked at what lay beyond.

Before them was a huge hole into the ground that extended out into the rough shape of a dome farther away from them. The distance across was impressive and it seemed like stepping out of the doorway would be like stepping off the edge of the world. Fortunately that would not be the case. There were wooden platform stairs descending down from the doorway to the depths below.

"Cor!" Grunda gasped. "Looks t'be the ground swallowed everythin' up."

"I guess we are going down from here," Kalise said with a sigh, to no one in particular.

Somewhere below them, the trickle of moving water could be heard as it echoed up in the cavern. An underground stream had been opened up long ago by the explosion that damaged the temple and created part of the hole in the ground. It now served as an internal water source for the Yuan-ti.

Long ago, a large pocket of methane trapped under the ground began to seep through the rock that had been weakened when the underground tunneling for the temple was done. It leaked into areas of the temple, some of which were completely missing now, and eventually collected into a sufficient concentration to explode. All it had taken was a simple torch flame and there was a blast greater than the oldest red dragon could ever hope to achieve.

The fire blast had rolled through the living quarters and instantly incinerated many members of the clan. A section of the temple and the rock around it was obliterated by the force. The rock below had heaved upward and partially buried the temple, leaving a hole of vacated rock, disintegrated temple areas and the natural cavern where the methane was trapped behind.

The cavern across from them was dark and they could see nothing. After the debacle with the golem, Verin and her sisters had doused all of the torch lights. They could now easily watch the approach of the intruders as they waited with their Yuan-ti army. Having an advantage of three sorcerers to one and far superior numbers, they now were depending on overwhelming force and isolation to defeat the group.

The group hopped down the platform stairs, level by level, descending deeper into the unknown. The sound of water became louder as they came closer to its source, though there was little to see but the platforms below them. Eventually their light revealed rock and what looked like a bridge.

"Is that a bridge there?" Kalise asked, pointing.

"I think so," Eleazaar said in reply. "It probably crosses the water source we hear."

"Ruddy bridge o'death it be then," Grunda added smartly.

"Cut the chatter," Yost said, interjecting. "Sound carries down here."

Before long they reached the bottom of the stairs and stepped down onto solid rock again. Indeed, there was a bridge at the bottom. It expanded more than one hundred feet across a gouge in the rock through which the underground stream flowed.

It did not seem particularly inviting. The bridge was made of wood planks, supports and of thick rope. It rocked slightly as Yost stepped onto it, testing it out for crossing.

"I hope no one has a weak stomach … or bladder for that matter," Yost said. "Follow me in single file. Hang on with both hands and walk slow and steady."

"You have a potion of flying in that little bag of yours, kid?" Barrister asked Eleazaar.

"No, I … I did not bring one," Eleazaar replied.

"Surprising," Barrister continued. "You seem to have a solution for everything else."

"I cannot carry everything," Eleazaar said, hesitating at the bridge. "That and I uh … I do not really like heights all that much."

"It is ok, El," Kalise said, putting her hand on him to reassure him. "Just do not look down."

"I had no plans to do so," Eleazaar replied, chuckling nervously.

The group started across the bridge, spacing themselves out as they crossed. No one could be sure how sturdy or how much weight the boards would hold, so they were not going to take chances. It also would have been a horrible spot to get attacked, if the Yuan-ti did not care that they fell into the water below. They were only able to cross the bridge safely because the Yuan-ti wanted them to, and Yost knew it.

"Be on your guard," Yost advised them. "As we get close to the other end ... draw weapons and be ready."

The bridge swayed a little as they crossed, making Eleazaar uncomfortable. He swallowed hard and just kept moving, trying to focus the feeling out. As each of them reached the last quarter of the bridge, where the sway was far lesser, they drew their weapons, except for Kalise, that is. She stopped and reached into a pouch as Grunda, who was behind her, looked at her with concern.

"Somethin' wrong, love?" Grunda asked.
"It is fine, Grunda," she replied. "Go on around me. I need to do something quick."

Grunda shrugged and eased around her, continuing on. Kalise removed a single, gray hair from the pouch and placed it in a small container she held, made from a carved and treated nutshell. She then sprinkled in a powder and a drop of some kind of thick, blackish-colored fluid she had in a vial. With a small, wooden stick that was rounded at one end, she began crushing, grinding and mixing the ingredients together.

"What is the hold up?" Yost asked, looking back from the solid rock of the other side.
"Nothing Manny," she replied. "I will be right there."
"What is she doing?" Yost asked Eleazaar in a whisper.
"No idea," Eleazaar replied simply. "Druid stuff ... maybe."

Kalise finished mixing and then banded and corked the nutshell, placing it into a pocket in her cloak. She hurried along afterward to the end of the bridge to rejoin the others. Before continuing, Yost scanned ahead of them, but they could still see little.

"I am surprised they did not attack us on the bridge, Manny," Barrister said. "They would have had us dead to rights."

"I know," Yost replied. "They did not have us where they wanted us yet."

"That is what I am afraid of," Barrister said.

"The first rule of battle is to pick the terrain that will give you the best advantage for fighting and make your enemy come to you," Yost added. "That is pretty smart," Eleazaar said. "We should try that sometime." "Wish we could cleric," Yost replied.

"They gonna wait 'till we gets right in the midst of them, they will," Grunda interjected.

"All bloody hell will break loose then, says I. That is what *me* thinks."

"Quite possibly," Yost acknowledged. "Spread out, everyone. Kalise to the left, the cleric to the right and Grunda covers the rear. Let us keep Stan in the middle where we can protect him the best."

The group positioned themselves in formation and Yost began leading them forward. The cavern was wide and their lights showed nothing but a generally smooth, rock floor beneath their feet and ahead of them. They advanced slowly, keeping their eyes scanning in all directions. Eleazaar could vaguely see the dome-shaped roof above them, just within range of his light.

"Definitely was some kind of pressure under the ground." he noted aloud. "Only something like that could cause a natural curve in the rock, I think."

"A cave expert too, now are you?" Barrister asked smartly.

"Naw," Eleazaar replied. "I just read it in a book once."

"Quit talking and focus," Yost said.

They all crept forward; despite knowing they had no chance of surprising their enemy. At the very least, Yost hoped they would see or hear something before it was too late and could react before the enemy attacked. But, Yost stepped on a crumbly piece of rock which crunched beneath his foot and a disappointed expression swept over his face. Verin swathed her clawed hand out before her and torches all along the wall in a semi-circle to the group's left burst into flame, lighting much of the rest of the cavern. Suddenly they all heard an odd, chirpy, guttural voice that came from seemingly nowhere and everywhere at once.

"Welcome, brave adventurers." Verin's voice boomed throughout the cavern. "It is a rare treat that we have guests to entertain us in our sanctum ... willingly that is."

"Considering the hospitality, I am not surprised," Barrister mumbled under his breath as he and the others looked around for the source.

Something resembling laughter rang out from multiple directions and echoed all around them, though the sounds seemed to originate from their left near the torches. It sounded closer to a chorus of frogs in a bog though, Kalise thought. Ahead to their two o'clock left, Verin rose into view behind the natural rock lectern-like formation that centered the left side of the cavern.

To either side of the rock platform on which it seemed to sit, Gresil and Sonnillon then emerged, purposeful in their dramatics. From behind them flowed a stream of Yuan-ti, all in various stages of the polymorph process. Barrister eased one of his fingers to his belt and uncorked a leather- wrapped vial.

The Yuan-ti pressed forward and formed a wall before the three sisters. Together, they all drew scimitars and took a step forward in unison, ready to attack. Barrister dipped his finger in the open uncorked vial, wetting it with an oily fluid as the others took a combat-ready stance.

"Sonnillon ... if you would. Please." Verin said.

"Graciously," Sonnillon replied.

Sonnillon lifted up a small, hollow piece of glass shaped like a short tube. She rubbed it vigorously with a piece of fur and pointed it toward the bridge. Swirling it around ever tighter in a shrinking circle, she cast the first spell of the engagement.

"Coupe de foudre!" she commanded.

The static charged tube of glass erupted from her clawed hand as a bolt of lightning. It struck the far end of the bridge with a thunderous clap, sending wood flying. The bridge shook and swayed before collapsing into the watery gouge beneath it.

"Will you not stay a while?" Verin said smugly, assured that they had the group defeated before the battle had actually begun.
"Remember that part where you said knowing there is a trap is the first step to avoiding it?" Barrister asked Yost, leaning over to him.
"Yeah. Why?" Yost replied.
"Oh, no reason," Barrister said. "I just thought maybe *now* would be a good time to tell me how that works exactly."

Yost rolled his eyes. Indeed, it was easier in theory than in practice. He decided to try and parlay, if for no other reason than to buy time to figure out some kind of plan. Parlay was not Yost's strong suit, however. He was much better at fighting.

"What is it that you want, o serpentish … lady?" he asked. "What have you done with the people from the village?"
"I am so pleased you have asked this question," Verin continued in her smug tone.
"Here it comes," Eleazaar thought to himself.
"You see, the great serpent … Heptmuz, called us here to serve him" Verin explained, "and he must be fed. Take heart, you shall provide rich nourishment for him."
"I knew it," Barrister said, as he shook his head in disgust.

"Oh, I am certain he will not eat you, Barrister." Eleazaar quipped snidely. "A sour prune like you would just give him indigestion."

"Nowt be the time f'makin' jokes, love." Grunda noted. "We be in it good this time, we be."

"Yep," Eleazaar replied simply, agreeing to the latter at least.

The ground rules had been laid out in pretty plain terms: kill the whole clan and you get to walk away ... do not and you get eaten by their god, whatever that meant exactly. In any case, it did not sound like anything they would enjoy. Yost largely drew a blank on how to parlay under such circumstances.

"So?" Yost began awkwardly. "What about the villagers?"

"Did I not mention the eating part?" Verin said, confused as she looked at her sisters.

"Covered that, yeah," Yost replied before whispering to the others. "Get ready ..."

"Heptmuz requires much sacrifice," Verin added for emphasis.

"Right, right ... I am sure he does," Yost said.

"I think we are as ready as we will get," Kalise said quietly to Yost.

"Hold onto your britches, folks," Yost told the others. "We are about to step into one big pile of serpent shit."

"Do it," Eleazaar encouraged him with a nod.

"It seems there is nothing for us to negotiate then," Yost said to the Yuan-ti as he looked at the mass gathered opposite of them.

"If you should like to plead for your lives now, we shall listen, of course." Verin said, amusing herself.

"Blow it out your slimy shit hole ... you stinking worm!" Yost spat back at her.

Verin was incensed, of course, hardly expecting to be provoked by such a perceived group of inferiors. The Yuan-ti had been largely isolated in their underground home for centuries, so their contact had been mostly limited to individuals. A trained group with fighting styles mostly unfamiliar to them probably deserved more caution, but Verin was not given to being cautious.

"Clan ... attack," she said, lowering her hand toward the group.

The wall of Yuan-ti warriors took a step forward in unison and began to charge, wailing a hideous sound that seemed like screeching birds that were choking on something. Kalise immediately started launching arrows into the oncoming mass. Eleazaar and Yost waited patiently in position as Barrister waved his left hand horizontally and flicked his wet finger out ahead of them.

"Sure no longer as before." Barrister said as he began his evocation. "Slippery has become the floor."

A tiny drop of something sparkled for a moment as it left his finger before hitting the cavern floor. It burst out with a flash and covered the cavern floor before them with a shiny-looking coat. The rushing Yuan-ti stepped onto the shiny area and began to slip and slide in all directions.

The Yuan-ti fell into and over each other in piles, or slid along awkwardly as if greased. As some of the Yuan-ti slid into range, Yost and Eleazaar began to hack at them, killing as many as they could as quickly as they could, knowing they were greatly outnumbered.

Kalise adjusted her targeting, firing right into the piles of Yuan-ti bodies for as long as her arrows would last. When she was able, she targeted their heads, but with all the slipping and sliding, hitting anything squarely was a bit of a challenge.

Grunda tried not to panic with so much going on. She stayed vigilant as she protected Barrister's spell-casting and watched the battle unfold before her. She had never seen or been in such a conflict before, so it was a very anxious moment. Watching the action from the other side, Sonnillon raised her hands in front of her and turned her palms downward.

"La lumière comme une plume." she began to chant. "Soulevée pour m'atténuer sur les quatre vents, je lévite comme une volaille montant sur l'air!"

Enacting a levitation spell, Sonnillon began to rise into the air above her sisters. As she did so, Gresil and Verin each took out a strip of leather and placed it on their left shoulder. They chanted together a protection spell.

"Cachez-vous de Heptmuz, la peau comme le cuir, protégez-nous maintenant!" they said.

A brief flash appeared to surround them and the strips of leather disappeared. A dim aura seemed to pulse around them and then simply faded away. For the moment, they reserved themselves from the battle as their eyes followed their warriors engaged with the group. They were going to be cautious for now and support their clan from the rear.

The Yuan-ti pushed their way through the slippery area en force at last and forced Yost and Eleazaar back by strength of numbers. Only two people were not going to hold back a horde of Yuan-ti for very long. Still, they put up quite the fight.

Eleazaar speared the sword arm of the Yuan-ti to his left with his hand scythe and, using it for balance, leaped into the air and kicked the one on the right in the torso with both feet. He twisted down to his left and brought his sword over the top. The Yuan-ti in front of him missed the block with his own sword and was gashed from his neck to his stomach by Eleazaar's blade.

As his feet came down, Eleazaar jerked his hand scythe back and ripped open the arm of the one he had hooked. He spun right with his sword and beheaded it as the blade came through and blocked another's attack from the front.

Yost had seen many battles in his days and was quite skilled as well, though his style was not quite as flashy. He had quick hands and his sword did most of the flashing for him. He whipped it from side to side, blocking the attacks around him and then he would strike unexpectedly in a different direction when he was ready.

He blocked to each side, spun right and slashed across the torso of the Yuan-ti to his left. When his body came around forward, a Yuan-ti was charging into him. He quickly ducked and went ahead into and under him, using the enemy's momentum to dump him over his own back to the floor. He blocked right and thrust his sword back down behind him, into the Yuan-ti on the floor.

Kalise, after running out of arrows, put her bow away and took out her scimitar. Wedging herself between and behind Yost and Eleazaar, she waited for Yuan-ti to pass though and take pressure off their backside flank. She made sure to stay close to Barrister though, not wanting to leave him too vulnerable.

While Kalise did her part, Barrister dug into his bag of tricks.

Assessing the situation, he took five pine tar-covered beads out of a pouch on his belt. He closed them in his hand and began shaking them like someone would shake a pair of dice.

"Beads of fire that burn euphoric;" he said as he began an evocational chant, "Streak up, strike down as meteoric."

He swung his arm out and opened his hand, tossing the beads high into the air above the Yuan-ti. The beads suddenly streaked down from above, propelled like fireworks, with each hitting one of the Yuan-ti. On impact, each of them exploded like a small fireball into the Yuan-ti warriors, blowing open their flesh and setting them on fire. They fell to the cavern floor where they died and burned away amidst the fight.

"Two can play that game, sorcerer." Gresil hissed from afar. "J'évoque maintenant, Heptmuz hear me! Noir tentacules!"

To Barrister's surprise, five black tentacles rose up from the floor around him and wrapped him up, binding him powerless. Grunda jerked with sudden panic as she saw the tentacles grab him. She ran over to him but was not sure what to do.

"Kalise!" she yelled.

Kalise turned her head and saw Barrister. The tentacles also had sharp claws that were digging into his flesh as they squeezed ever tighter. Barrister screamed out as blood began to run from the claws cutting into him.

"Help me!" he shouted.

Following Kalise's lead, Grunda began hacking at the tentacles, trying not to do more harm to Barrister in the process. They were not too hard to cut, but that made cutting them more difficult as their blades could pass through and cut Barrister just as easily. As each was cut in two, the tentacles disappeared into nothing again.

Verin had something of her own for the three of them though. Just as it seemed Barrister's problem was taken care of, Verin dug into her spell components. She took out a hard little ball of bat guano and rolled it in a sulfur powder. She drew back her arm and hurled the ball at Barrister, Grunda and Kalise.

"I like mine well done," Verin sneered. "Puissant boule de feu!"

The little ball of guano and sulfur suddenly expanded into a large sphere of fire. As it burst into flame, it looped down at the three of them from above. The light it cast caused the three of them to look up.

"Fireball!" Kalise shouted. "Scatter!"

"Cor!" Grunda said, shaking with panic as she took a few quick steps back.

The fireball was coming in fast, so Grunda turned away and leaped, rolling herself into a ball as she crashed to the stone floor. Kalise took a step away in the opposite direction and dove headlong, quickly covering her head as she hit the floor. Barrister though was on the ground after being squeezed and cut by the tentacles, and he fumbled to get up and move away.

Unable to get up and run and with the fireball closing on him, he crab-crawled backward for a moment, not able to think of anything else. The fireball was going to hit him whether he liked it or not, so as a last resort, he threw his robes over his head and curled up, burying his head beneath his arms. The fireball dropped and exploded in a thunderous blast above him, covering him in a sea of flame and shaking the whole cavern.

The blast took the breath from Kalise and she sat up coughing, trying to get air back in her lungs. Her cloak was on fire, so she quickly slipped out of it and stamped out the flames. Grunda's beard was singed and flames danced on her padded armor. She began rolling around; trying to put them out before her armor was destroyed.

Kalise looked over and saw Barrister lying there with his robes on fire. He was not moving and she could see blackened skin exposed. She rushed over with her cloak and covered the flames burning on him to put them out.

Kneeling beside him, she pulled back her cloak and saw the crusted flesh. It smelled distinguishably bad too, as only burnt flesh can. Fearing the worst, she pulled back the remaining material of his robes from his head and checked for a pulse.

Barrister opened his eyes as his body jerked and made a sound that was hardly audible. With Eleazaar locked in combat and unable to help, she was going to have to do any healing that was to be done all by herself.

"For the love of Youja." she said despairingly. "Gott der Natur und aller lebenden sachen. Von der erde, fleisch heilung!"

Her healing skills were adequate, but not nearly as skilled as a cleric's. The druids traditionally relied more on slow, natural healing with herbs, balms and extracts. Her hands glowed as she finished her healing prayer, though she could not see much change in his condition. She hoped there was healing more on the inside that she could not see.

She possessed only a single healing potion that she had saved back for an emergency. Considering Barrister's condition, that seemed to qualify at the moment. She took out a vial from its protected cache around her waist and uncorked it.

"You son-of-a-wench." she said, looking at him as she prepared to use her potion. "This had better count for something."

He was burned so badly, she was almost afraid to touch him. It looked as if his burned flesh could flake right off in her hands if she pressed it too hard. She carefully dribbled some of the fluid onto his lips and color seemed to return to them. She gently opened his mouth and began to trickle the potion of healing into it, letting it help the process along.

Normally, a potion of healing vial contained about three doses. As it were, she was going to have to administer the whole thing to him if there was to be any hope of getting him back in this fight. Grunda crawled over to join her, on the opposite side of Barrister.

"Sure looks pitiful, lyin' there he does," Grunda said. "Anythin' mes can do t'help?"

"Protect us until I can get him up … if I can get him up again," Kalise said gravely. "Keep them off my back, Grunda."

"Ah do that." Grunda replied. "Not to worry, love."

"Maybe pray a little." Kalise mumbled, mostly to herself as she continued to feed the potion to Barrister.

Yost upended one of the Yuan-ti, sweeping his sword under its legs. He blocked the scimitar of one to his left and slashed down, striking the legged Yuan-ti to his right in the thigh. His sword cut to the bone and locked there in its leg. He yanked at it voraciously, dumping the Yuan-ti on it back in the process but the sword would not pull out.

As he stumbled awkwardly in fighting to free it, he was attacked again from his left. He saw the attack coming, but there was little he could do. At the last moment, he twisted his body to avoid it but the blade caught his left hand.

"Damnit!" he yelled, as he drew his hand back quickly.

Blood ran down his arm from the gash where his pinky finger used to be. He tucked it against him to slow the flow and at last ripped his sword away from the Yuan-ti's leg. His sword blocked the return strike by the one that had wounded him and he thrashed it back, blocking another attack from ahead of him as he stumbled back and away.

Eleazaar hooked the scimitar of the Yuan-ti in front of him with his hand scythe and stepped to his left, bringing his sword under and around on his right. He slapped the flat of the sword on the back of the Yuan-ti that had gotten behind him and yanked on his scythe, driving the two into each other. The sword of the one in front ran through the abdomen of the one that had been behind him and he spun around to his right, driving his sword into the back of the other.

But, he did not account for the one to his left. He saw its blade coming too late and arched his back, trying to avoid it. The blade pierced his splint armor and flayed into his side, just above the hip.

"Uuuuunnnggghhh!" he blurted out in pain before knocking the blade away.

Blood oozed out his side and ran down, coloring his armor with a dark red. A blade from behind slashed across his back, but the splint mail kept it from cutting his flesh. He ducked down and used the bodies of the two he had run through as a shield to reposition himself. Then, Gresil ripped a strip of red cloth and placed a goopy substance upon it. She rolled it up tightly together and threw it into the air.

"Peste de Heptmuz, envoyer des entrailles de la frange monde!" Gresil commanded for her summoning spell. "Nuee d'insectes!"

The rolled, goopy cloth exploded into a dark, undulating cloud above her. She raised her open hand to it and cast it forward at the embattled group. A loud buzzing-like sound filled the air as the undulating cloud of locusts sprang ahead toward Yost and the others.

In readjusting his position, Eleazaar had also readjusted his weaponry. Awkward as it was, he had switched out his hand scythe for his mace and was trying to use it to create better space for fighting. He hurled it around him on one side, and then attacked opposite to give him more time to recover. Though he had not sustained a life-threatening injury, his side stung badly when he moved and it was slowing him down. Eleazaar was the first to hear the sound with his keen elven ears. As he hurled his mace around, he looked up to locate the sound's origin. Spotting the movement against the shadowy backdrop of the roof of the cavern and recognizing what it was, he called out for help.

"Kalise!" he shouted over his shoulder.

Kalise was just now helping Barrister sit up. She turned to Eleazaar's voice and he pointed up above before engaging a Yuan-ti. Kalise looked up and recognized the dark mass too. Similar to Gresil, Kalise immediately dug into one of her bags and retrieved a rolled cloth that was already pre- prepared. She pulled the cloth open and inserted a small, organic ball into the goop inside before rising and heaving it into the air toward the mass that was now descending upon them.

"Die erde mutter," she began, calling out a summoning of her own, "gottsanbeterin verschlingen!"

Kalise's roll of goop exploded into a mass of its own; a mass of praying mantis.
Kalise waved her hand at the incoming swarm and the two swarms collided with each other. The mantises intercepted and devoured Gresil's locusts, then disappeared from sight into the darkness.

"Aaawwwk!" Gresil screeched as she looked at Verin. "The girl has sorcery too!"

Chapter Fifteen

PUKTAH

"This is quite unexpected." Sonnillon added as she hovered above the other two Yuan-ti sisters. "Verin?"

"Yes, they are full of surprises." Verin replied. "My turn, sisters. Greve son, fleche de la magie!"

Verin clasped her hands together around a thorn and opened them upward as she raised them. There was a brief sparkle in the air over her hands and then an arrow magically appeared, hovering above them. She waved her hand toward Kalise and the magic arrow took flight, wisking away and striking her in the right shoulder.

The blow toppled Kalise over and she fell to floor, but it was only a flesh wound. The arrow disappeared after impact, so it took her a moment to realize what had hit her. Barrister, who was getting back to his feet finally, had seen the arrow strike and cleared up the confusion for her.

"Just a magic arrow." he said to her. "I will get that bitch ... you watch. Three on one is hardly fair, now one for each will make us square."

Holding three thorns, Barrister extended both hands out from his chest as if releasing doves or offering a hug. That was hardly his intent, however. He cast the thorns ahead of him into the air and three magic arrows exploded from his hands like missiles with a radar lock on each of the three sisters.

The levitating Sonnillon attempted to fly up and away from the arrow's path, but it followed her and struck her in flight, sending her spinning in the air. The second arrow hit Verin at the stone lectern, knocking her down on her back. Gresil tried to hide behind the lectern, but the magic arrow just curved around over it and struck her where she hid below.

"I will get that wizard." Gresil snarled.

Eleazaar was overpowered by three Yuan-ti and knocked to the floor. He thrashed violently as they tried to pin and kill him. One of the Yuan-ti swept his scimitar down as another grabbed hold of his legs. Eleazaar rolled to his right side as he kicked with both feet and all of his strength. The Yuan-ti's blade clanged against the floor less than an inch from his side. Eleazaar broke a foot free and kicked the Yuan-ti holding his legs in the torso, knocking him back. Grunda saw him on the ground as the Yuan-ti tried to encircle him.

She rushed toward him, but one of the Yuan-ti saw her coming and kept her back with his flailing scimitar. She waited for it to swing again and she did a summersault forward, coming up and driving her short sword into its abdomen. She drew her sword out as she crawled quickly through its legs toward Eleazaar.

When she rose up to her feet again, she accidentally ran into the back of the Yuan-ti behind Eleazaar, knocking it forward. Eleazaar flipped his sword up and thrust it back at the one falling forward, spearing him in its snake-like abdomen area. He drew away his sword quickly and, as it swung around to the other side, it slashed another Yuan-ti across the buttocks that was chasing after Grunda. The Yuan-ti leaped in the air from the sting and Eleazaar spun up onto his feet, slashing in a circle around him to clear space and reorient his position to the enemy as Grunda retreated.

Despite losing blood, Yost continued fighting voraciously. He tried to keep his hand pressed against him, but it was not easy. The Yuan-ti flooded at him from all sides, despite the efforts of Grunda and Kalise. Seeing that he was clearly in trouble, Gresil seized her chance to unbalance the defenders. She placed a clump of matted hair before her on the lectern, then sprinkled a powder upon it and waved her hand over it. The clump of hair burst into flames, and she thrust her clawed hand out toward Yost.

"Orycterope!" she commanded for her summoning spell. "Je vous somme d'honorer votre serment!"

Out of thin air, four bugbears suddenly appeared not far from Yost. Under the command of Gresil, they spotted Yost amidst the pack of Yuan-ti and charged right in at him. Yost saw them coming as they pushed Yuan-ti out of their way to get to him.

"Right." Yost mumbled in frustration before calling out to the others. "I ... I need some help!"

Eleazaar heard and turned his head toward Yost. He could see the bugbears coming as they were taller when upright than the Yuan-ti. He knew exactly what they were since he and Jayden had once had a run-in with them as kids. There was nothing he could really do to help Yost, however. He was largely surrounded and fighting on all sides himself.

Kalise saw what was happening too and quickly realized she was the only one who could offer any help to him now. She reached down into her pocket and removed the little nutshell container she had prepared and filled earlier while on the bridge. She popped it open and dumped the contents into her mouth.

"Die erde mutter." she said. "Versipellis faolain hombre lobo!"

Almost immediately her body began to convulse and her eyes drifted back into her head, showing only the whites. Her body grew pale as if ill and then it began to contort and stretch oddly. Her head elongated and her arms grew long with sharp claws extending from her fingertips. Then, hair began to burst through her skin, covering her body in fur. Her hands became paws and she dropped down on all fours. She growled deep and menacingly as she looked over and spotted the bugbears bearing down on Yost. Kalise had polymorphed herself into a werewolf.

She sprung forward and charged at the group surrounding Yost. With a mighty spring, she leaped into the air into the surprised Yuan-ti, biting and tearing at them with her claws. As she tumbled to the ground with two of them in her clutches, she leaped again onto the back of one of the bugbears. She bit into its neck and ripped away a chunk of its flesh. As blood spewed from the hole, the bugbear fell and disappeared.

The werewolf Kalise leaped again into the swarm of Yuan-ti, clawing and biting in all directions as she fought her way to the next bugbear. Yost was doing his best to do his own part. He spun the opponent's sword and cut off the head of the Yuan-ti to his left. Yanking the sword back, he clubbed another at his five o'clock left with the hilt. He thrust his sword back forward and stabbed two of the oncoming bugbears in rapid succession.

Kalise pounced on the third bugbear and began ripping into its backside. It flailed wildly, tossing her about but she held onto it tightly with her teeth as her claws continued to slash at it. As the bugbear fell and disappeared, she was hit by the scimitar of one of the Yuan-ti and blood began to ooze from the cut to her side. She turned on it and leaped atop it, driving it to the ground.

Yost turned and plunged his sword into one of the Yuan-ti behind him and swung it back across the front, blocking the claws of one of the the bugbears. Then suddenly, his body lurched forward and his mouth opened in surprise. He looked down and saw the blade of a scimitar jutting out from his just below his ribcage.

"Damnit." he said with disgust.

His vision grew blurry and he wobbled as the scimitar withdrew. The two bugbears knocked him to the ground and pounced upon him. They drove their beaks into his flesh, ripping him apart.

"Excellent work, sister." Verin praised Gresil.
"Naturally." Gresil hissed with glee in return.

Verin placed two pouches, a vial and a small bowl on the lectern. She sprinkled calcium powder, dried protein and poured a syrupy fluid into the bowl. She took a short, thick stick with a rounded end and began to grind the ingredients together. Once the mixture was smooth, she drank it up.

After a few moments, Verin began to grow larger and larger until she was over ten feet tall.

"Play time is over." she said smugly. "Bigger *is* better."

Barrister was not about to give in so easily, regardless of the loss of Yost and the seemingly eventual futility of their situation. His components bag had largely escaped damage from the fireball, so he dug around inside it for the items he needed to cast the next spell. He retrieved a small, crystal tube and rubbed a cloth against it rapidly.

"Sizzling light ... electric shine," he said in evocation, "send that overgrown bitch a little of mine!"

He held up his hand with the crystal tube, opening it and aiming it at Verin. With a sudden thunderclap, the tube disappeared and a bolt of lightning shot forth at the super-sized Yuan-ti ringleader.

The bolt snapped Verin with an earth-shaking boom, toppling her and sending her crashing to the stone floor. Undeterred as she watched her sister knocked to the ground, Sonnillon immediately floated forward to the foray and spotted the werewolf Kalise as she shredded through the Yuan-ti warriors.

"Such a pretty fur coat." Sonnillon said aloud to herself as she rubber her fingertips with sulfur and oil. "L'obscurite enfer flammes je te convoque, de brulure des mains m'habiliter!"

Flames burst forth from her fingertips and she lowered her hands, aiming them at Kalise. She gritted her teeth in a hateful sneer and squinted her eyes before a flamethrower-like burst erupted from her hands. The flames engulfed Kalise and the bugbear she was battling. Kalise's werewolf fur caught fire and burned against her as it did the bugbear's. Even a few of the Yuan-ti nearby were singed by the flames, but the bugbear, already wounded by Kalise, fell away and disappeared into nothingness again.

Kalise rolled frantically as she tried to stop herself from burning, but the Yuan-ti warriors swarmed upon her. Eleazaar could see everything, but still could not do anything to help her. As he slung his mace around with his left hand to knock the Yuan-ti away from him, it was jarred out of his hands and slid away across the floor. He immediately grabbed Jayden's sword that still hung from his belt.

Out of desperation to help Kalise, he hurled his own sword through the air with all of his strength at Sonnillon. What he thought it would accomplish, he did not know. He was lost in that moment and that was the first and only thing that came to his mind. He just needed to do something, anything.

The sword spun through the air around and around. Perhaps guided by Youja Shilud or by fate, the sword hit Sonnillon on the arm and abruptly flipped up, slashing her across the throat. Surprised and panicked, she grabbed her bleeding throat and retreated back behind the lectern.

Eleazaar lost sight of Kalise among the swarm of Yuan-ti, but he had his own problems to remedy before he could help anyone else. He was basically alone now, holding back the Yuan-ti by himself. He tried one last thing to open up a path to her.

"Vinciret ego imperare angelos malos alligaverit!" he commanded, grasping onto one of the Yuan-ti with an invisible, heavenly force.

Summoning the assistance of an angel to bind the Yuan-ti, he tried to sling it around like a battering ram into the others and make a path that would get him to her. He did manage to cause a pile-up of bodies, but not the opening he had hoped for. He was left to hope that Kalise could somehow survive on her own as he continued to fight for his very own survival.

Grunda had to protect Barrister and his spell casting all by herself now, which was no easy task. She was small, quick and had become a fierce little dwarf in the past day, but there were still a lot of Yuan-ti left opposing them all and Eleazaar could not fight them all. They pushed him back farther and farther until finally he was fighting alongside of Grunda.

"How do you like the adventuring life so far, Grunda?" Eleazaar said smartly, trying to keep his own spirits up.

"Bollocks," Grunda replied simply as she blocked a Yuan-ti attack.

"Pretty much," Eleazaar agreed.

"Great fires of mantle burning hot below;" Barrister then said, evoking a spell, "come to me now and with fury explode!"

"You wizard types seriously need to work on your poetic prose." Eleazaar called out, overhearing Barrister as he fought. "It is a total load of rubbish."

"Hmph!" Barrister grunted dismissively in return.

Barrister let loose his own small ball of guano which bloomed into a big fireball, landing in the midst of the oncoming swarm. The fireball exploded and the whole cavern shook from the blast as singed Yuan-ti and parts of others flew about in all directions.

Verin then raised a thorn and launched another magic arrow, this time at Barrister. His body twisted as it impacted him but he held his ground stoutly and continued preparing for his next spell. He took a pebble from a glacier and dribbled water from his wineskin upon it before hurling it into the air above the Yuan-ti warriors.

"Frozen desert from skies that fell." he commanded. "Icy shower of cold that is straight from hell!"

There was a whitish burst in the air above and a thunderous clap. Seconds later, sheeting bands of freezing sleet and hail rained down on the Yuan-ti in a bitter cold and swirling wind. Even Eleazaar caught some of it as he was packed in tight fighting them. The bare, scaly skin of the Yuan-ti was poorly equipped for such cold by comparison, however. Eleazaar got a little dose of frostbite to his hands and face, but that was minor by comparison.

Those Yuan-ti along the edge of the affected area near Eleazaar were slowed by the cold and had trouble moving their extremities in an effective way. At the epicenter, some of the Yuan-ti were even frozen solid, dying where they stood or crashing into a million pieces upon the floor. It was a huge boost to Eleazaar nevertheless, and he eagerly hacked through the Yuan-ti around him almost at will.

Gresil and Verin watched the sudden turn of the conflict with frustration and shock. In particular, the evoker Barrister had proven to be much more powerful than they had anticipated and he just continued to wreak havoc on the clan. The time had come to commit everything to the fight and either finish the intruders off or die trying. The Yuan-ti was so close to winning, but had left themselves no amicable alternative if they were to fail.

"We cannot wait any longer, Verin." a worried Gresil urged. "The boy is slaughtering our warriors."

It was true; Eleazaar knew the cold would not last and the effects were already wearing off for some of those who had only been slowed by it. He struck as fast and as far into the mass of them as he could, hoping to prevent them from surrounding him in huge numbers again. Verin was no fool though, so she did not hesitate to go all-in.

"Do it." Verin said. "Then, get the boy out of the way. Let us finish this once and for all."

Gresil nodded her head and turned, disappearing briefly behind the rock platform. She returned moments later holding a large horn with a wide end. She put the horn to her mouth and blew a long, reverberating blast, before placing it down next to her on the platform.

"Oh, great and mighty Heptmuz!" she bellowed as loudly as she could. "Come to us now and you will feast grandly!"

There was a bit of a disconcerting tremor in the ground beneath Eleazaar's feet. With the acoustics of the cavern, he had heard the words of Gresil clearly enough that the two things put together had him a little worried. If something was making the ground tremble, it must be pretty stinking big.

"Oh … that cann*ot* be good," he said aloud to himself.

Off to the right of the platform with the stone lectern, something was rising up from the cylindrical pit. A giant, human-like face on an otherwise massive snake head and body, erupted up from below and slithered out onto the cavern floor. Its long body was a massive eight or perhaps even ten feet thick and colored in black and purple splotches. All three of the remaining party members; Barrister, Grunda and Eleazaar, stood for a moment in awe.

"Sweet fanny adams …" Grunda said, almost breathless in awe.

It turned out that the cult had mistaken a dark naga for their snake god, Heptmuz. While that much was probably a relief to Eleazaar, he knew from what he had read in books that a dark naga was a very powerful and dangerous creature in its own right. Notwithstanding its size, obvious strength and propensity to eat things, it was highly intelligent and could sometimes wield various magic as well.

To the isolated and somewhat primitive society of the Yuan-ti, it was easy to see how the dark naga could be mistaken as their god. It was intelligent enough it seemed, to have realized that it had found a good thing here. It got to be worshipped and had its food brought directly to it.

Surely it must also have figured if the food ever ran out, it could just eat the clan and they probably would be too afraid of their 'god' to fight it. Once the dark naga had emerged, a confident (and enlarged) Verin leaped off of the platform and bounded ahead toward the battle.

Gresil dug into a sash and retrieved a sticky ball of rolled up spider webs.

"The boy has impeded our devices for too long." Gresil said. "Now bind him with spider silk in a web that is strong. Toile d'araignée ecclésiastique!"

Gresil placed the ball of sticky webs on the fingertips of one of her clawed hands. With a powerful exhale, she blew the ball up into the air toward Eleazaar, who had moved away from the rest of the group as he tried to kill as many Yuan-ti as he could. The ball took off with a flash of light, heading right at him.

By the time Eleazaar saw it coming, it was far too late to do anything about it. The ball exploded into a giant web and hit him, sweeping him up off of his feet. It carried him backward through the air until he hit the back wall of the cavern, near the far corner.

For a moment, he was knocked silly by the impact against the stone. He shook his head around as his vision blurred and twisted. When he focused his eyes, he realized he was in a whole world of trouble.

"Fiddle," he said in disgust.

If there was one, redeeming bright spot about his situation, it was that the place he got stuck to was at an angle that prevented a particularly nasty creature from getting at him: Puktah. The cave fisher that lived above the ledge on the back wall had a good attack range with its harpoon, but it could only attack at straight trajectories. Eleazaar had a seam of rock between him and Puktah's harpoon, though he was not yet aware of his good fortune.

Despite that, Grunda and Barrister were left all alone now against the Yuan-ti warriors, the mage sisters and the dark naga too. Eleazaar knew that they could not possibly last very long alone. After struggling to no avail to free himself, he pounded his head against the rock, desperate to think of something, anything that could help them. He also was well aware that once they went down, he was in for a horrible end.

Barrister though was dumping everything he had left into the fight. Once the dark naga appeared, he immediately began preparing his next spell. He took a sticky ball of magnesium powder and sulfur, and pressed a string into it. He then pinched the string between his fingers and tossed the ball into the air.

Fires of chaos, sphere from below, I command you come to me under my control," Barrister chanted. "Prodocju plamena!"

A flame seemingly burst forth from his fingertips and moved quickly up the string to the ball. There, it burst into a sphere of fire and he moved it back and forth at his leisure as one might swing a simple, if very long sword. He immediately used it as such, battering nearby Yuan-ti to help Grunda keep them at bay for as long as it would last. He figured it could be used effectively against the dark naga as well.

"Yeah! Excellent choice," Eleazaar cheered from his web restraints. "Get them, Barrister."

"I can do that too, sorcerer," Verin snarled with a scowl. "J'invoque la flamme de Heptmuz, sphere d'incendie!"

Using similar components, Verin produced an almost identical weapon of spherical fire. As she continued to advance toward them, the two engaged their flaming spheres in a strange battle above the heads of the others. The naga had ideas of its own though. Impatient and eager to feed as promised, it assessed the situation before it and intervened. It reared back and emitted an ear-splitting scream that was disorienting to the party, but not so much to the Yuan-ti who had mostly lost their human-like ears. It was so powerful that Barrister lost his hearing.

He wobbled as his equilibrium went out of balance and his spell failed him, causing the sphere of fire to disappear. The dark naga began slithering forward toward the remnants of the group. Verin, at a complete advantage now, swathed the sphere of fire back and forth at Barrister. She drove him farther and farther back. Grunda continued to do her best to keep the Yuan-ti away from him, but that was not the threat of most concern.

Eleazaar watched in dismay at the situation, thinking that surely they all were done for now. Then, ever sensitive to creepy, crawly things, he caught movement out of the corner of his left eye. He turned and raised his head forward above the rock seam, which was about the only body part he could move much, and at last saw the cave fisher. He had never seen one before, but it looked enough like a spider that he knew it had to be a threat to Barrister. He began screaming at Barrister, thrashing wildly in the web as he tried desperately to get his attention. Barrister could not hear him, however, and was fixed on the threat he could see. His hearing was gone and blood ran down from his ear from his burst eardrum.

Grunda did hear Eleazaar screaming, however. She could not understand at first what he was screaming about and was a little busy trying to keep from getting killed. But, the screaming did not stop and she focused on what he was saying at last. A shudder passed through her when she finally was able to turn and look behind them.

At that point, Grunda began yelling at Barrister too and tried to wave her arms to get his attention, but to no avail. Eleazaar was screaming so hard now he was in tears, desperate and knowing he was powerless. A sudden burst of Puktah's harpoon and Barrister's body lurched forward.

Grunda screamed at him as she disengaged and took a stride toward him. Barrister looked down at the bony harpoon as hook-like claws exploded out of the end of it into his flesh. Open mouthed, he began to shake before he was suddenly ripped up into the air by the cave fisher, retracting its harpoon.

His flailing body bounced off the edge of the rock ledge as it was reeled in. It drew him screaming to its bony mouth and clamped onto him. With a sickening crunch, the screaming stopped.

Eleazaar felt sick and was angry as tears rolled down his cheeks. It was just he and Grunda now, which meant it, was really just Grunda; he was completely useless in his current state. He wished now that he had never brought her into this mess.

"Damnit!" he screamed out to God, cursing for the first time in his young life. "Why? Why did you not just let me die with my parents? Why?"

He was in despair at that moment and understandably so. A simple dwarven beggar was all that stood between him now and a quick, terrible end to a short life. He was surrounded by people that had polymorphed into snakes, a massive naga and the alternative of a bony, spider-like creature to finish him off. But then again, he remembered something that he had forgotten to this point in that traumatic moment. Grunda was not such a simple beggar after all.

There was the thing she did with the stolen item and he recalled the stories she spoke of; the things she sometimes had done when she got emotional. He needed a miracle if he was to see another day and frankly, any kind of miracle would do. Maybe … just maybe, there was a much more profound reason that Grunda was here at this time and place after all.

On an otherwise mundane day of catering to his mentor, he had felt compelled to drop a coin to a poor beggar in a simple act of compassion. The seemingly innocuous choice he had made began a chain of events he had never imagined. Sent to the jail to meet with Yost, he again encountered her and had made another choice; it was a moral, albeit gutsy choice, which had combined with his other choices and led to this moment.

Had he not made those choices he would surely still be where he was, but now it seemed he still had another choice before him. He had always been taught that the choices we make define us and determine our destiny.

What that destiny could be he had no way of knowing for sure, but for now, Grunda and he were still alive.

He went through it all again in his head as Grunda backed up continuously towards him, careful to stay out of Puktah's range. Puktah had returned to the ledge and was watching too, eager for another meal. It had spied Eleazaar as well and was keeping its eyes on him, hoping for a clear shot to present itself.

Eleazaar was staying mindful of Puktah too. He knew if he somehow ever got out of that trap, he would have to be extra careful to get safely out of its range. Before that was even worthy of consideration, however, he somehow needed for Grunda to accomplish the impossible.

"Sod all!" Grunda exclaimed, turning to look at Eleazaar. "Whit me's to do?"

"I do not know, Grunda," Eleazaar called back to her. "What I do know is that you are one amazing little dwarf. In my heart, I want to tell you to run away and live out your life, but there is nowhere to run for either of us. You are the only chance we have now and I am sorry it came to that."

"T'were not yous fault, love," Grunda replied, feeling bewildered.

"I do not know if there is a fault, but here we are," Eleazaar said. "I put you into God's hands and the will of Youja Shilud. He made you all of those unusual things that you are for a reason; maybe this was the reason ... I do not pretend to know that. What I do know is that now would be a good time to bring out some of those gifts, my little friend. Give them a taste of the nasty ... I believe in you, Grunda."

Grunda turned her head again and looked at him strangely. She could not remember anyone ever speaking in such an encouraging way to her before, certainly not to be expected when their life was hanging in the balance. He was a good young man, she thought and, maybe he was right. Until today, her life had seemed almost meaningless to the world in which she lived. She had often longed for an answer as to why her life was of such misfortune, forced to carry the burden of her bizarre abilities in filth, rejection and poverty.

If there was ever a reason to the lot one has in life and a purpose lain out by some god, then maybe this really was her moment of truth. For that one moment, it all seemed to strangely make sense. A twisted, angry look swept across her face and she turned back toward Verin, shaking a stubby little finger at her.

"Y'know, me's ruddy tired being pushed round alls the time," she said. "Gots me brassed off now y'do, and me gots a cure f'that! Picked the wrong dwarf f'some aggro y'didst!"

Grunda gritted her teeth and her eyes began to sparkle. Eleazaar was not at all sure what was happening at that moment, but she seemed to become almost transparent before him and then faded away altogether.

That is to say, all faded away but for her sword, which hung seemingly from nothing there in midair. Once he realized that she had turned herself invisible, he thought to remind her of what had not become so.

"Grunda!" he shouted. "Your sword!"

There was no reply, but the sword simply dropped and clanged upon the floor. What followed was a sound he would never forget, but one he had vaguely heard before. When they had first entered the temple and encountered the millipede, he had heard a sound like that as well. It was a metallic sound, like metal grating against something and snapping into place. She was transmuting her arms into weapons again and he had no doubts that she meant to do it this time. He was not so sure he would want to see what happens when she got angry, except under the dire circumstances of this moment.

"That is right, Grunda," he whispered, thinking out loud. "Get angry."

Chapter Sixteen

THE CHANGE WITHIN

The Yuan-ti, mistaking Grunda's disappearing act as an escape likely perpetuated by the cleric in a last act of heroism, all advanced ahead to take Eleazaar. They were understandably certain that they had won and had no fear of the possibility of some invisible little dwarf running around. Verin and Gresil both marched with them, eager to gloat before the clan and their false god.

That sense of security would change very quickly. There was an awful sound above the relative quiet that had fallen over the cavern; the kind of sound that only steel can make as it plunges through flesh and bone. Two of the Yuan-ti warriors wobbled and fell in half upon the floor before the eyes of all; split in two by an invisible Grunda.

"What is *this*?" Verin exclaimed with surprise. "What is happening?"

"Gaaaaaa! The dwarf!" Gresil shouted out in panic. "Where is she? Stop her!"

Grunda may have been mostly illiterate and largely uneducated, but she was smart in many ways too. To survive alone on the streets, one had to learn many things to make it as long as she had. Using her small size, she wove her way through the confused Yuan-ti and headed straight for Verin.

Figuring Verin was the key to order amongst the Yuan-ti rank and file, she went straight for the proverbial throat of the clan. Verin had actually made it easier for Grunda with her giant size, as she was able to move quickly about her. She first rushed around Verin's snake-like lower half and slashed her across as she sped past behind her.

"Awwwwk!" Verin screeched as the blade slashed through her flesh. "Help me!"

Verin flailed her sword wildly about, trying awkwardly to strike her hidden opponent. Gresil stood frozen out of fear, unwilling to move until she could spot the dwarf. But, Grunda moved fast and kept moving.

Despite knowing that the Yuan-ti could not see her with their infravision when it had been exposed to the light, she was not going to take any chances. She ran at Verin from behind and leaped unnaturally high into the air. She crashed onto Verin's back and locked her sword arms across Verin's throat in a V-shape as Verin gasped in sudden terror.

"Now;" Grunda said matter-of-factly, "give us a bell when y'gets t'hell."

Grunda drew her sword arms back and pulled away. Her blades sliced through Verin's neck and spine, decapitating the Yuan-ti leader. Grunda dropped onto the ground and fell, rolling in her fluffy padded armor as Verin shrank to normal size again and collapsed into a blood-spurting heap on the floor. Grunda was quick to get back to her feet, but the Naga had managed to see her. With much more acute vision than the Yuan-ti, the Naga could see the movement as a distortion; like that when heat rises up from the ground. It began to move toward her position slowly as it caught glimpses of her.

A shudder ran through Gresil at the sight of her sister and she took into a panicked flight, running away from the area. The Dark Naga, however, moved into her path to block her. It had come to feed and would not let anyone run away until it had been given the tribute that it was promised. Catching her wits, Gresil turned back and took up a defensive stand as she tried to locate the surprising dwarf. The Dark Naga had another weapon in its arsenal; a sharp, spike-like bone tail. As it slithered and curled around, scanning for glimpses of Grunda, it raised its spike high into the air. If it could lock onto her for a moment, it was intent to try to end the chaos in one fell strike.

"Watch out for the Naga, Grunda!" Eleazaar yelled.

Grunda stopped for a moment to look at him and nodded, despite the fact he could not see her do it. As she took a step forward, the Naga's spike slammed into the stone floor, just missing her. It was a clear awakening that she was not as invisible as she thought.

"Ooooh!" Grunda squealed, a little frightened by it.

Gresil reacted to the squeal, which came from somewhere in front of her. She stepped forward and thrashed her sword about but Grunda had already moved away. She ran laterally and then zigzagged her movements back toward Gresil. Then Grunda did something even more bizarre. Not wanting to stop and let the Naga zero in on her, she elongated her neck away from her running body and swung it around behind Gresil's shoulder. She cleverly thought to use the situation with the Naga to her advantage.

"Here me is," she whispered just to the left of Gresil's head.

The Naga locked onto Grunda's head and slammed its stinger down again, close to Gresil. Gresil Swung around wildly trying to catch the dwarf, but she had withdrawn her head away, back to her body already. It was close, but Grunda needed to get closer to make her plan work. As the Naga continued to follow Grunda's movements, she stopped in front of Gresil and waved her arms to get the beast's attention.

The Naga locked onto her and brought its spike down. With the spike tracking her, she ran and slid just below Gresil. Gresil looked up and saw the stinger coming down fast, but it was too late to move. Her mouth opened in surprise and the stinger plunged right into it, ripping through Gresil's body. Her body quivered and fell limp around the spike as blood oozed out from all over. But, the spike caught Grunda in the shoulder too. It easily pierced her soft padded armor and ripped open her shoulder. Though it hurt, she was quick to get up and stumbled up to her feet, ready to run again.

The other Yuan-ti warriors could not see her either, so they had become bystanders more or less and watched helplessly from afar. With Gresil dead, however, the web spell holding Eleazaar now failed. The web disintegrated into nothing and he dropped down to his feet upon the cavern floor. At last, he was back in the fight. The Yuan-ti warriors turned and looked at Eleazaar, who rolled his neck and shoulders.

"Oh yeah," he said, looking back at them. "Bring it."

Mindful that the cave fisher was watching and waiting, he started to rush forward and then stopped abruptly. The creature's harpoon snapped just in front of his chest, just a little too close for comfort. He quickly ran ahead out of its range before it could retract its harpoon and try again.

With Jayden's sword in hand, the only serious melee weapon he still possessed, he leaped into the crowd of Yuan-ti that remained. He then grabbed the hand scythe from his belt to use as a blocking weapon as he spun and dodged amongst them. The break had done him some good and he felt full of fighting spirit once again.

Gresil's impaled body was stuck on the Dark Naga's tail-spike. No matter how it tried to shake it free, it had pierced bones and was not coming off. Not terribly put out, the Naga took Gresil's body in its teeth and pulled it loose. Not wanting to waste anything, it then swallowed Gresil whole and the problem was solved.

The Naga lost track of Grunda in the meantime and she was all too happy to put some distance between it and her. She ran back toward Eleazaar and attacked the Yuan-ti by surprise from the rear. It was hardly a fair fight, as they could not see her and their attention was focused on Eleazaar. Of course, nothing had been much of a fair fight since it all began; at least now it was unfair in their favor for a change. Eleazaar blocked the scimitar of the Yuan-ti to his right and spun it around, temporarily locking the swords together.

Then he caught the scimitar of the one on his left with his hand scythe and hooked the hilt. He kicked the one on his right, knocking it back a few steps, as he yanked down on the sword he had hooked to his left. As the Yuan-ti holding it was pulled forward, he stuck it in the throat with his sword and ripped his scythe away. He spun back to his right and reengaged the first Yuan-ti once again as the other fell, trying to cover its throat and stem the flow of spurting blood.

Rid of Gresil, the Naga reassessed the situation and began to slither in. At this point, it no longer cared who would win as it figured it would win either way and would just eat everyone. Grunda seemed to be the only serious threat as she was hard to see, so it focused on finding her first.

One of the Yuan-ti lunged at Eleazaar with the tip of its blade, but he met it with his hand scythe and redirected it beneath his arm as the warrior crashed into him. Eleazaar planted his feet and lowered a shoulder into the charge, which still knocked him back. He kneed the Yuan-ti in its relative abdomen and brought his own sword down into its back. The sword plunged through to the front and he stepped back, letting it fall to the floor as he yanked his sword back out.

Grunda leaped up from behind and scissored a Yuan-ti in half as another one tripped and fell, stabbing Eleazaar in the foot. He immediately tripped forward as he yanked the foot back and crashed into another warrior who was looking for Grunda. As both tumbled to the floor, Eleazaar spied his mace lying not far from him.

Eleazaar hopped to his feet and was struck in the back by a scimitar, opening up a three inch gash that stung pretty good. He stumbled away toward the mace and fell again, but he was able to put away the scythe and reach out to grab his mace once again. The Yuan-ti slithered over bodies after him and raised its sword up. Eleazaar swung his mace up and struck it across the face, sending teeth and blood flying in a spray.

Grunda severed the leg of a Yuan-ti and it fell over in a spatter. She drove her arm sword into it and looked up at the last of the Yuan-ti. It was very alone now and stressed to locate her. Eleazaar arose once again and stepped tenderly on his bloodied foot. It was cut well, but it did not seem like anything important had been damaged. It was a clean cut and just burned a little.

He spied the last of the Yuan-ti and grabbed his weapon tightly as he walked toward it with a menacing look upon his face. He was covered in blood and hobbled as he walked towards it. He raised his weapon as it backed away from him, but then suddenly, he just stopped and stood there before it. The terrified Yuan-ti looked all around frantically, expecting Grunda to surprise him before his body suddenly jerked forward.

"Let us do lunch," Eleazaar said smartly as he looked upon it with little emotion.

The claws in the end of Puktah's harpoon exploded into the Yuan-ti's flesh. It was yanked up into the air screeching as the harpoon was recalled. It crashed into the rock ledge and was drawn over, flailing all the way. The sickening crunch of snapping bone ended the terrified screeching.

"Cor ... look out, love!" Grunda suddenly yelled.

Eleazaar turned quickly and saw the Naga coming up on him fast. He had momentarily forgotten about it in his relief of vanquishing the Yuan-ti. He took off running away from Grunda toward the spot where the bridge had been.

"Do the opposite of what I do!" He yelled back at her.
"Whit d'that mean, love? Grunda asked, puzzled. "Ah dinnea understands whit t'do. Gaaaaaaaaaa!"

She saw the spike of the Naga coming down and took off running. She was so busy worrying about him, she did not see the Naga change course for her. She scolded herself internally for forgetting to keep moving.

"I mean attack," Eleazaar yelled back to her. "Attack from the opposite direction as I do. If we make it fight two ways at once, it will make it harder to defend against us."

"Right;" Grunda said, "gaein'ta try, me will."

Eleazaar took a deep breath and exhaled. He had no idea how or even if they could kill the monstrous Naga. He felt beat up, and he was, but he could only imagine what he would look like when the armor finally came off. He really needed stitches in a place or two, but he figured they would probably rip out fighting the Naga and he did not have time for that anyway. What he did have was one last dose of healing extract potion left. He took out the vial and was about to tip it up to drink when he spotted Kalise lying upon the floor, still in werewolf form.

"Oh, God …" he said, awash with emotions he had set aside until now. "Grunda! Keep the Naga occupied for a minute. I found Kalise!"

"What?" Grunda called back. "Take that ruddy big thing all by meself? Cor! Chivvy along wit'it then. Must be off me ruddy carriage!"

Eleazaar felt bad about it too, but he had to know if she was still alive. He ran to her and fell to his knees next to her. He took her werewolf head in his arms and he felt a breath against his skin.

"Great God, you *are* alive," Eleazaar said in disbelief. "I am so sorry, Kalise. I could not get to you. I … I have a dose of healing left … let me …".

"Too late…. for that," she said in a weak voice, amidst coughs. "Waited for y … you as long … as I could. I am only … alive be … because … I have not shifted … back to hu … human form yet. In … juries beyond … healing now."

"No." Eleazaar replied. "Do not say that. I *will* heal you."

"No … you will not … my young prince," she said as a tear dripped from her eye.

"Gaaaaaa!" Eleazaar heard Grunda squeal as she dodged the Naga's attack on the other side of the cavern.

"You cannot die here," he said, his face turning red, "not like this. Not … I have all these feelings about you and I cannot … I do not know how … what to do with that."

"I know," she said, sadness flowing freely in her voice. "We will meet again … one day … my sweet … sweet young prince … in your far away … kingdom, perhaps."

"Take that, y'brute!" Grunda yelled, echoing across the cavern. "Gaaaaaa!"

"I will h … have … only a mome … a moment," Kalise said. "When I become human again. Kiss me … like you di-gnhhh … did … the first time."

Eleazaar nodded that he understood as tears streamed down his bloodied face. He held her head close to him as she began to shift her body back to its true form. She opened her eyes as a human woman again and he pressed his lips to hers, never breaking the eye contact between them. Her eyes fluttered for a moment and then shut, never again to open and look upon him. She went limp in his arms and he began to sob, unable to hold it back. He rocked back and forth with her as he sat there in despair, kissing her face and squeezing her head tight against him. His body trembled as emotions raced through him in total chaos. His eyes burned and his heart pounded inside his chest. He finally lay her head down and rose to his feet,

"I am taking you home," he said, struggling to say the words.

He turned away and looked over toward the Naga. Grunda needed his help in the worst way and he had asked too much of her already. He sniffled and took a deep breath to calm himself as he wiped his face with his arm. He stared at the ground before him, but could find no peace inside himself; there was only anger left inside … and hate. He had found a dark place within himself and, that would have to do. His hand squeezed tightly around the hilt of Jayden's sword, and he took out his hand scythe again, re-holstering his mace.

Hatred swelled up within him and pulsed through his veins. He sprang forward and began running as hard as could, straight for the Naga. He hurdled bodies as he ran and leaped into the air, burying Jayden's sword into the Naga all the way to the hilt. He hooked his scythe into the Naga too and used it to hold on as he thrashed the sword in and out of its flesh violently. The surprised Naga threw its head back in pain, never seeing him coming as it was so intent on Grunda.

The Naga swung its head down and rammed it into Eleazaar, knocking him and his scythe loose. He flew a few feet back and crashed into the Naga's side before tumbling to the floor. Jayden's sword remained stuck in the Naga's side and it grabbed it in its mouth, pulling it out and tossing it aside. Eleazaar still had a brass dagger he never really used much, so he pulled it out and began stabbing the Naga's winding body repeatedly with it. As the Naga turned its head toward Eleazaar again, Grunda stabbed it with her sword arms from the other side.

The Naga was indecisive now but turned its spike on Eleazaar so it could keep its eyes on Grunda. It would look quickly at him and strike, but could not quite seem to get him. Then it would bite at Grunda, trying to catch her in a wrong movement, but neither effort was being very effective. If anything, it was hitting itself with its spike and little else. Eleazaar kept on or close to the Naga for that very reason, but the Naga would not be tricked like that for very long. It switched its tactic and turned the spike back at Grunda while it tried to clamp down on Eleazaar. It logically concluded if it could eliminate one of them, it would eventually get the other.

Thus, it went snapping voraciously after Eleazaar, trying to get him in its mouth so it could swallow him. Eleazaar however, had become a whirlwind of violence. Several times the Naga got a hold on one of his legs, but the mindless aggression of the young cleric always freed him somehow. He would hook right into the Naga's head and pound his dagger mercilessly, over and over and over again in a wild rage. The constant pricking pain caused the annoyed Naga to throw the boy repeatedly off. As he tumbled, slid or bounced across the floor, it came at him again and the same series of events repeated themselves. The Naga only cared to keep Grunda busy for now; the boy had made enough trouble of himself and had to go.

Eleazaar was trying to get up behind the Naga's head and hold on, where he could stab it most effectively without getting eaten. The Naga was always moving and thrashing about, however, snapping quickly at him with its large mouth. He thus hooked into it and stabbed as long as he could until it threw him off again. His scythe hooked into the side of its face as it got his legs again and the Naga shook its head violently trying to jar loose his hold. When that did not work, it drug him into its own body to knock him off.

The force of the blow hurt Eleazaar immensely, but he still held on, stabbing it near the mouth with his dagger.

Grunda ran up while it was occupied and plunged both of her sword arms into the Naga. It gave a mighty whip of its head and sent Eleazaar spinning through the air to the floor. It turned its head angrily toward Grunda and stabbed its spike at her faint image, but missed and quickly abandoned her to go after the cleric again.

As Eleazaar began to rise, he saw Jayden's sword lying upon the floor where the Naga had tossed it. The Naga turned its head and saw him looking at it also. Eleazaar put the dagger away and sprung towards the sword to grab it up. As he did, the Naga sprung at him to intercept him before he got to it.

As Eleazaar's hand grabbed the hilt of Jayden's sword, the Naga struck his midsection, but could not clamp down on him. He bounced off of the hard edge of its mouth and tumbled forward. He swung Jayden's sword around as he fell and struck its mouth, but the Naga was undeterred. It snapped at him and rolled him across the ground as it tried to get him in its mouth. Grunda again charged forward and speared the Naga with her sword arms, but it ignored her and the pain she inflicted this time.

She speared it again and again to no avail, trying to draw it off of Eleazaar. Eleazaar battered the Naga's face with his sword as he fought to stay out of its mouth. It was hard to get an angle to stab with a long sword in his current position, so he did what he could in the hope of hurting it enough to somehow get a moment of escape. But, the Naga was relentless and was determined to get him.

And get him it did. It finally got enough of him to flip him up into the air and snap down on him. He fought inside its mouth as it threw him to the back of its throat, trying to swallow him. Eleazaar was not about to go down the gullet of anything so easily, however. He hooked his hand scythe into the back of the Naga's throat and held on for dear life as the contracting muscles tried to pull him down. He still had Jayden's sword in hand too, so he plunged it into the opposite side of its throat and worked it back and forth.

It caused the Naga to choke and it threw its head around violently, trying to make the painful sting stop. Unable to swallow Eleazaar and choking on the sword stabbing inside its throat, it whipped its head violently into the air and expelled Eleazaar. Eleazaar tumbled into the air above it and looked down at the Naga. Free of his blades in its throat, it opened up its mouth below him, intending to catch and swallow him quickly as the cleric fell into it.

Eleazaar began to fall toward the open mouth and as he did, he hurled Jayden's sword down before him into it. The long sword spun around and around as it fell into the Naga's mouth and the tip of the blade stuck in one side of its throat while the hilt fell and hit the other side. As the Naga's throat muscles involuntary contracted, the sword was jammed horizontally in its throat. The Naga instantly began choking again and shook its head violently from side to side trying to dislodge it.

As Grunda stood there watching it all, a strange sensation came over her. As Eleazaar fell toward the floor now, a golden glow began to emanate from her eyes. She became visible again and the glow became like beams of light, scattering out about her eyes. A deep, welling of energy swelled up inside of her and the sword lodged in the Naga's throat began to glow red as the molecules comprising its steel moved ever faster and became hot.

"Detonate," a distorted, heavy voice erupted from Grunda's mouth.

Jayden's sword turned white hot and exploded outward into fragments of hot steel. The fragments blasted out through the Naga's flesh in all directions, taking flesh and blood with it. The Naga's body slithered about as its head wavered and began to drop. Eleazaar hit the undulating body of the Naga and, on the way down, was swatted aside. He crashed upon the floor and rolled into a heap. The Naga's head slammed down against the stone floor and bounced before settling and becoming still.

Its body moved briefly before easing over onto the ground and becoming still also. At last, the Naga was dead. Grunda ran around the body of the Naga looking for Eleazaar as an eerie stillness fell over the cavern.

She looked around frantically for him across the sea of bodies that cluttered the cavern floor, but could not see him anywhere. Then, there was the sound of metal grating upon the stone of the floor.

She looked out toward the sound and saw movement at last. Eleazaar moved slowly, trying to get up as his vision spun from impacting the stone floor with his head. He was dazed and confused as he twisted and tried to get up. Only when his eyes began to focus did he realize the Naga was dead. He flipped over awkwardly and fell against the floor again. Grunda began to scurry toward him as he struggled again to get up. He wobbled to his feet and swayed as he looked around. Spying the natural stone lectern on the platform, he began to stumble toward it.

"Wait, love!" Grunda called after him.

Her little short legs were challenged by the mass of Yuan-ti bodies and that of the Naga she had to run around. It was easy enough to dodge amongst them, but a straight line after someone else through them was not quite so easy. Eleazaar stumbled forward faster and faster as she tried to catch up to him. At the end of the cavern, behind the stone lectern, Sonnillion sat quietly holding her bleeding throat.

She dared not make a sound or look out to see what was happening, hoping to be forgotten and escape their detection. Eleazaar had not forgotten about Sonnillon however; not after what she did to Kalise.

He trudged on ahead, closer and closer to the platform with only one thing on his mind. He was going to find the last of the Yuan-ti and kill it, or die trying. He was so overcome with hatred and grief that he was not even certain of what he felt about anything anymore.

"Cleric?" Grunda yelled after him to no avail.

Eleazaar reached the platform and fell against it. He planted his arms against it and tried to flip his knee up on one of flat spots in the rock. He got it up there on the second try and began to pull himself up on the platform. Grunda raced up behind him but the edges were too high for her to climb up and he was already atop it. Frustrated, she scurried to run around to one of the sides of it, to find another way up.

Eleazaar paused to catch his breath and pushed himself back up on his feet. He swung his head around and spotted Sonnillon cowering upon a rock behind the platform. He began walking toward her with a slow dreariness about him.

He stopped before her and stood there for a moment. One of his eyes was swollen and his face was smeared with blood and dirt. He scowled at her with a tired, emotionally bereft look about him.

"Mercy," Sonnillon pled, shivering and weak from the loss of blood.
"I will grant you mercy," Eleazaar replied in a raspy, strained voice, "just as you did to Kalise."

Eleazaar thrust the blade of his hand scythe into Sonnillon's abdomen and ripped it up through her torso. Sonnillon's body shuddered and then fell limp against the rock. Eleazaar then pulled his scythe free of her and placed it into the holster on his belt. He stood there for a moment before his knees buckled and he collapsed upon the stone platform.

"Verge trimmed, Jayden," Eleazaar said weakly as he began to fade.

Grunda, surprised at what she had just witnessed as she ascended the platform, ran to him. His vision grew hazy and the voice of Grunda seemed to echo distantly as she called out to him. Grunda knelt at his side and shook him repeatedly until he at last responded to her.

"Come on now, love. Y'hasta gets up. Y'be alrights now." she said.
"No," Eleazaar said weakly. "I will never be alright."

A short time later, Eleazaar was sitting up at last. Under his guidance, Grunda had bandaged the worst of his wounds in his foot, his left side and his back beneath the right shoulder. Blood was already beginning to show through, but the bleeding had slowed at least. He was pretty sure now that he had at least one broken rib, maybe more.

He had to return home for proper treatment of his wounds, so resting there for a few days was out of the question. If disease set in, he was sure to die there. Thus, he and Grunda set off searching through the underground cavern for the means to get out another way or at least back across to the platform stairs that would take them to the surface. As he paused with pain during their search, he caught a glimpse of something metallic wedged between a split in the rock of the floor. He got down and wedged it up, careful not to lose it down the crack. He lifted it up with two fingers and saw that it was a very unusual ring.

A lover of unusual things, he looked it over and pocketed it securely in a pouch on his belt. He rose again and continued searching for a way home. Eventually, they found a way to effectively cross the deep gouge of flowing water and Eleazaar went to retrieve Kalise's body. He knelt beside her and just stared at her for a moment.

"I said I am taking you home ... and I am ... to the garden. That is where you will find me," he said.

Eleazaar lifted Kalise's limp body into his arms and carried her away. He carried her across the flowing water, up the platform stairs, through the levels of the temple and eventually out through the trap door atop the hill in Satoochie Forest. Jayden's body was nowhere to be found.

Despite her protests to him bearing the burden all to himself, Grunda stayed close and steadied him as he trudged through the forest with her. Three days after they all had entered Satoochie, Eleazaar and Grunda stepped out into the late afternoon sunshine just outside of the town of Luitgarde. There, the rangers met him with amazed looks.

They had all held out little hope for the group's return after so much time had passed.

Though they offered to help him, he refused and continued walking with her in his arms. The rangers stood aside respectfully and watched him pass, following along behind him with Grunda. News quickly reached the constable's office and both he and Captain Silger ran to the edge of town to see it for themselves.

"He went into that forest as a boy;" Ranger Bo observed aloud to himself, "but, he has come out a man."

Eleazaar carried Kalise into town and shortly, the whole town seemed to come out and swell around him. From the way he looked, it was clear to all he had been through hell. He stopped at the cart in front of the constable's office and laid Kalise's body down in the back of it. Then, he sat down beside her with a blank look upon his swollen face. Constable Spillman and Captain Silger came to him as he sat there. They had to know what happened, but were loathing to ask. Eleazaar looked so broken and distant, and they were not sure they really wanted to know.

"Were you able to eliminate the problem?" Captain Silger asked gently, to which Eleazaar simply nodded.

"Did you find anyone? Some of the missing … alive?" the constable asked.

Eleazaar stared off at the ground and after a moment, shook his head no. Though he had returned to Luitgarde and would soon be home to Warfall once again, it seemed that a part of him had remained behind in that buried temple. He had purposely kept both he and Grunda away from the Naga's pit afterward because he had known what they would have found down there. He had enough to carry with him already and did not want that to haunt him also.

"Leaves him be, all of yous," Grunda said. "If y'gots questions t'ask, tell it like it was, me will."

Grunda told the story to the whole town in rather dramatic fashion as only a dwarf could, though surely minimizing her own courageous role, as was her way. Father Kluge tended to Eleazaar and both the rangers and some of the townsfolk walked with the wagon for the first mile as it bumped along the road back to Warfall. It was a long, sad ride but Eleazaar scarcely noticed.

Upon returning to Warfall, they were met by a mass of priests and staff from the St. Gustav von Claus Seminary School. Eleazaar met with the priests privately to discuss the plight of Grunda, her unusual gifts and the burial of Kalise. They were unanimous in their support of her burial in the seminary gardens, but his other request for her was not something they agreed upon.

Eleazaar could not bear to just bury Kalise and close the door. He was adamant that they perform the reincarnation ritual upon her at burial. Some thought it was foolish, probably would not work after several days of death and that he was doing it simply for himself. But he remembered her affinity for life and particularly animals, so he refused to take no for an answer.

After what had happened down there and with the encouragement of Father Mannesh, the order acquiesced to his demand. The ritual was performed and she was interred in the garden where Eleazaar spent his time meditating so often. Much more of his time was spent there from that point on. Often he would bring a book to read and even read aloud at Kalise's grave on occasion.

But, mostly he meditated and reflected on the events surrounding his experience at the temple. The seeming insignificance of his compassionate gestures to a beggar had changed his own fate in ways he could have never imagined. By now he had come to realize an important paradigm that would change the rest of his life as well: what he dubbed the insignificance paradigm.

While each individual choice he made or would ever make would be largely insignificant by itself, they each were significant in the larger scheme of the world around him in which he lived. Like a droplet of water falling into a pool, the ripple effect touched every part of the water or, more clearly put, affected the entire fabric of life.

Through the efforts of the order, Grunda was sent to a special school for *the gifted*, where she could be with others like herself. She seemed excited about it as Eleazaar saw her carriage off that would take her there. Built in a remote location, she would finally be someplace where she would be accepted and away from those who would not understand how wonderful and special she truly was. Eleazaar often found that he missed her in the days that followed though.

About a year later, as Eleazaar sat in the garden just after dusk, a young wolf appeared to him. He watched it as it studied him and it finally came over to him where he sat. The wolf sniffed him and he gently held out his open hand to it. It let him stroke its ears and the wolf lay down beside him, putting its head against his leg. The wolf returned many nights and came to him there. He often brought food with him and fed the wolf as they sat there in the silence under the moonlight. He named the wolf Kalise.

www.ingramcontent.com/pod-product-compliance
Lightning Source LLC
LaVergne TN
LVHW041758060526
838201LV00046B/1036